Death Through a Dark Green Glass

Julia Buckley

A WRITER'S APPRENTICE MYSTERY BOOK 6

To my sister Linda,
A generous and invaluable editor.

For all the readers who wanted this series to go on,
Thank you for loving the Blue Lake Crew.

Mystery Novels by Camilla Graham

The Lost Child (1972)
Castle of Disquiet (1973)
Snow in Eden (1974)
Winds of Treachery (1975)
They Came from Calais (1976)
In Spite of Thunder (1978)
Whispers of the Wicked (1979)
Twilight in Daventry (1980)
Stars, Hide Your Fires (1981)
The Torches Burn Bright (1982)
For the Love of Jane (1983)
River of Silence (1985)
A Fine Deceit (1987)
Fall of a Sparrow (1988)
Absent Thee from Felicity (1989)
The Thorny Path (1990)
Betraying Eve (1991)
On London Bridge (1992)
The Silver Birch (1994)
The Tide Rises (1995)
What Dreams May Come (1996)
The Villainous Smile (1998)

Gone by Midnight (1999)
Sapphire Sea (2000)
Beautiful Mankind (2001)
Frost and Fire (2002)
Savage Storm (2003)
The Pen and the Sword (2005)
The Tenth Muse (2006)
Death at Seaside (2008)
Mist of Time (2009)
He Kindly Stopped for Me (2010)
[a four-year hiatus]
Bereft (2015)

Written with Lena London:

The Salzburg Train (2016)
Death on the Danube (2017)
Death at Delphi (2018)
Danger at Debenham Station (a work in progress)

Press Packet Document One

Dateline Blue Lake, Indiana - For Immediate Release:

PR Genius Sasha Hardwick has announced what she calls her "Biggest Event Yet" that is sure to intrigue every mystery lover in America.

THE GREAT AMERICAN MYSTERY CHALLENGE will bring together four famous mystery writers--Camilla Graham, David Canfield, Gloria Gale, and Oliver Lord—to compete for supremacy by solving a real mystery.

"All four writers are friends of mine," Hardwick said of the event. "I wanted to bring attention to their amazing books, all of which are routinely on the best seller list."

Camilla Graham, originally from England, has carved a career in America as a writer of romantic suspense, and *The New York Times* dubbed her "The Reigning Queen of Suspense" last year. Graham's most recent titles have been written with newcomer Lena London.

David Canfield is a Seattle writer who has won acclaim for his broody police procedurals. He claims both Elmore

Leonard and Michael Connelly as influences. Canfield's tormented detective, Ross Gamble, has won his way into the hearts of readers.

Gloria Gale writes "ingenious" mysteries according to the *Los Angeles Times*. Her novel *"Within These Walls"* was made into a movie starring Emma Thompson and Colin Firth last year. Gale was a model in her youth, but she soon found that writing was her real passion, and her first novel, Bitterroot Street, shot to number three on the NYT Bestseller List. Gale resides in Connecticut.

Oliver Lord, whose thrillers have kept readers on edge since 1988, has garnered several writing awards in the last two decades, and his third novel, *Midnight Blood*, was adapted for film in 2019. *One Night* stars Catherine Zeta-Jones and Idris Elba. Lord lives in San Francisco, California.

Hardwick adds, "The contest will be all in good fun, but there will be a simulated crime with carefully constructed clues, and one writer will win. We will cover the competition on a website and blog created for the event. May the most brilliant writer win!"

"When friends come together after long separation, there is both magic and mystery in the reunion."
--from *They Came from Calais*, by Camilla Graham, 1979.

Sam West frowned at me as I zipped my suitcase. "How long will you be gone, again?"

"Just the weekend. Camilla is super excited; she hasn't seen some of these people for years and years."

"Mm-hmm," he murmured, stroking my hair. "It's gotten so much longer, since I first met you. Long, dark, silky." He pressed a kiss on my temple and tangled both hands in my locks. Then his blue eyes met mine. "Why do you have to go? I can hire a driver to take Camilla."

"Because I'm her writing partner." I narrowed my eyes at him. "Did you think I should just sit in the house and ponder the joys of being your fiancée? Just that, and nothing more, forever?"

"Sort of," he said, and I laughed. I understood his unwillingness to watch me drive away. We had not been apart for even one day since becoming engaged, and we both liked it that way. In addition, Sam's room was warm and cozy, a crackling fire in his hearth helping to blot out the winter gloom and chill. The day was standard January fare, but being inside, with Sam, did in that moment seem more appealing than going outdoors.

I touched his nose. "You know I'll miss you, but it will be good for us. Besides, don't you have some big man adventure planned with Cliff and Doug?"

He shrugged. "I can think of a man adventure I'd rather have, right here in the bed. I would do man things, and you would do woman things, and it would be an adventure."

I giggled as his hands roamed over me. "I don't know if we have time for that kind of adventure, but I can promise you one when I get back on Sunday night."

He sighed. "All right, all right. I know you and Camilla want to have your girl adventure, as well. And this will give me a chance to help Adam with some of the two-man tasks he's been wanting to accomplish around the house." Adam was Camilla's brand new and doting husband.

"Don't let Isabelle hear you calling it a 'girl' adventure," I warned.

"I'm so sorry. I should say your 'womanly excursion'."

"No, definitely don't say that." I smiled at him. "Anyway, you'll be playing in the snow today?"

"Yes, Cliff has finally convinced us to go cross-country skiing with him. We may share some genes, but Cliff has all the explorer DNA. He claims it's fun, though."

I saw the fondness in his face as he talked about his

half-brother, a sibling with whom he had only recently been united. "Even if you just go through the motions, you know you'll have fun with those two. You always do."

He nodded and followed me out of his bedroom (I divided my time between Sam's house and Camilla's) and down to the main floor. "Speak of the devil," I said. Through the front window we saw a car pull up, and Cliff Blake unfolded his tall form from the driver's seat. He crunched purposefully over patches of ice and snow and went to his trunk. He opened it and rummaged around, emerging with some skis and poles. He met my gaze through the window and grinned at me. How much like Sam he looked, I thought with a burst of love for them both.

Cliff came in the house and thrust his equipment at Sam. "I'm just leaving," I said. "You boys have a good time."

"Don't go yet," said Sam with a woebegone expression, clutching the skis like a boy on Christmas who had received the wrong present.

"I think you can live a couple days without your woman, Sam," said Cliff in a superior tone.

I smiled at him. "Isabelle texted me and said she had to push you out the door. She has to work a shift, helping the animals of Blue Lake, but her boyfriend wanted her to stay home with him."

Sam and I looked at Cliff, whose superior look had vanished. "Women lie," he said weakly, and we laughed.

Sam clapped a hand on his shoulder. "The problem

is that we're in love with amazing women. But if you can break away, I guess I can."

I kissed Sam on the cheek and waved at Cliff. "I'll see you both in a couple of days." Sam dumped the skis on his couch and helped me put on my coat. Cliff still wore his padded parka, looking like a big red traffic cone.

"Make sure you're there by noon," Sam said. "It's supposed to snow."

"It's supposed to snow a *lot,"* Cliff added. "They're talking blizzard."

I frowned at him. "Don't get Sam all worried. Camilla and I will be fine. I'm a very safe driver."

Sam did look worried. "I need you intact for a certain event which shall happen on the fourteenth of next month." Sam, ever the romantic, had selected Valentine's Day as the date for our wedding after we'd considered several options. Now the date was imminent, and we were both a blend of excitement and anxiety.

"I will be present at the event, as Camilla would say, with bells on, and no one will be able to stop me." I wound my scarf around my neck and picked up my suitcase. "Because I love you, Sam West."

He followed me out onto the porch. "Lena," he said.

"Hmm?"

"I love you, too. Be careful."

I nodded. "Bye, Sweetheart."

I navigated down his driveway and made my way to the little road that led up the bluff and to Graham House, Camilla's stately Victorian home. She was tucking her bag into the trunk of my car, which sat waiting in front of her porch. Ever attentive, Adam leaned in with her, rearranging her packing and looking generally bereft. What spell had we cast on the men of Blue Lake? I grinned, but felt a touch of chagrin at the thought of Sam in the house behind me. I told myself that coming home would be extra special, and then there would be the wedding to think of . . .

"Lena," Camilla said briskly. "Right on time. Do you have everything you need?"

"Yes, I went through my list, and I'm all set. Are you ready for what Sam is calling our Girl Adventure?"

Camilla looked at me with her amazing violet eyes. "I am indeed. Although poor Adam is feeling quite left out."

Adam tried to look dismissive of this idea and failed. "I'll manage. I have my friends down the road, after all."

When Camilla and I climbed into the car at last, Camilla holding a folder and a bag of treats from her chef, Rhonda, I started the engine and laughed. "Does Rhonda know our journey will last less than an hour?"

Camilla smiled. "You know Rhonda. And I see some breakfast muffins in there. I actually haven't eaten yet. I confess I'm a bit excited."

"I'm sure you are! I don't know who's happier about this event—you or your publicist."

Camilla nodded, digging in the bag for her muffin as I drove down the driveway. She sent a last wave to Adam and then turned to face the road, her expression bright. "Oh, definitely my publicist. You know Gabby. She thrives on things like this. But I am excited, too. It's such a clever idea Sasha had."

"Sasha" was Alexandra Hardwick, a well-known figure for her own career in P.R., but also for being the daughter of Gavin Hardwick, a wealthy entrepreneur who had left his only daughter his fortune. Sasha and Camilla had met because of the former's love of mysteries. She'd gotten involved early on in the planning and running of mystery conferences, and Sasha was, Camilla told me, one of the first people she'd met at a conference in California, a type of event Camilla rarely attended. Camilla had been forty-five and Sasha thirty-three. "We spent time together then, Sasha and David and Gloria and I, and then two years later, at Sasha's next conference, we all met Oliver. We four had great fun together, mainly at conferences." She smiled out the window as we merged onto Green Glass Highway. "Although we did all fly out for Oliver's first wedding. If only he had stayed with Jenny. She was so good for him."

The names Camilla threw around casually were names that I had seen only on the spines of bestsellers: David Canfield, known for his broody police procedurals; Gloria Gale, a master of the locked room mystery; and Oliver Lord, who wrote thrillers. "I will be spending the weekend with actual celebrities," I said, not hiding my awe.

She waved a hand. "They don't see themselves that way." She grinned and added, "Well, maybe David. But if he acts superior, we'll soon sort him out."

"You seem thrilled at the thought."

She nodded, still smiling. "It's just so wonderful, the thought of seeing all these friends again, and not even having to leave Blue Lake. How lucky is that? Especially in this weather."

It was true; Gavin Hardwick had owned a large estate on the outskirts of Blue Lake, called Green Glass Manor. A rather pretentious place, Camilla said, but lovely, and a bona fide tourist attraction. Sasha lived there when she was in town, but she also had places in New York and California.

Camilla pulled out a flyer from her folder. "This is the latest advertisement. Sasha e-mailed it to me this morning."

I glanced over. "Ooh, these are great pictures. You look gorgeous." I looked back at the road, a gray ribbon winding forward under looming snow clouds. "I can't read it—tell me what it says, please."

Camilla read aloud. "A Puzzle for the Greatest Minds in Mystery." She paused. "That's the headline. Then it says, 'Camilla Graham, David Canfield, Gloria Gale and Oliver Lord will gather in a secluded mansion to solve a murder mystery. May the best writer win!"

"And I assume Sasha will have the press swarming all over this?"

Camilla nodded. "Yes and no. She has invited a hand-selected crew of journalists to come and take part in the event. That giant house of hers is full of bedrooms, and I think her goal is to fill them all."

"And she knows I'm coming, right? I'm not going to be an unpleasant surprise?"

She shook her head. "She specifically invited both of us. And I know Oliver travels with an assistant, who is also coming. Not that you are an assistant."

"I know what you mean. There will be other sidekicks of various kinds."

"I think so, yes. Gloria has a personal assistant who travels with her. I think he also happens to be her lover, despite their age difference."

I felt my brows rise. "How large an age difference?"

"I would say, twenty or more years."

"Good for you, Gloria."

"Well, you've seen her. She has always attracted men like a modern siren. And in some cases, she has, in fact, been their destruction."

"Wow. I'm going to get some good gossip at this event, aren't I?"

She adjusted her knit hat. "Undoubtedly."

A thought occurred to me. "So, Green Glass Manor. That must relate somehow to the very road we are driving on."

"Indeed, it does. Gavin Hardwick was a prominent person in Blue Lake, and for a long time he was on the town council. Everyone deferred to him when the new road was built, decades ago, and he made his decision the way he made all his decisions: in deference to his wife. Her name was Selena Hardwick, and he was smitten with her from the moment they met until the day she died. A storybook romance, really. Selena was drawn to the color green, so he proposed with a huge emerald that everyone in town had seen. He filled the house with antique emerald glass lamps and specially made stained-glass windows in varying shades of green. She loved it. So of course, Green Glass Highway was an inevitability."

I shot a quick reproving glance at her. "And how is it that you've never told me this story before?"

Camilla shrugged. "Every story I've told you has come up naturally in conversation. Somehow this one didn't, until now."

Slightly mollified, I turned back to the road. "Look at those clouds. The snow can't be far away."

"No." Camilla's voice sounded concerned. "I do hope we don't have to drive in a blizzard."

"We'll be fine," I assured her. "So—this Green Glass Manor is not even an hour away. Why have we never visited it?"

"I suppose because you and I have been quite busy since you arrived in town. And I thought it would be polite to wait for an invitation from Sasha. She used to invite me now and then, when she and I were both in town. But those meetings became harder to arrange, and we fell out of the habit. Now, here we are, bound for Sasha's house and a grand game."

"Sam told me he heard about this event on the news this morning. Sasha the public relations guru lives up to her reputation."

"Oh, yes. She's always made promotion look effortless and fun. I dislike it, especially now, in the era of social media. Thank goodness my dear publicist handles most of the promotion."

"Mm," I agreed. "Isabelle told me that your event was a trending topic on Twitter yesterday. People were forming alliances: Team David, Team Camilla, Team Gloria, and Team Oliver."

Camilla frowned. "I do hope I held my own in the standings."

"You had the most votes."

Camilla was not a vain person, but the look she gave me after that remark was somewhere between smug and jubilant. "That's good, then."

"I do believe you are competitive, Ms. Camilla Graham Rayburn."

"Certain people bring out my competitive feelings, yes."

"And, am I about to meet those certain people?"

"You are, indeed."

I grinned out the window. "Well, what's a little rivalry between friends? It's not like it will lead to actual murder."

I squinted out the windshield. "I think we're about ten minutes away—maybe more, considering this weather." The snow had begun to fall when we merged onto the highway, just a light fairy dusting of flakes, but now it was coming down in earnest, hindering visibility and barreling out of the sky. The snowflakes were big and fat and spiky, like little, white, weightless Koosh balls.

"There's always a storm, isn't there?" Camilla murmured. "At the beginning of the mystery."

"I suppose so. Or at the climax of one. It was storming the day I met you, remember?"

"Of course, I do, dear. You and the dogs got quite soaked. And right afterward you spied a dead body on the beach."

I shivered at the memory. Back then, I hadn't known

anyone in Blue Lake. Doug had been a stranger, Sam had seemed sinister, Cliff hadn't even been in town. I had only Allison, the friend who had lured me to the idyllic town which had become my home.

"Storms don't have to be sinister," I said with forced brightness. "Let's sing 'Let it Snow.'"

I had never asked Camilla to sing with me, and she darted an amused glance at me before pointing. "That's the turn, Lena. By that giant Cypress tree. You can just make out the branches—"

"I see!" I said, relieved. I wanted to be out of the weather now, despite the beauty of the snowfall.

"We are now in unincorporated Blue Lake. Mostly forest, but a few homes dotted here and there."

"By homes you mean mansions," I said, making the turn and sliding slightly on the slick road.

"Some of them. Certainly, Sasha's place. It will be picturesque in winter, I'm sure."

I drove slowly down a wooded lane, peering into the quiet thunder of flakes, looking for a driveway.

"Sasha said she'd put out a large red welcome sign. Even in the snow we should be able to find that."

"That will be very helpful."

Camilla cleared her throat in a dainty sound. "I should mention that Sasha said there would be television cameras. Though I doubt the news hounds will make it out in this weather."

I bit back a distressed moan. When she had said "journalists," I had been picturing print media. Why television had not dawned on me, I don't know. I didn't love the idea of doing anything in front of a camera. I was scowling slightly when I spied the red sign and turned onto a private drive through stately iron gates.

We drove through a Narnia-like cloud of snow until eventually a very large house came into view: through the snow it looked like a gray and black blob, but eventually it evolved into a charming, elegant, and inviting building.

I parked the car and sat, staring, my mouth slightly open. "It looks like Downton Abbey's little brother."

Camilla giggled. "And we shall be living in it for two days." She patted my arm encouragingly. "Let's escape the snow and have some of Sasha's tea."

"Deal," I said.

Camilla and I were walking toward the main entrance when several dark figures loomed out of the snow and began lurching toward us. A small scream escaped me in an instinctive monster-fearing reflex, but then another scream followed when I realized that they were reporters.

"It's Camilla Graham!" one of them shouted.

Another lunged forward with a microphone, and her cameraman was a step behind. "Camilla, welcome to Green Glass Manor. Are you ready for the Great Mystery Challenge?"

Camilla, looking rather darling in her blue snowsuit with white faux-fur lining, spoke sweetly, looking directly at the camera. "I am very excited to see several old friends, and to reminisce in this beautiful setting."

The reporter persisted. "But do you think you'll win?"

Camilla waved a gloved hand. "I know I'll win, dear. I have a secret weapon, a partner in crime, who stands here beside me. Never underestimate the intellect of Lena London."

They were on me then, reporter and camera. "Lena, you've written with Camilla for more than a year now. What's it like to partner up with one of our greatest mystery writers?"

The answer came before I thought about it. "It's been the greatest honor of my life, and I've found a wonderful friendship, as well."

"And is Camilla right? Will the two of you win this challenge?"

I shook my head. "Camilla doesn't need me to win. She could do it all by herself. I'm on Team Camilla as well, just like all those fans out there. They won't be disappointed."

The reporter was loving this. It wasn't clear how long she'd been waiting in the snow, but her own hood had fallen back, and the snow had settled heavily on her blonde hair. Still, the soundbite was worth it to her, if her expression was any sign.

Still sweetly, Camilla said, "And now we must go in, dear, before we catch a chill."

Camilla, the sturdiest person I knew, was playing the delicate old lady card, and it worked. The reporters stepped backward and we made our way to the grand stairway that led to the main entrance. The stairs had been salted, I was relieved to note, as the pellets crunched under our feet, preventing slips and tumbles.

We reached the massive wood door, in the center of which was a beautiful piece of stained glass in shades of only green. Of course.

I was about to knock when a man appeared out of nowhere, a tall man in a wool coat, dark haired and dark-eyed. He grabbed Camilla around the waist with big blue gloves and hoisted her right into the air. "Submit or Die!"

I stood, dumbfounded, about to scream, but I stopped when laughter bubbled out of Camilla and she cried, "Put me down, you oaf!"

The man set her down, and they grinned at each other. "Oh, David, it's so good to see you!!" she cried, and they shared a giant embrace.

The camera appeared at the foot of the stairs and filmed this personal moment without any apparent reluctance.

I glared at them and purposely moved between Camilla and the camera.

Camilla turned to me. "Lena, this is David. David, this is my lovely Lena."

I shook David's gloved hand and said, "You came out of nowhere."

He grinned wickedly. "I am not to be trusted."

Camilla laughed again. Her face was youthful, too, along with her laughter. She was like a young woman again, reunited with one of her first mystery friends.

"Go in, go in," David said, turning the doorknob to reveal that the door was unlocked. "We can chat inside."

I followed Camilla, walking past David and noting his assessing glance. Camilla had described him, quite fondly, as "rather a wolf."

I peeled off my gloves and scratched my cheekbone with my left hand, displaying my engagement ring like a talisman meant to ward off evil.

David laughed. "That's an impressive ring, Miss London."

It was my turn to smile sweetly. "Given to me by an impressive man."

A red-haired woman appeared, bustling around to take our coats and hang them on a nearby coat stand. We left our boots by the door and turned to the woman, who was quite young and pretty. "Ms. Graham, Ms. London, welcome to Green Glass Manor. Sasha will be down in just a moment. I'm her assistant, Zoe."

"Don't I get a greeting?" David asked with a theatrical pout.

She sent him a chiding look that hid something else. Attraction? A secret? Annoyance? I couldn't tell, but something was sparkling in her eyes. "David, it's always good to see you," she said smoothly.

She turned back to us. "If you'll follow me, Sasha has hot tea ready in the lounge."

She turned and began walking down the hall. Thanks to the green stained glass, the hallway had a greenish tinge, as though we were meeting underwater. Camilla followed Zoe, chatting about types of tea. David gestured broadly with his hand, saying, "After you, Lena."

I nodded and followed Camilla. Suddenly I wondered if I'd left the car keys in my coat, and I spun around to look back at the coat tree. In the process, I caught the expression on David's face, but pretended that

I hadn't. Instead of the jolly, fun-loving expression of the last few minutes, his face bore an almost calculating look.

I turned back and stumbled after Camilla. The car keys could wait. David, in that brief moment, had not been thinking about some lighthearted mystery challenge. He had been harboring some negative emotion, and just a glimpse of it had left me shaken.

I shook my head as I moved down an elegant, polished wood hallway. How silly. Of course, he was thinking about the game. What else were we all here for?

I gave a mental shrug and moved deeper into Green Glass Manor.

Two

"It's hard to win a game when you don't know all the rules."
--from *Sucker's Bet*, by David Canfield, 1999.

No sooner had we been seated, than Sasha Hardwick, all expensive perfume and elegant salon hair, swooped in to hug Camilla, David and me. We were gathered at a long glass table in a lounge with two walls of windows that made it seem we were sitting outside in the snowfall.

"Camilla, it's been too long," she enthused in a sultry voice. "And this is going to be so much fun! David already got the tour, but I can take you around after you check out your room and have a rest."

"But first, tea," Camilla said appreciatively as an aproned woman came in with a large pot, and a male server gave us each a plate with elaborate-looking tea sandwiches.

"Wow," I said. "It's not even eleven o'clock."

Sasha's laugh was sultry, too, and I noted that David's eyes had been on her since she had swooped in.

"David," I said, "Camilla said that you had an assistant?"

He looked at me, slightly distracted, and said, "Yes, Eva. She's not here this weekend. She's working on my manuscript, getting it ready to submit to my agent."

Camilla turned to him, pouring milk from a white China pitcher into her tea. "Oh, what a shame. Eva is always such an interesting conversationalist."

David shrugged. "Yes, well, couldn't be helped. Now I'll turn all my flirting in your direction," he said, admiring Camilla's violet eyes.

"Camilla recently married, did you know?" I asked, trying to keep my tone light.

Camilla and David both laughed. "Don't worry, Lena. David is all talk. Once Gloria gets here, he can flirt with someone who likes and expects it." She said this fondly, and David laughed again.

"You are so right. Where is Gloria, anyway?"

Sasha, finished fussing with place settings, dropped into a chair at the head of the table. "She texted me about five minutes ago. She should be here within the hour. And Oliver has landed safely at O'Hare, but he's got a long ride ahead of him. Even longer than expected, I suppose, in this stuff." She gestured toward the lacy curtain of snow that sheeted down on two sides of us. "It is gorgeous though, isn't it? Normally I'm in California at this time of year, but when I miss the seasons, I come back to the Midwest and just hang out in here, working in the home office."

Sasha's assistant, Zoe, glided in from the hall and

went to Sasha, murmuring something in her ear. Sasha said something back in a low tone, and Zoe turned away.

"Will you be joining us, dear?" Camilla asked.

Zoe grinned and slipped out of the door.

Sasha looked after her with apparent affection. "No, and Zoe's work is never done. She sneaks her meals when she can. But she loves it, the whole PR gig. She tells me so all the time."

"How did you happen to find her?" I asked.

Sasha shrugged. "She applied. I was in New York at the time, and looking for an assistant. Zorana "Zoe" Taylor applied and had great references. That won her an interview, and she aced that, too. She's been invaluable."

David slurped his tea. "No one is paying attention to me," he complained, and Camilla's giggle sounded again. She got a real kick out of this guy. I had to admit, he was kind of funny, in an over-the-top way.

"Mr. Canfield, I've read several of your books. They're very exciting," I offered.

David's dark brows rose. "First of all, it's David. I have no intention of calling you Miss London." He grinned, softening the rude comment. "Second, I encourage you to read them all. Did you start at the beginning of the series?"

"Of course," I said. "I am a linear reader."

"Good. So do you like my hero, Gamble?"

I lifted a little sandwich. I spied cucumbers poking out of one side. "I didn't at first. He grew on me, though, especially when he began to admit to his own flaws. Claudia is a saint to put up with him."

He grinned. "He has bad habits, but he's physically compelling."

I nodded. "But that only lasts so long. I hope I won't find out that he drives her away in some future book."

David studied me with momentary interest. "You, young lady, are a romantic."

"I won't deny it. That's why I love Camilla's books. She may put her characters through some trauma, but she lets them be happy in the end."

David waved a hand in the air. "Happy endings are overrated."

Sasha grinned from her host's seat. "Yes, yes, get out the competitive spirit. You'll need that tomorrow."

"Please don't say we have to hunt one another in the woods," David said, gazing at the snow and belying his words with an eager expression.

"Of course not," Sasha said. "You'll be right here in the house, using your little gray cells, as Poirot taught us. By the way, the TV cameras are limited to the outdoors. They are allowed exterior shots of the house, and footage of each author's arrival, and then they will be asked to skedaddle. I have Mondo out there, and he is no nonsense."

"Mondo?" Camilla and I said together.

"Is that your Doberman?" David asked.

"Sort of," Sasha said, smiling. "He's in charge of my security. Ex-Navy Seal. The guy is a wall of muscle, and he smiles only once a year, on Christmas."

We laughed, and just then a man, I assumed, stalked past the window in a green parka and a Balaclava that made him look like a terrorist. "Ah!" I screamed.

"That's Mondo," Sasha said. "He's harmless. Unless

you try to break in here. I know, because someone did once. Some poor druggie who was just looking for some stuff to steal, I think. I wasn't home at the time, but some of my staff were, including Mondo, who works here all year long. He pressed the silent alarm and then went to confront the intruder. The kid wasn't armed, thank God, and Mondo just barreled in, picked him up by his collar, then bellowed into his face until the poor guy was almost crying. Then he put plastic ties on his wrists and ankles and waited for the cops."

"Very efficient," I said. "Camilla has two German Shepherds and a very protective husband. They have all saved us from some scrapes."

"We all need protection in a violent world," David said, rather solemnly for him. "I spent a fortune on a state-of-the-art security system, and it has paid for itself many times over."

I was about to ask him how often people tried to break into his house when there was a flurry of activity in the front hall. Sasha jumped up and said, "Excuse me for a sec." She jogged out on expensive-looking heels and returned, two minutes later, with Gloria Gale and a man of thirty or so. Gloria was one of those people, Camilla had told me, who really was as glamorous as her book jacket suggested. Now, as the young man helped her off with her white wool coat and she shook snowflakes out of her hair like a model at a winter photo shoot, I saw what she meant.

"Hey, Glor," David said, rising and giving her a hug. She squeezed back enthusiastically.

"Dave, you old Devil, I'm so glad to see you!!" They

grinned into each other's faces, and I admired Gloria's tumbling blonde hair and slender frame. She wore a white knit turtleneck sweater and winter white slacks, accented by a long necklace of silver links and some sort of glinting stones. She turned to the man behind her. "Charlie, you remember David, don't you?"

The young man, his face reddening slightly, leaned forward to shake David's hand.

Gloria spied Camilla and ran around the table with a gleeful expression. "Cammy! My sweet partner in crime!" Camilla stood, and I watched another reunion. I glanced at the man Gloria had called Charlie, and he rolled his eyes good-naturedly. I smiled at him.

Camilla said, "Gloria, I'd like to introduce my dear Lena. She and I are joined at the hip these days. I don't think I could function without her."

I stood and offered my hand, but Gloria Gale, her beautiful face twisted into a faux-scowl, pulled me in for a hug. To give her credit, it was a real hug, warm and maternal and fragrant. She let me go and said, "Oh, you are lovely. To have silky hair like that, I tell you." She fluffed her own generous blonde locks and said, "I get so tired of my hair."

Camilla and David laughed and the latter said, "Like hell you do. You're the vainest person I know."

Gloria looked slightly hurt, and Charlie gave David a cold look. "Gloria doesn't have a vain bone in her body."

Gloria recovered quickly and sent Charlie a megawatt smile. "You're so sweet," she said, and the two of them exchanged a glance that could have melted some of the snow outside.

I shifted my gaze to Camilla, who was studying her friend and the young man with open interest.

Sasha sat back in her chair and said, "Please have a seat, both of you, and we'll get you some tea and sandwiches. How was the journey, Charles?"

Apparently only Gloria called him Charlie. "It was a bit dicey for the last twenty minutes or so. But I'm from the Midwest, and I still remember how to drive in this stuff."

"Oh, yes, my Midwestern Charlie. He's so practical and earthy, with his solid middle-American upbringing. He's just what I need to counter my Delusions of Grandeur." She grinned at this last quote, but Charlie, clearly besotted with her, disagreed.

"They aren't deluded. You live life on a grand scale, and it suits you. You're a glamorous person."

Gloria stroked his cheek and he blushed. Gloria Gale was fifty years old, but she could pass for thirty-eight. Her skin looked young and blooming. Her hair was plentiful and thick, and her figure was shapely and youthful-looking. She didn't look like a person who'd indulged in endless plastic surgery. She was one of those people, Camilla assured me, who simply aged well—and slowly.

Sasha cleared her throat. "So now we wait for Oliver, and then I can explain the whole lovely game. Thank you to all of you for coming out for this adventure."

A figure moved past the door, and Sasha said, "Bob!

Can you come in for a minute?"

A red-haired man walked in, smiling deferentially around at the group.

"This is Bob Preston," Sasha said. "He's going to be taking pictures for my blog, and there will be a couple other photographers later on. I told Bob not to start shooting until all four of you were here. We want to feature the whole group."

We nodded and waved at Bob, and he made his way out again.

To my own surprise, I had finished all of the sandwiches on my plate. They had been delicious. I saw Camilla smother a yawn. "I think we're ready to see our rooms now, Sasha. Maybe rest a bit before the big tour."

"Of course!" Sasha said. "I should have realized you'd all need some down time after that treacherous drive. Come on up, you two, and I'll show you the rooms. David and Gloria, I'll get you next. Just catch up for a while."

We left the room to the sound of Gloria chattering happily about the last time she'd seen David. She made sure to include "Charlie" in the conversation.

Camilla and I followed Sasha up a sweeping staircase, at the top of which was another green glass window, multi-tone and giant. The sun shone through the glass and cast mysterious light on the stairs. On the landing, Sasha turned right and led us down a hallway with a multitude of doors, some of which were open and revealed little lounges and libraries, restrooms and storage spaces. Others were closed, including the two she pointed out to us. "Lena, this is yours. You and Camilla have an adjoining door in case you need to reach each other without having to knock via the hallway. Camilla, here is your room. You'll both find a key inside by the lamp that you can use to lock the door once you settle in. Just keep that with you for the whole weekend, and then leave it on the table when you check out."

She opened my door onto a surprisingly large room with a king-sized bed and a floor-to-ceiling window beside it. The snow pelted down, looking poetic and almost other-worldly. Sasha put an affectionate arm around my shoulder. "There's a mini-fridge over there with various drinks, in case you get thirsty. There are a few bakery snacks in that little kitchenette there. And of course, you have your own obligatory green glass room."

She led me further into the room, and I saw that there was a small hallway near the tall window, and this too was lined with clear glass, but green glass ornaments were everywhere: along the windowsill, hanging down as suncatchers, resting on a small display table in the center of the space. There were glass vases, glass animals, glass crosses and infinity symbols and fleur-de-lis patterns. Even in pale sunlight, the tiny space was like a light show.

"It's magical," I breathed.

"My dad," she said fondly. "Quite the romantic. My mom made the mistake of saying she loved green, and he never stopped giving her green." Her eyes looked bright with tears for a moment, but then she was smiling and turning to Camilla. "Your room has a green skylight, my dear."

"Oh, my," said Camilla, and we walked through the

adjoining door to another immense room. Camilla's bed, like mine, bore an elaborate quilt with squares of blue, green, and white, giving a homey air to an otherwise palatial space. A brown Teddy Bear that looked like an antique sat against Camilla's pillows.

"My brother collected the bears," Sasha said. "They're valuable, I suppose, but we keep them for their sentimental value. I think they're all from Germany."

I turned and met her eyes. "I didn't know you had a brother."

"Once, long ago," Sasha said. "He was killed in a car accident. He was only twenty-three."

"It was hard on Sasha," Camilla said. Now it was she who looked ready to cry.

Sasha gave her a quick hug. "Long ago, as I say. But I do miss him. We were thick as thieves, back in the day, Aaron and I."

Before I could offer my own condolences, Sasha looked at her watch. "Oh boy! I've got stuff to do. I have to find Zoe. If you have everything you need, I have to run for now. But I'll give you the tour in an hour or so. Sound good?"

We agreed that it did, and she moved swiftly out of the room.

I turned to Camilla. "This place is something."

"A rather vague understatement," she said, smiling at me.

"Would you like some resting time? I can busy myself in here. There's a huge bookshelf on one of those closety areas of my room. I can look at books for at least an hour. And I want to text Sam."

She nodded. "Yes, a brief lie-down will be perfect, even if I only watch the snow. And I'll call my husband, too. We are of the telephone generation."

I laughed and gave her a hug. "I would never see places like this if I hadn't met you," I said.

"And if I hadn't met you, I would have little interest in seeing places like this," she said. "Now I like to see things through your eyes."

I squeezed her hand, then said, "I think you're right about Gloria and her Charlie."

"Oh, goodness, yes. "

"And David? Is he married?"

She sighed. "He was, long ago, but like Oliver, he spent too much time on his career and not enough with his wife. I thought he might be planning to marry Eva, but he opted not to bring her, which seems odd."

"Hmm," I said. "Mystery upon mystery. And we'll be distracted by other puzzles tomorrow."

"Yes. Go enjoy your books, Lena, and tell Sam I said hello."

I went back to my room, full of luxury and whimsy, and took photos of it all: the tall windows framing falling snow, the green glass museum, the little kitchen, and the giant bed. Then I texted Sam: *Look at my room.*

Thirty seconds later his response came: Where the heck are you? Narnia?

I laughed. *It feels as alien, I must say.*

That's a giant bed.

Yes. I wish you were here.

Me, too. We gave up on the skiing when it started coming down, and now we are drinking beer and telling lies.

I laughed and typed back. *I love you.*

I love you more.

Doubtful.

Sam sent a picture then, taken surreptitiously, of Doug and Cliff embroiled in some beer-infused argument. They were pointing at each other, obviously in high spirits.

These idiots. Sam wrote.

Don't forget about Adam. He's lonely, too.

He's on his way. He said he's bringing lunch.

Mmmm.

You know what I'm looking forward to?

Lunch? I joked.

Marrying you.

A burst of love and desire went through me.

Me, too. I sent a bride emoji, several heart emojis, and even more kiss emojis.

He sent back a groom, about twenty hearts, and as many kisses.

Always trying to out-do me., I typed with a smile.

I never could.

I have to go. But I'll text in a couple of hours. You'll be around?

Not going anywhere in this maelstrom. I'll be snug at home. Waiting for you.

We said our goodbyes, and I set down my phone, grinning stupidly. I wandered over to the tall built-in bookshelf that sat in another alcove, and I began perusing spines. For me, if I couldn't be with Sam or Camilla, there was no better way to spend the time.

Oliver Lord arrived in the afternoon in a blast of snow and personal magnetism. I had always admired Lord on his book jackets: his tall, lean form, his square jaw, his nearly bald head which somehow accentuated his masculinity.

He swept into Sasha's foyer, his arm around his rather shaken driver, a middle-aged woman in a ski suit and a pink pom-pom hat. "This is Carla," Oliver said. "She's had a rough go of it, getting me here, and I assured her she's not going anywhere else tonight, right, Sasha?"

Sasha glided forward and took control of the stunned woman, murmuring about a glass of whiskey and a hot bath and her own room for as long as she needed it. "Zoe?" Sasha said, and her assistant appeared to escort the woman to the kitchen for some warming fluids, and on, I supposed, to the promised room.

Oliver grinned at all of us, studying each of our faces in turn, and I was struck by the power of his charisma. He had a friendly smile, but his gray eyes held one's attention, warm and searching as they were. When those eyes rested on me, my pulse fluttered slightly and my stomach felt weak. Suddenly I missed Sam.

Camilla grinned at me as she moved forward to greet Lord.

"Ollie, it's been such a long time," she said, hugging him.

"And you're still gorgeous, my girl with the amethyst eyes." He kissed Camilla's hair and hugged her back with obvious affection. "How are things in the Heartland?"

Camilla stepped away, but held on to his elbows as she studied him. "It's charming. You should come to visit."

"Don't think I won't, my pretty. There's a conference in Chicago in six months, and I might just stay with you on the way back."

"That would be wonderful! Make sure you do."

Sasha took Oliver's coat and said, "Dinner is at six. After that, we learn the rules of the game. Before that, my friend Bob is going to take some awesome photos so that we can publicize the hell out of this."

"That's our Sasha," Oliver said. "Can I see my room?"

"I'll take you there now." She turned to us. "Camilla, Lena, don't go far. Pictures in half an hour."

There were so many pictures that we could have been mistaken for a wedding party. First Bob and the local press posed the four famous writers: walking up the stairs, filmed from the back, four abreast; walking down the stairs, smiling, four abreast; standing in Sasha's giant library, holding magnifying glasses; wearing trench coats and looking mysterious, the women and men standing in back-to-back pairings; bundled up and walking down a forest path in heavy snowfall. All of the pictures would be amazing, I knew, but I thought the one in the snow would be the best. It looked the most mysterious because of the dark outlines of the trees and the limited visibility of the path.

We sidekicks were photographed, too—Charles with Gloria, I with Camilla. Bob the P.R. guy tended to have the creative ideas, and the other photographers snapped away, pleased with his poses.

Camilla and I were posed at an antique typewriter, Camilla sitting in front and I standing beside her, leaning against the desk. Her hands were on the keyboard, but she was looking up at me, and I was chatting with her about wedding plans, trying to forget about the cameras.

After that, we were posed in the kitchen because Bob foresaw a headline that said, "These Two Are Cooking Up Something New," or something like that. Camilla and I were given aprons, each of which bore a skull and cross bones (Sasha had thought of everything) and posed in front of a giant mixing bowl. Finally, Camilla was seated in a giant red armchair that resembled a throne, and I sat on a pretty ottoman in front of her. Bob said this was for an "at the foot of the master" sort of picture.

When we finished the monotonous photo session, Camilla and I returned to our rooms to freshen up and dress for dinner. I sent a quick love note to Sam from the privacy of my room, along with a photo of the bear in my room. Like Camilla's bear, it was an antique, with faded fur and hand-stitched paws. After that I wrote "I can't bear to be without you."

Same sent back a photo of his cats, Geronimo and Arabella, sitting in front of the heat vent in his kitchen and looking smug. "All three of us miss you."

I sent a heart and several kisses, then put down my phone and went through my bag. I hadn't known what to pack, but Camilla had advised a couple of formal looking things, considering the glamour of the place we were to visit. I didn't have too many fancy clothes, but I had splurged on an outfit at a store in Blue Lake the previous year. I had thought I'd be dining with my father, but I was actually attending my own surprise birthday party. I realized in a burst of memory that the proprietor, too, had been named Sasha. That dress hung on a hanger in the generous closet, as did another dress I had bought at Sasha's—the same Blue Lake store. This second dress was black with emerald green edging along the collar, cuffs, and hem. Camilla had lent me one of her brooches— "In honor of the house," she'd said, before handing me an elegant emerald brooch—and I pondered both choices now. The first was brown and gold, and had a regal look. The second was elegant and, in a practical sense, much warmer than the first. I decided to pay tribute to Mr. Hardwick and his beloved wife. I slipped into the black and green sheath, along with some black tights and shoes. I pinned on the emerald brooch and put some tiny gold earrings in my ears. After brushing my hair, I stepped back to survey the result: it looked nice, understated yet impressive. I had no wish to show up the glamorous Gloria or the effortlessly attractive Camilla. This was their event, their special time, and I was happy to be a bit player.

I knocked on the adjoining door. "Come in," Camilla called. I entered to find her in a violet cashmere creation. The color accented her bright white hair, and her eyes seemed to glow.

"You look perfect," I said.

"As do you, my dear. Let's go have fun with my friends."

We headed for the kitchen, already feeling more familiar with the house, and found our way to the dining room, where little cardstock nameplates alerted us to the seating plan. I was placed between Gloria and Oliver, while Gloria's besotted companion, Charles, sat between Camilla and David. Sasha, once again, sat at the head of the table, and Zoe sat opposite her at the other end. The press had gone, Sasha informed us over a salad course served by a young woman we had not seen before, and we would have the place to ourselves.

"What became of Oliver's driver?" Camilla asked. I had forgotten about the woman, but nothing got past Camilla.

Sasha grinned. "She was chatting with Mondo and Bob, and the three of them wandered down to the basement bar. We have a lovely bar down there, and Mondo makes a mean drink. We also have a bowling alley, and I think Mondo talked her into a game. He's a terrible flirt, Mondo is."

I watched Camilla, who processed this information with a slight smile. I wondered if she thought that we were already getting clues for the next day's mystery. Perhaps we were, though I had not considered it until now.

David said something to Charlie and Camilla, and they turned their attention to him. The young woman came and took my salad. Moments later, she was back with a bowl of soup, a delicious pea and scallion puree that I probably ate too quickly. When I looked up from my feasting, I saw Oliver looking at me with a gleam in his eye.

"I like a girl who enjoys her food," he said affably.

I laughed. "I can't deny it. I enjoy eating. I'm getting a bit too close to thirty to be called a girl, though." I said it lightly, but gave him a reproving glance.

"Sorry. Old habits. I even call my mom a girl, and my sisters. It's not a sexist thing, just what we grew up calling each other."

"They call you a boy?"

"Absolutely." He grinned, and once again I reacted physically to his charisma: my stomach grew ticklish, and I felt slightly dizzy. Someone came to take my soup bowl, and I realized it was a different girl, but she looked very much like the first one.

Oliver saw me looking. "I already asked. They are sisters, and they live down the lane. They were able to hike over in their snow boots, and intend to do the same going home." He smiled at the girl with the soup bowl, and she froze in place, smiling shyly back at him and apparently forgetting the rest of the world. "You're Linda, right? And your sister is Laura."

She nodded, amazed. "People never get us right!" she cried.

"Mystery writers have to be observant. Isn't that right, friends?"

David smirked. "That's why we're all here. To observe, and to dig up secrets. And some of us have already started exhuming secrets." He winked at Camilla, as though they were in cahoots. The P.R. man, Bob, and the limo driver had appeared in the kitchen; apparently, they had been told that dinner was ready. The driver looked less cold now, but her straw-colored hair was still smashed down from her winter hat. She and Bob peeked in from the kitchen doorway, and David winked at her, too. Lord, these men and their need to prove their virility. I noticed that David glanced briefly at Oliver, perhaps to gauge his reaction to David's amazing way with women.

Gloria said, "Sasha, how about if you fill us in on the plan?"

Sasha shook her head, grinning. "No way. Dinner is for socializing. Then we'll get down to business." She paused, glancing around the table. "But that doesn't mean you can't start observing now."

This was a dangling carrot that did not sit well with me, given my level of curiosity about the whole event. I met Camilla's eyes and saw that she felt the same way. I had also seen, though, that Camilla was observing, and had been since we arrived. Even as she smiled, laughed, and listened to her friends sharing their memories, her eyes would drift to a person at the other end of the table, or to an object on the sideboard, or to a painting on the wall. Others might not notice that she was doing it; I only did because I was trying to follow her lead, and to be at her side when the mystery was solved.

My eyes went back to Oliver, serenely buttering a roll at my side. He looked up to see me watching him, and my face warmed slightly. "I'm guessing you were an only child," he said, surprising and disorienting me.

"I—why do you think that?"

He studied me for a long moment. "I'm not entirely sure, but I thought it the instant I saw you: only child. You have an aura of loneliness about you, for one thing. And a desire to please people."

I found this vaguely insulting. "I am an only child, so you win the stuffed animal. But I can't say that I'm lonely, or that I really want to please anyone besides Camilla."

"Hmm," he said, with a smile that could only be described as sexy.

"And you?" I asked, feeling bold. "Are you an only child?"

He set down his knife and took a bite of his roll, swallowed appreciatively, then said, "Not at all. I am one of five, and the eldest."

"Ohhh," I said. "That explains a lot." And it did—the air of authority, the confidence, the lack of shyness around others.

He laughed. "You have me figured out, huh?"

"Only as much as you have me."

He raised his glass in my direction, then took a sip of red wine that shone in the light of the chandelier with the allure of rubies.

For one instant, a millisecond, I had a strong presentiment of undefinable menace. Oliver's wine made me think of blood, and nauseated me; the faces around the table looked sinister and conspiratorial, and when Laura or Linda set down my main course, I felt a burst of real terror that it had been poisoned. Then, as though I had wakened from a nightmare, everything became innocuous again: Gloria, in a beautiful blue dress, was making eyes at her "Charlie"; Zoe was surreptitiously checking her phone and then exchanging inscrutable glances with Sasha; David was watching Zoe, with the eyes of a detective or a predator; Oliver, still serene, took a bite of his salmon and winked at Camilla, as David had done minutes earlier. Who winked anymore? I studied Oliver, wondering suddenly at his intentions. Were he and David condescending to Camilla with their ridiculous winking? Or were they trying to ally themselves to her? Surely, they couldn't be underestimating her after knowing her for all these years. If they were, they had a surprise coming.

A man entered; it took me a minute to figure out that this was Mondo, no longer in his terrorist-in-a-movie attire, but in a pair of jeans and a button-down shirt in an interesting shade of green. He went straight to Sasha and bent to say something in her ear. Her skin grew pink as he murmured, his lips almost touching her skin. His hand was touching hers, as well, and for the first time I saw Sasha Hardwick in a less-than-authoritative position.

So, I thought. Sasha and Mondo, sitting in a tree . . . I shifted my gaze to Camilla, who had seen it, too, and told me so with her eyes.

Sasha nodded when Mondo finished speaking, and then she said, "For those of you who haven't met him, this is Albert Mondragan, our chief of security. Around here he's known as Mondo."

Mondo acknowledged the faces around the table with a friendly but unsmiling demeanor. I realized that he, too, was quite attractive, and around Sasha's age.

Oliver pointed with his fork. "Why do you need a head of security?"

Sasha sighed. "Good question. This isn't a castle, and there are plenty of other expensive houses on this street. But we've had enough incidents, going back to when my dad and mom were living here, that it became necessary to have a protective presence." She smiled at Mondo, and for her he summoned a return smile that made him less a mysterious former Seal and more a regular guy.

I turned back to the table to find David and Oliver frowning at one another as though they had jointly received bad news. I had the surreal sensation that I had lost track of what was reality and what was a part of the mystery game. It was an unpleasant feeling, and it lingered through the meal and into dessert. The sisters had served a rich chocolate mousse that briefly cheered me and made me miss Allison, my BFF in Blue Lake who shared my passion for chocolate. Camilla shared it, too, and we sent each other a secret glance of appreciation.

Eventually Zoe stood up. "Hi, everyone. For any of you that haven't met me officially, I'm Zoe Taylor, and I'm Sasha's P.A. Sasha has worked really hard on this event, and it's been a labor of love for her author friends, since the goal is to get them some good promotion." We all clapped for Sasha, and she nodded.

Zoe continued, tucking a strand of blonde hair behind her ear. "When you've finished dessert, we'll ask you to gather in the drawing room so that we can lay out the rules for this event." Zoe seemed to be enjoying her moment of authority; I imagined it was a lot of work being Sasha's assistant, but it was most likely exciting, and often glamorous. I noticed that Zoe's hair was highlighted in a way similar to Sasha's. Surely there was some hero worship involved in the equation—similar, I realized, to the relationship of Camilla and me. "So, enjoy your dessert, and we'll see you in the drawing room in twenty minutes."

Zoe left the room, as did Sasha, with Mondo at her side. Had Mondo been involved in the planning, I wondered?

I finished my mousse in a leisurely fashion, then found my way to Camilla's side as people began to migrate to the gathering place for more information. I noticed that Bob, the photographer, had re-appeared to take some pictures of the game's beginning.

As a group of us shuffled through the doorway to the drawing room, a voice in my ear said, "May the best woman win."

I turned, surprised, to see that it was Charles, looking smug and confident. He seemed to be implying that the contest was really only between Camilla and Gloria. I grinned at him, nodding. "Absolutely," I agreed.

And then I turned back to follow the group into the room where we would learn about a murder.

Three

"There is something sinister about snow."
--from *Fear of Freezing,* by Gloria Gale, 1994.

One window in the room had no curtains, only a wide wooden casement, and we could see that the snow still fell in the velvety dark. A strong wind had entered the equation, and the snowflakes were falling at a diagonal in a dizzying effect. The wind howled audibly and regularly, as though an army of angry ghosts shouted their misery from the surrounding woods.

"Perfect weather for a mystery," Gloria said. "Especially the kind I write."

David nodded. "You and Agatha Christie both! The perfect locked room scenario."

Sasha looked pleased. "I couldn't have asked for better cooperation from Nature. So, everyone have a seat and we'll begin."

I followed Camilla to a long couch, but the seats beside her were quickly claimed by Oliver and David, so I sat on a loveseat with Gloria and Charlie. Mondo stood against one wall, and Zoe stood at Sasha's side.

Bob the photographer was already snapping away.

"As you know," Sasha said, "this is meant to be a challenge for the greatest mystery minds. When you wake tomorrow, you will descend to find a crime scene somewhere in this house. It will be up to you to find it, identify the victim, preserve the scene, and solve the mystery. Once you think you have solved it, you will find me and present your evidence. If you are correct, I'll tell the others that you have won. If you are incorrect, I'll send you back to continue playing. Any questions, before I go on?"

David sat back and folded his arms. "Let's say you've told us we are wrong in our theory. Will you identify which elements are correct and which are not?"

Sasha shook her head. "Nope. You have to go back not knowing where you went wrong, just like your detectives have to do when a theory doesn't pan out."

David nodded, acknowledging the fairness of this.

Sasha went on, "You can begin to gather clues before the crime occurs. There are some to be found, but I realize that is rather nebulous information. When you all go off to bed, I'll ask you to remain in your rooms until at least eight tomorrow morning, but you don't have to lock down until midnight."

A moment passed while people rumbled in conversation about this. Zoe said, "You are not allowed to work in teams, but only as individuals. However, that only applies to the four mystery writers. If, say, Lena or Charles or Mondo wanted to compare notes, that would be fine."

"So, you're saying that someone other than the four mystery writers could solve the crime?" Oliver asked, winking at me.

Sasha shrugged. "I suppose that's conceivable. But my money's on the four. You guys have thought about crimes for far too long not to be able to solve one."

I thought she was probably right, and nodded my agreement.

Camilla, tucked snugly between the two men, set us straight. "I have a question." Everyone went silent. Camilla was able to command a room that way, despite the softness of her voice, and the gentleness of her slight British accent. We all looked at her.

"I wonder," Camilla said, "If we have been made privy to all of the suspects?"

Sasha's brows shot up. "What do you mean, Camilla?"

"Who made our dinner? Who served it? Are there other employees in this house, moving silently in the background? As you know, these people are often the perpetrators in our fictional worlds. They are effectively invisible."

Everyone was impressed by Camilla's questions, as attested by the nods and murmurs.

Sasha smiled affectionately at Camilla. "My brilliant friend, you make an excellent point. But for our purposes, the only suspects are in the room with us now. I do have a cleaning crew, and a chef, and some girls who helped with the serving. They are either going home or staying in some apartments in the basement. The lower floor is off limits for our purposes. Please do not disturb the staff."

Zoe stepped forward, looking important. "The only places you will look for clues are this floor and the upper floor, with the exception of occupied guest bedrooms. Those are also off limits." She was wearing a very short skirt, and she tugged it down every few moments. Her pretty face was flushed, perhaps with the excitement of her authority, and her blonde hair sat in a perfect bell around her shoulders. "As Sasha told you, the rule is that you must stay in your rooms between midnight and eight A.M. To enforce this rule, we have set up cameras in the hallway, and Sasha and I will receive a notification if anyone emerges before then."

"You've thought of everything," said Oliver with a strange smile, his eyes on Sasha.

"We hope so." Sasha looked around the room, and I sensed a tension in the air. A scan of the faces around me showed nothing out of the ordinary, but there was something in the room, something disturbing that made my heart beat a bit faster.

Zoe spoke again, smoothing her perfect hair. "Are there any other questions?"

Gloria looked thoughtful as she raised her hand. "Just hypothetically, what if one of us had to leave our room?"

Sasha observed her with interest. "Why would you need to? Everyone has an in-suite bathroom and a mini kitchen stocked with the basics. What other reason might there be?"

Gloria shrugged. "Emergency of some kind, I guess. Appendicitis, fire in the room, poisoned gas blown under the door …."

Everyone laughed, including Gloria, and Charlie gave her a spontaneous hug. I noticed, though, that she looked briefly troubled, as though her question had been prompted by a genuine concern.

Bob darted forward from his shadowy corner. "If everyone's ready to go, I'll just take a few photos. This first one will be captioned 'Challenge Issued.'" He took a few shots of the four writers exchanging one big handshake. Then he had Camilla and Gloria tucked against one another, folding their arms and keeping their backs to the men in the same pose—a visual gender challenge. When he was finished, he said, "The initial shots are already on Sasha's website, as well as Twitter, Facebook, Instagram, basically all social media. And the posts are getting a *lot* of attention," he said.

Once we got upstairs, I intended to check out the posts at length, and to alert Sam to the fact that he could be following our progress by watching it online. Thinking of Sam made me want him at my side. I wondered if I could wander away, leaving the writers to their detection while I chatted with my fiancé on my bed.

Camilla appeared before me, smiling. Despite all the reunions with friends and the attention she was receiving, she was wearing her same old practical expression. "I have an extra little notebook," she said, handing it to me along with a tiny pen. "Apparently we can't work together, but I am confident we'll reach the same conclusions."

I took this as a giant compliment. "So—are you starting now? Just wandering around and jotting notes?"

She looked surprised. "My dear, I began the moment we entered the house. I don't know what the crime will be, but I do know stage setting when I see it."

My heart sank. I hadn't seen a single thing that looked amiss. Or had I? I would have to think back over everything that had transpired and use my little notebook that way. "I think I'll go up to the room for a while," I said. "Make some preliminary notes."

She nodded, her eyes watchful, as she scanned the people in the room. "That's fine. Adam told me that the men have started a Lonely Hearts' Club."

I sniffed. "Doug and Cliff aren't lonely. Belinda and Isabelle are right there with them."

"Apparently Belinda is at a library convention, and Isabelle has to work a double shift."

"They're all professional men. They have jobs to keep them busy."

Camilla smiled. "They are fools for love."

I started to respond, but Mondo loomed up, looking intimidating. "May I offer you an after-dinner drink?"

I shook my head, as did Camilla. "We have to stay sharp, Mr. Mondragan. But thank you for offering." He bowed his dark head in a nod.

"Smart choice. Happy hunting."

"Mondo," I said. He turned his attention to me. His eyes were a deep brown. "Have you heard any sort of weather forecast?"

His face turned grim. "Snow throughout the night,

tapering off by morning, but then a high chance of more snow tomorrow."

"Ugh." I wanted to be able to return to Sam on Sunday. The thought of postponing our reunion was not appealing to me. "Well, thanks. Let's hope this area is spared the heaviest of it."

He scratched his left shoulder with his right hand in what seemed an unconscious gesture. "This part of Indiana doesn't get spared much when it comes to snow."

I knew this, having lived in Blue Lake for more than a year. I thanked him again, and he moved away. I met Camilla's wise gaze. She knew what I was thinking—she always knew. "I'm sure the roads will be plowed well by Sunday," she assured me, touching my hand.

"I suppose." I summoned up some excitement. "Well, you should be on your way, Hercule Poirot. I don't want Sasha to accuse you of conspiring."

She sniffed. "I am surely more of a Miss Marple. And Sasha knows I don't conspire." But she had her notebook out, and she looked ready to hare off in search of clues.

"I'm going upstairs. I'll meet up with you later," I said, giving her a half-hug. "Happy sleuthing."

Camilla opened her notebook and turned some pages. There was plenteous writing in it already, and the sight made me suddenly heady, as though I'd drunk Mondo's postprandial offering: Camilla was going to win. I waved her off; she slipped quietly down a hallway, and I climbed the stairs in quest of Sam.

I didn't expend much energy looking for clues. This was

Camilla's challenge, after all, and I was merely here to support her. I lounged on the bed for a while, perusing Bob's posts on social media. The contest was indeed getting a lot of attention, with thousands of comments from fans of one or more of the writers. A visit to Amazon told me that sales were climbing for all four of them. Well, well. Sasha truly was a public relations genius.

The pictures were all fabulous, but my favorite, aside from the ones of Camilla and me together, was the one in which the four writers walked into the snowy landscape. The shot was moody, mysterious, almost frightening, yet it suggested a bond between them, a "team of rivals" aura that said they would conquer this together. Whatever "this" was. I set aside the computer and contemplated the ceiling. What would the crime be? It would have to be fairly impressive, something worthy of the notables that she had lured to Indiana from places far and wide. I assumed it would be a murder, but how did one collect clues from a fake murder?

I sighed and picked up my phone. I had sent a picture of our dinner table to Sam, and he had sent back a picture of the spot I usually occupied on his couch, now filled by his cats, Geronimo and Arabella. Geronimo, once a tiny kitten that Sam had rescued, was now a giant marmalade-colored beast, and Arabella his daintier, smaller sister. Sam had written, "Not an effective replacement for my usual evening companion."

I sent back a heart emoji. "This event is all over social media. You can see pictures of it all. I'm even in some of them." I sent him some links, suggesting that he check them out later.

"I have my own favorite pictures of you," he wrote, with a wink.

I sent him a picture of my left hand, engagement ring winking in the bedroom light.

He sent one of a black bow tie, something I hadn't seen. The image had the surprising impact of filling my eyes with tears. Our wedding was really going to happen, at long last.

"I'm excited," I wrote. "And I'm ready."

"Feel like eloping in the snow?"

I laughed. "Feel like risking murder at the hands of Allison and Tabitha?" My best friend and step-mother, respectively, had been instrumental in the planning, and had labored more than was necessary to make our wedding dream a reality.

There was no response, but a moment later my phone rang. "Sam?"

"What are you wearing?" he joked, and I giggled. "What are you doing now?" he asked.

"I'm just relaxing on my bed. This is really a gig for the four famous people. I've kind of lost interest because they made a rule that the writers can't collaborate. So much for Camilla and me as the dream team."

"That's a shame. But you can be on my dream team. You're already in my dreams, you know."

"Yes, I know."

"No, really. Last night I dreamt you were on a train, and I was trying to run up the aisle toward you. It was one of those old-fashioned trains, like the kind in the movies. I couldn't get to you because there were too many people in the aisle, and then you disappeared. I looked out the window and saw that you'd jumped off and were running into a forest."

"Wow. Super-Lena."

"Yeah. And I pushed past the people and jumped after you. It was terrifying-I just leaped into space and it wasn't clear where or how or when I would land. Then I was running after you into the forest, but the path kept narrowing, and then it finally ended. I was in a copse of trees, and you were nowhere in sight."

"And that's how it *ended*?"

"Sort of. But then later, in another scene—do dreams have scenes? — I walked past a sort of farmhouse, with peeling paint and no glass in the windows. I looked in and you were there, at a kitchen table, drinking a cup of coffee and crying."

"Sam! All this because I went away for the weekend?"

He laughed. "It was sad, though. I talked to you through the window. I said, "Lena, come with me now. I've been looking for you." He paused, remembering. "And you cried and said that you couldn't come with me. You pointed down, and I saw that your legs were in chains. Really big chains, heavy ones, and we both knew that there was no getting you out of those in time."

"In time for what?"

"I don't know. I woke up. It was a disturbing dream."

"I'll say! Well, I'll have you know that I am not a prisoner, and I fully intend to come back to you, although not via train. I am worried about the snow, though. The forecast is dire, and I'm afraid they won't plow enough."

"If need be, I'll come and get you."

I cuddled against the pillows, picking up the Teddy Bear with one hand. "I love you, Sam West."

He was quiet for a moment. "You saved my life, Lena London."

I set down the bear and wiped at my eyes. "How about if we just agree that after this, neither of us will go away, ever again?"

"That sounds like a good policy. We'll write it into our vows."

A tap sounded on my door. "Oh, someone's knocking. I have to go, Sam, but I'll text you later. I love you."

"Be safe," he said, and we ended the call.

I set down the phone, wondering at his use of the word "safe," and I opened the door to find no one there. On the carpet at my feet lay a piece of folded paper, which I picked up and took back into the room. I unfolded it and read, "Don't trust Oliver Lord. He's not what he seems."

I stiffened, then relaxed. Apparently, some of the "clues" were being hand-delivered. I tossed the note on a side table and went back to the bed, tucking the bear back in place against the pillows. I was restless, vaguely troubled, perhaps because of the forecast, or Sam's odd dream, or the note. I focused on the bear, lost in thought, and recalled Sasha's poor brother, the collector of the antique bears. It seemed odd, in a way, for an adult to collect bears, but then again, Sasha had said they were valuable.

Suddenly curious, I found my laptop and searched for the name "Aaron Hardwick."

Several links appeared, one of which was his obituary. It read:

> *Aaron Ellis Hardwick, 23, passed away on February 21, 1992. He is mourned by his loving parents, Selena and Gavin Hardwick of Blue Lake, Indiana, and by his devoted sister Sasha, 25, also of Blue Lake.*
>
> *Aaron Hardwick was a graduate of St. Thomas High School and Columbia University, New York. He was the founder of the "Fine Minds" appeal, a crowdfunding effort which raised money for worthy students to pay their college tuition. Hardwick helped to raise more than one hundred thousand dollars toward this effort.*
>
> *A fine businessman and a budding entrepreneur, Hardwick was in the process of starting his own company, called The Sustainable Life, which sold products meant to be sustainable over a long period of time. Hardwick was concerned about America's growing garbage and recycling problem, and suggested that not enough was being done to address the mountainous landfills that spoke of waste and a lack of creative thinking.*
>
> *The Hardwick family asks that in lieu of*

> *flowers, mourners donate to the Fine Minds Initiative at Columbia University.*

I thought about this. What a fine person Aaron Hardwick had been. Smart, wise, future-focused. Despite his own advantageous circumstances, he was moved to think about others. What a terrible loss for Sasha and her family.

If Hardwick had died recently, I would have been tempted to search his social media for more context, but of course he died before social media was really a thing. No Twitter, Facebook, Instagram in 1992. I doubted that many people even had a home computer.

I closed the link, and saw another that said, "Hardwick lawsuit." I clicked it, and read another story, dated 2006.

> *Blue Lake notable Gavin Hardwick was in court today, testifying in a lawsuit involving his late son, Aaron. The trial was closed, and the judge has declared that the transcript will not become public. When asked for comment outside the courthouse, Hardwick said, "I miss my son every day, and it saddens me that there are people out there who would sully his memory in an attempt to lay hands on his inheritance. The judge agrees with me, and that is all I have to say on the matter." The judge has put a gag order on all parties involved.*

"Well, that's a non-story," I said. Clearly, it had been written to evoke speculation, and I was indeed speculating. In what way might someone have tried to "sully" Hardwick's reputation? Did it have to do with his fundraising? His business? His family?

I went to the window and peered out at the snow. The wind had died down, but I saw its handiwork in giant drifts that climbed the garage walls and a brick fence that separated the manor from the woods. The landscaping lights were covered in snow, but still shining, throwing a misty, surreal brightness into the snowfall.

I heard Sam's voice in my head, saying, "You saved my life, Lena London."

I drew a heart in the condensation on the window.

It was eleven o'clock when I heard Camilla return to her room. I knocked at the door, and she answered, still looking surprisingly alert. Did the woman never tire?

"Did you need anything from me, Camilla? I'm going to turn in soon."

"No, dear. You relax in that pretty room."

"Have you solved it yet?" I joked.

She smiled. "Since we don't know what "it" is, I can't comment. But I do have some intriguing notes."

"And did you also get a note on your threshold? I think some elf has been delivering clues."

She raised her eyebrows. "What do you mean?"

I went back to my room and retrieved the note, which I handed to Camilla. She read it, but didn't smile. "And this was outside your door?"

"Yes. Someone knocked, and I went to the door. No one was there, but this note was lying in front of it."

"Hmm," she said, her brows furrowed. "Come with me."

Surprised, I followed her as she marched down the hall to the last door on the right. She knocked, and the door was opened a moment later by Oliver himself. His charisma still emanated from him like a glimmering cloud, and he sent me the obligatory wink, to which I was becoming immune.

"Ollie," Camilla said crisply, "Have you been toying with my young friend here?" She held up the note, and Oliver laughed.

"You caught me. How did you know?"

Camilla practically rolled her eyes. "I recognized your handwriting, Oliver."

He smiled again, pulling her into a hug. I realized that he was a bit inebriated. Camilla was going to wipe the floor with these simpletons, I thought with sudden disdain. "Oh, Cammy, I've missed you so."

"I thought maybe it was Zoe who wrote the note," I said.

Oliver looked at me, his smile weakening. "Who? Why?"

"I thought maybe you'd had an affair. Maybe she wanted some revenge."

Oliver Lord straightened and studied me, then laughed. "Oh, God, there are two of you. And please don't spread that around. It was a one-time thing."

Camilla was still frowning, and he held up a hand. "I know, she's my daughter's age. That's why I put an end to it. You won't believe me, Cammy, but some of these young women can be very determined about seduction. I wouldn't have made a pass at all, but she—persuaded me."

"When was this?" Camilla asked.

He shrugged. "A year ago. At a conference. It was a brief diversion, and then it was over. We were both unattached, both adults."

"Yes, well, that's your business," Camilla said, relenting. "As long as you don't intend to prey on any young women this weekend." They both looked at me, as though I were a lamb cavorting in the fields.

I laughed. "I think I'm safe, Camilla."

Oliver feigned a wounded expression and pretended to have an arrow in his heart.

"I'll say goodnight, then," I said, and I walked back toward my room, leaving them to discuss Oliver's boyish prank. I was suddenly exhausted, and not in the mood for what had excited me earlier.

I got to my door and glanced back to the end of the hall, where Camilla and Oliver Lord were still speaking in low tones. In the dim light, they looked almost conspiratorial. But this was Camilla, after all, which meant it was my mood that was coloring things in a sinister light.

Back in my room, I felt a wave of loneliness. My phone buzzed in my pocket—a text. I swiped the screen to see that Adam had sent me a text. Surprised, I clicked on it and saw only a picture of my own dear cat, Lestrade, lying luxuriously on the living room windowsill and watching the snow. He looked fuzzy and funny and utterly perfect. I texted back, *"Thanks, Adam! I was in need of a Lestrade pick-me-up, and this was perfect. See you soon! I know your wife is going to win.* 😊 "

For twenty minutes, I puttered around my room, then donned pajamas and brushed my teeth. I briefly opened my laptop to send an e-mail to Camilla's publicist (I had promised her updates). I was about to close it when I saw that I had two e-mails, one of which was marked urgent. I clicked on it. The sender, apparently, was me. This made me think it was one of those spam things that use your own e-mail to get your attention. I was about to dump it into the trash when I saw a word in the preview window: Camilla.

I hesitated, then clicked on the e-mail, which was quite short:

You are a good friend to Camilla, but you don't know what you're getting into. Call yourself a car and leave now.

I stared at this for a full minute. Was it supposed to be a warning? The way Oliver's note had been a warning? My lip curled, and I clicked out of the e-mail. The other one was from my bank. They were all excited about interest rates, but I was not. I closed the laptop, set it on the side table, turned off the light, and snuggled into the very comfortable bed. The Hardwicks, I had noticed, did not spare any expense on being good hosts. Although "the Hardwicks" translated now to just Sasha, I assumed her parents, and even her brother, had made a lot of design choices.

I lay on my pillow, looking at the ceiling. I had fallen into that ironic trap of being exhausted, climbing into bed, and then finding myself wide awake. I pondered life in Green Glass Manor. How different life was for people who had money. And how little rich people knew about the struggles of those who did not. I thought back to my own struggling student days, before I met Camilla—too proud to borrow from my father, but too poor to sustain a writing career—and recalled some of the lean times. I had struggled, but I hadn't been without friends or resources. I wondered about people who had nothing, and no one. I wondered about children who grew up hungry. What would they make of the meals I had eaten today?

"Oh, God," I murmured, wishing that I could talk to Sam, or one of the cats, or even one of Camilla's dogs. When I slept at her house, they occasionally wandered into my room to check on me. I left my door open a crack so that they could do just that, and I listened for the click-click of their nails on the wood floor of the hallway as a part of my Graham House experience.

But I had no Sam to kiss, or cats to confide in, or dogs to tuck me in. I was unusually melancholy and depressing myself with thoughts of hypothetical suffering. What was wrong with me?

I sighed and closed my eyes, and sleep arrived so suddenly that I never felt it coming.

A bang woke me at three A.M. I sat up, my heart pounding. The noise had sounded very much like someone pounding on my door, just one loud crack against the wood. Was this part of the game? If so, it was like a hazing. I did not like it, and I was going to tell Sasha as much in the morning. "Hello?" I called. There was no response, and after a moment, I flopped back down on my pillow. I think I was asleep a moment later.

I was awakened again when it seemed only one minute had passed. A bleary look at the glowing numbers of a bedside clock told me it was five forty-five A.M. "What the heck?" I said to the empty room, and a ringing sound brought me to full understanding: I was getting a phone call, and the ring tone had awakened me.

Who would be calling at this hour? I felt very grumpy as I fumbled for my phone in the dark and swiped the screen "Hello?" My voice was bleary and disbelieving.

"Hi! Is this Lena London?"

"Yes. Who is this?"

"I'm Harry Pratt? They were expecting me before six."

I scratched my head. "Who was expecting you? How did you get this number?"

"Well, Miss Hardwick and her assistant weren't answering, so I had to see if anyone from the website was in the white pages, and I found you."

I sat up, trying to disentangle the ball of yarn that had replaced coherent thought. "So—you were trying to reach Sasha Hardwick? Can I take a message?"

"Well, no, Ma'am, because it's pretty cold out here, and I was hoping someone could let me in."

"You're outside? Outside Green Glass Manor?"

"Yes, Ma'am. Miss Hardwick said I wouldn't be paid if I was late, so I wanted to make sure I got here in plenty of time. But it's freezing—"

"And you said no one is there to let you in?"

"No. I've been ringing the bell."

That was weird. "I'll be right down," I said. Never mind that I didn't actually know who this person was, or why he needed access at five something in the morning. As he pointed out, it was too cold to leave him out on the porch, whoever he was. I got out of bed with the optimistic thought that I'd be climbing back in soon and hunted for my slippers, tucking my feet into their warmth. I had no robe with me, but Sasha had hung white fluffy robes in the guest bathrooms, clearly trying to emulate the fine hotels. I retrieved mine and put it on.

At the door to my room I stopped, remembering the rule about leaving before eight. I would be caught on the camera leaving my room. Then I shrugged and flung wide the door. If Sasha wanted to penalize me, I would inform her that her mysterious visitor had awakened me from a sound sleep to let him into the house.

I marched down the stairs in quite a snit, feeling resentful of Sasha and Zoe and this whole project. It had seemed so glamorous to me, and now it seemed so stupid, just a crass exercise in promotion with the goal of lining the pockets of everyone involved.

I got to the front door and saw the shape of a man through one of the beveled green windows. "Mr. Pratt?" I called.

"That's me." I could hear his teeth chattering even with a door between us.

I opened the door, and he moved gratefully onto the welcome mat. The air behind him was free of snow, but

Harry Pratt seemed to be covered in the white stuff.

He saw me glancing at his coat and said, "I walked under that elm and it dumped a whole bushel of snow on me."

"Why don't you give me your coat, and you can come in here by the furnace." He relinquished his wet coat gratefully and followed where I pointed, settling into a chair in the warm room.

"I'll just get Sasha, and she can give you whatever instructions she has for you." I assumed he would have to be a butler or a footman or whatever wealthy scenario would suit her mystery. I hurried out of the room and moved down the main hallway to the back of the house. Only Sasha had a bedroom on this floor, Camilla had told me, and apparently the entire back of the house had been rebuilt as Sasha's living quarters. I passed the dining room where we had eaten both brunch and dinner. The door was closed. It looked odd, somehow, because I had only seen the room with an open, welcoming doorway.

I moved closer, peering through the green glass window in the top of the door. Things on the other side seemed to shimmer and undulate, distorted by the thick glass. Something was off, though, something I hadn't noticed when I'd been in the room earlier.

I turned the knob, not sure if it would be locked, and the door opened easily. The room was dim, though it was growing light outside. I flipped the light switch beside the door and scanned the room until I found the object that seemed out of place was not an object at all, but a person, lying sprawled on the carpet with a knife protruding from their back. My brain registered this fact in a robotic way, but that was all. It ran through possibilities: I was seeing things, or I did see something but it looked like something other than what it was, or it was what it looked like, but it was part of Sasha's crime scene.

Of course! Sasha had said there would be a crime scene. The guy at the door was probably supposed to be a policeman or something.

I grinned, squatting down next to the actor on the floor, but then my brain registered several things at once: the body was very still, and very stiff; the face, which looked truly dead, belonged to Sasha Hardwick herself; and the knife had created some very real looking blood, more black than red, some of which had sprayed the wall in front of us and had run down a decorative green glass window.

I bit back a scream and took my phone out of the pocket of my fluffy robe. I pressed one of my speed-dial numbers and listened to the ringing on the other end.

"Doug Heller," said a sleepy voice that immediately brought some calm to my thoughts.

"Doug," I almost whispered.

"Who—Lena? What's up? Why are you calling this early? Is something wrong?"

"Doug. I came down to answer the door. No one was around to let in this guy who had been hired—"

"Lena. Slow down. Take a deep breath. Good. Now, take another one."

I did as he said. "I came down, and our host, Sasha, wasn't around. I started looking for her, and I found her in the dining room. I'm kneeling in front of her."

"I don't believe it," he said. "She's dead?"

"Yes."

"And it's really her, not some wax doll or something? This whole weekend was meant to be a big ruse, right?"

"Yes. But—there's blood, and it smells like blood. Metallic and—I feel like throwing up. And there's another smell. Like—bad meat."

"Shit."

"I'm scared," I breathed.

"Lena. Did you touch anything?"

I thought about it. "The doorknob and the light switch."

"I want you to stand up now and back out the way you came in. Shut the door and put some kind of sign on it saying no one can go in, police order."

"Okay."

"Then go wherever people are sleeping and wake them up. Tell them what happened. Tell them no one can leave until the police get there."

"They couldn't if they wanted to. I just looked outside, and the drifts are higher than my head. I doubt they've plowed much yet."

"That works for me, because my murderer is in that house, right?"

I swallowed. "Yes, I think so."

"So, I want you all together. There's safety in numbers, and you will watch each other. We'll be there as soon as we can. Okay?"

"Okay. Thanks, Doug."

"Lena. I'm sorry this happened. I know how excited

you were."

I was backing into the hall, the way Doug told me, but I felt nervous in the dim hall alone. "I'm going upstairs now. I'll leave my phone on so we can text each other."

"Good." I could hear Doug moving briskly around. Bless him. "I'm going to hang up so I can call some people, okay? You call me if you need anything. See you soon."

"Yes—thanks."

We ended the call. I went into a nearby room that had a desk in it and scrounged around for paper and a pen. I wrote "Closed by Police Order. Do not Enter." I found a roll of scotch tape and taped the sign on the door.

I returned to find that Harry Pratt had fallen asleep on the couch, a slight smile on his face.

It seemed safe to leave him to his dreams, and I desperately wanted to be off of this floor.

With winged feet, I turned and ran up the stairs.

Four

"It's the shock that keeps you moving when the terror would paralyze you. It's the shock that keeps you from admitting that you've looked the Devil in the eyes."

--from *Evil at the Door,* by Oliver Lord, 2001.

I didn't bother knocking on Camilla's door; instead, I dove into my room and through the connecting door. The dawn light had begun to filter into her room, and she was still asleep. She lay on her side, her hands tucked under her check, the way people sleep in cartoons. Any other time I would have laughed, but now I approached her bed, my hands trembling. I knelt down.

"Camilla," I croaked. I cleared my throat and said, "Camilla."

Her eyes opened and looked at me. In an instant she seemed to understand that something was wrong. She sat up, looking grave. "Is it Adam?"

I squeezed her hand. "No, no! Adam is fine. But—something has happened."

"This isn't part of the game? Sasha didn't enlist you to--?

"No." I took a deep breath. "Someone has—committed murder. For real. I'm so sorry, Camilla—Sasha is dead."

She drew in a breath and briefly covered her face. "This has been confirmed?" she said into her hands.

"I found her myself. She's lying in the dining room. There's a knife in her back."

She dropped her hands and turned toward me, her eyes brilliant in their anger. "An appropriate method, considering that whoever it was betrayed her mightily." She sighed. "Did you call Doug?"

"Yes. They'll get there as soon as they can. The weather—"

She was out of bed now, heading for her little bathroom. "I'm going to take a one-minute shower. I assume we are supposed to tell the others?"

I nodded.

"I'll meet you in two minutes, dear." She went into the bathroom and shut the door, quietly.

I took her lead and returned to my own bathroom, taking what Sam called an "army shower" and hastily drying off. I threw on some jeans and a cable knit sweater, along with some thick socks. It was comforting to put on warm clothes after a shock. I tapped at Camilla's door and she opened it, fully dressed in turtleneck and slacks. I gauged her mood to be sad, but determined. "Let's go," she said.

We moved down the hall, informing Gloria, David, Oliver. Gloria pointed out Zoe's room, at the opposite end of the hall, and we moved to her door together.

When she did not answer on the third knock, we began to worry. "Could she be--?" David asked hoarsely.

Oliver knelt to study the lock. "This old thing won't stand up to much tampering," he said. "Give me a sec." He looked around on the floor, then at the women in the group. "Anyone have a hairpin or something?"

We shook our heads, but then Camilla said, "I have a paper clip in my pocket. Probably from when I last sorted mail." She handed it to him, and he bent it into the shape he wanted, then went to work on the lock.

I studied the group surreptitiously and found that no one looked particularly murderous, but everyone looked tired. Gloria's blue eyes were filled with tears, and she clutched Charlie's hand tightly. David and Oliver had exchanged some inscrutable glances, but they didn't seem sinister as much as resigned.

"Got it!" Oliver stood up and turned the knob of Zoe's door. It swung inward, and we saw what seemed to be a figure lying in her bed. A hand slid into mine. Camilla, seeking or giving comfort.

"Let Charlie go," Gloria said. "He's a doctor."

Everyone turned to stare at Charlie. "I didn't know you were a doctor," David said. Clearly, none of us had known. Shame filled me as I realized that I assumed he was some sort of boy toy and hanger-on. What a terrible presumption!

Charlie moved across the floor and approached the bed. He spoke quietly to the form, then lightly shook her shoulder. Nothing. He lifted her wrist, apparently taking her pulse, and then he lifted one of her eyelids, leaning close to study her pupil.

He walked back to us over plush blue carpeting. "She's been drugged. Or she took drugs. I don't think she's in danger, but we won't get any information from her for hours, I'm guessing. I'll keep checking on her."

We thought about this, standing clumped in the hall like a blood clot in a vein. I said, "I called the police about half an hour ago. They'll be here as soon as they can, but Detective Heller said that no one is to leave, and he wants us all to be together in one room."

David raised his brows. "We need to see who else is here. Has anyone seen Mondragan? Or that guy Bob?"

"Sasha said they had rooms in the basement." Camilla's voice sounded clipped, almost brittle. "Perhaps one of you can go down, and maybe ask the chef how we can go about making coffee."

"I'll do it," David said.

I held up a hand. "Detective Heller said everyone should move in pairs. He doesn't want anyone isolated."

David nodded, then smiled grimly. "We're trapped in one of our own damn books. Sasha would have loved this." His voice broke on the last word, and Gloria gave him a hug. "Charlie and I will go with you."

The three of them moved to the stairway and descended.

Camilla, Oliver, and I remained in Zoe's open doorway. Oliver looked thoughtful. "We should check her for blood."

"What?" Camilla said.

Oliver turned to me. "Was there blood spatter? Where you found Sasha?"

The dark blood on the green glass, a testament to violence . . . "Yes," I whispered.

"If Zoe did it, there will never be a better time to check, will there?"

Camilla and I stared at him, saying nothing. He shrugged and walked into the room. We followed. Oliver went to the bed and flung back the covers, peering at the sheets, at her clothing, at her fingernails. "She's still wearing her clothes," he said. "Looks like she barely fell into bed before she conked out."

"Or someone carried her there," Camilla said.

"I don't see anything," Oliver said, sounding almost disappointed. "Everything's clean."

"Same for her room," Camilla said. She had been walking the periphery, studying the knick-knacks on Zoe's dresser, and on a table by the snow-spattered window. A jewelry box, a framed photo of Zoe hugging a gray-haired woman who might have been her mother, a few bottles of perfume. I was standing near the dresser, which held few items aside from her phone, a set of keys, and another framed photo of a young man that I took to be her brother. He had Zoe's fair hair and square jaw. Hopefully Zoe's brother was alive and well, unlike Sasha's unfortunate kin. With a pang, I realized that the Hardwick clan was now entirely wiped out. Had whoever killed Sasha wanted to achieve that nullification of a family?

I posed this question aloud to Oliver and Camilla. Oliver shook his head, his eyes somehow remorseful. "I don't know. Let's go drink some coffee and figure out what the hell we're going to do."

Five

"In the aftermath of murder, many things go unseen."
--from *Stars, Hide Your Fires,* by Camilla Graham, 1981.

We sat in the living room, the entire group, including the four writers, Charlie, Mondo, Bob, and Harry Pratt, who had awakened to a room full of people and had been handed a hot cup of coffee.

Sasha's cook, a Mrs. Barnard, had come upstairs to make the coffee and some breakfast. She had been crying softly since she heard the news. At one point I ventured into the kitchen, asking if she needed any help.

"No, dear," she said. "But thank you."

Her hands shook slightly, and her eyes were rimmed with red. "Do you need a hug?" I asked, to my own surprise.

The second surprise was that she said, "Yes!" and threw herself into my arms. I hugged her tightly, suddenly needing the embrace of another human being as much as she did. Something evil had been done, and we both sought something normal, something kind…

Emerging from the kitchen, I saw that Oliver had found a rolling whiteboard in one of the office spaces and had brought it into the living room. He sighed and looked around at all of us.

"Here's how I see it. We don't know when the police will get here, but they will be here. We didn't touch anything, but David and I did look in the dining room, and Lena was very right. There's nothing fake about that crime scene." He cleared his throat, looking briefly emotional. "David and I took the liberty of turning off the heat in that room, for—obvious reasons."

"Good thinking," said Gloria dully. She wore no make-up, but her skin looked luminous, and she was actually more youthful this way, though her face was sad.

Oliver looked around the room. "The reality is that someone plunged that knife into poor Sasha, and that someone is in this house. Most probably in this room."

We looked furtively at one another. The misery washed over me again, the same misery that had plagued me the night before. Had I sensed that something was wrong? Had everyone sensed it?

David joined Oliver at the whiteboard. "We don't want to sit here wasting time, and we want to be helpful to the police. We owe it to Sasha to figure out what happened here."

Oliver nodded. "So, we're going to go through every single person's possible motives. We'll hash it out in the hopes that something valuable will emerge."

Bob had his phone out, and Oliver pointed at him. "There is a gag order on EVERYTHING that happens in here. Bob, or anyone, have you informed anyone about Sasha's death?"

Bob shook his head. "I'm just texting my wife to say that I'll be delayed," he said, holding up his phone.

"Let's keep the outside communication to a minimum," David said. "And everyone be ready to surrender your phone if we have a question about your texts or calls."

"Who put you two in charge?" Mondo said. "I'm the security here." His eyes looked red, as well, and I wondered again if he and Sasha had been in a relationship.

"You're welcome to join in," Oliver said. "Everyone is welcome. We simply brought in the whiteboard so that we can be transparent about all of our thoughts. We're in this together, folks, whether we like it or not. In case you didn't hear, the detective in charge has told us to stay out of the dining room and to stay in the house, together. So why not do our best to solve this?"

We sat quietly, and then Camilla said, "You can start with me. Shall I offer up bullet points of information?"

Oliver nodded. "Thanks, Cammy. You do that. When you finish, anyone else can add their thoughts to the list."

Camilla sat up straighter in her chair and picked a little fuzzball from her sweater sleeve. "I've known Sasha for twenty-five years. We met at a mystery conference and began a friendship. I was forty-five years old when we met, and Sasha was thirty-three."

Oliver wrote rapidly on the board, bullet-pointing for brevity. Camilla said, "Sasha grew up here in Blue

Lake, but that wasn't where I met her. Isn't that funny? But once we became friends, we would meet here once in a while, for a meal or an event. I don't think we ever had a disagreement."

Gloria raised her hand "We're supposed to add on, right?"

"Be my guest," Camilla said graciously.

Gloria smiled, apologetic. "I'm just going through the motions so we can see how this works. And I'll add that I do remember one argument between you and Sasha, Camilla."

"Oh?" Camilla looked less guilty than she did curious. "When was this?"

"Oh, way back. We were at a conference in Seattle, and you had brought James with you. Sasha had never met him, and she ran across him in the hotel lobby and started some major flirting. You know how Sasha was. She could have taught college courses in flirting."

Camilla smiled sadly, remembering. "Ah," she said.

"Anyway, you can all guess the rest. Camilla came in from chatting with someone outside the hotel and found Sasha draped over her husband like a mink stole." Gloria laughed a little—a rather miserable laugh. "I just recall James looking really uncomfortable. But Cammy, I'd never seen you angry before. Your eyes were like two glowing amethysts in your head. You walked up to Sasha and said, 'Perhaps you'd be so kind as to take your hands off of my husband.' It was crazy. Super uncomfortable." Gloria looked at Camilla. "But also sort of awesome."

People laughed at that. Camilla made a wry face.

Oliver said, "Well, if we go with the theory that Camilla was holding on to a two-decade grudge and decided, while a house full of people and the press were watching, that she'd plunge a knife into Sasha and see how it played out."

David nodded. "Everyone goes on the board. So, Camilla's motive: jealousy."

Oliver's marker hovered. "Anyone have anything to add about Camilla? Anyone see her lurking around the halls in the wee hours?"

I raised my hand. "If any one of us was in the hall, it would be on the camera, right? The camera that was going to monitor our doors between midnight and eight."

Gloria looked at Mondo. "You have access to that footage, don't you?"

Mondo raised his brows. "Yeah, actually. I can access it on my phone. If I can take it out?" he asked, with a touch of sarcasm, looking at Oliver and David.

They nodded impatiently, and Mondo took out his phone and pressed some keys. We all gathered around him and watched the image of the upstairs hallway. Almost every door was in view, as was the stairway. The video started at about eleven o'clock, so we were able to watch everyone going to their rooms at different times during the hour. Gloria and Charlie were the last to arrive, but they didn't look as though they'd been sleuthing as much as if they'd been kissing in some dark corner of the house. Gloria was giggling, and Charlie was smirking, his hand around her waist.

They disappeared into their room, and then—the link went dead. "What the heck?" Mondo said. "Let me fast-forward."

He couldn't, though, because there was nothing to scroll through. The camera had simply stopped recording.

Mondo had offered his phone to Oliver for inspection, and now he held up his hands. "Don't look at me. As far as I knew, the thing was recording fine."

"Who would be able to tamper with the feed?"

He shrugged. "Sasha, Zoe, and I could stop it from our phones or computers. But anyone else could just have tampered with the camera itself. It wasn't hidden. It's just drilled into the wall up there."

David said, "We need two people to go and look at the camera."

"I'll go," said Bob. "I know something about cameras, as you'll recall."

Oliver nodded. "Who'll go with him?"

Charlie raised his hand. "I will."

"Thanks, guys," David said. He pointed at the whiteboard. "If we're finished with our case against Camilla, I'll take a photo of our notes, and we'll start over."

He took a couple of shots on his phone, and then Oliver erased the board. "Who's next?"

Mondo raised his hand. "You can do me. I've got nothing to hide."

"Okay," said Oliver. "Start us off."

Mondo coughed into his hand, looking self-conscious. He was perched on a window seat with dainty linen cushions. "As you know, my name is Albert Mandragon. I'm retired Navy, twenty years served. I met Sasha at an event she was directing, raising funds for veteran charities. We got to talking, and we hit it off. I told her I was currently unemployed, and she said she could use security at her big house in Indiana. I told her no thanks, and then she named a price. I couldn't believe the salary she was offering, just for me to patrol a house in the woods."

He shook his head, remembering. "As it turned out, the job was pretty challenging. I've been here for seven years. And ultimately, I failed her." One sob escaped him, and he bent his head until he had it under control. "You should also know that Sasha and I were—involved with each other. We weren't necessarily exclusive, but—we mostly were. Neither of us found someone we liked better." His brown eyes were so sad I almost began to cry myself.

Oliver had been diligently bullet-pointing. "Thanks, Mondo. Anyone have something to add?"

Camilla said, "Sasha told us that people had tried to break in before. Is it at all possible that someone did, in fact, break in last night?"

We looked at Mondo, who slowly shook his head. "I've got alarms on all the doors and windows. I set them myself last night before I turned in."

I pointed at Harry Pratt, who sat in silence, watching the proceedings as if they were a movie. "But I let him in this morning before six, and no alarm went off."

Mondo frowned. "I can't explain that. I checked the

system when I woke up, and it indicates that everything is still working. However," he added thoughtful.

"However?" David prompted.

"Individual alarms can be turned off manually. You would just have to be familiar with the system."

"So, you wouldn't necessarily have to live here to know—"

Mondo shook his head. "Nah. And actually you could probably look up the system online, if you cared enough."

Oliver made a note of this on the board. Then he said, "So if we suspected Mondo, his motive would be--?"

"Jealousy again," Gloria said. "If Sasha was seeing someone new."

"Did she say anything to you?" Oliver asked her.

"No. I'm just saying, if there was a romantic relationship, then love can be at the root of anger, or—violence." She looked uneasily toward the dining room, where our hostess lay, excluded from society in her own giant house.

"It would be, yeah, if there was any sort of argument between Sasha and me. But there wasn't. Even last night—" he stopped, looking at the floor.

"What about last night?" David prompted.

"She came down to my apartment at about ten. She said Zoe could handle things for a while, and she needed a break."

"So, you were—together?" Oliver asked.

"Yeah. It's always been very natural and comfortable with us. It was never like she was some grand mistress and I was a servant. I worked for her, and she was the boss, but at the end of the day we left that behind. Sasha was just a nice person."

Camilla studied him. "Do you know, Mondo, I think you put that very well. For all her family money and her career success, Sasha never put on airs. She was actually quite generous."

Gloria shivered. "I can't believe we're talking about her in past tense."

We all looked toward the dining room. We were all being civilized, considering the fact that there was a murderer in our midst. How many times had I read this kind of scenario in an Agatha Christie novel and found it satisfying? There was nothing cute or cozy about this situation.

David pointed at the board. "If there was someone else in Sasha's life, or she had broken up with Mondo, then obviously he would have motive. The old, 'If I can't have you, no one can.'"

Mondo shrugged. "A lot of hypotheticals, but sure." He wiped at his reddened eyes and went silent.

Bob said, "If it had been Mondo, and it was a lover's spat, I don't see a knife in the back as his method. That's kind of cold and calculated, not a crime of passion. And, based on what I've been told, it was a very precise blow. The kind that would require some knowledge of anatomy." He looked pointedly at Charlie, who raised his brows.

"I don't like your implication. I barely knew Sasha. But I agree that the knife was precisely placed. Only a pathologist can tell you the details, but I would guess she died instantly, after one hard thrust."

Camilla gasped, and he sent her a remorseful look. "Sorry."

"It's good to know, though," Oliver said, still holding his whiteboard marker. "Bob makes a good point. This doesn't seem like a crime of passion. And the fact that someone picked this weekend . . ."

I looked suddenly at Harry Pratt. "Harry, what exactly were you supposed to do when you got here this morning?"

Harry looked surprised, and slightly blurry, as if we'd awakened him from a magical sleep. "Oh, I thought you all knew. I was supposed to be the dead body."

This announcement brought a heavy silence. Finally, Camilla said, "So—what was the plan?"

Harry cleared his throat. "Well, Miss Hardwick said she would let me in and tell me the basics. Her assistant would then take me somewhere to give me make-up, and then I was essentially supposed to play dead for a few hours. She was going to pay me a really generous amount . . ." His face fell as he realized that might not happen now.

Oliver walked over to him and patted his shoulder. "Show me the amount she offered. I'll cover the bill."

Harry murmured his gratitude, and Gloria sat up. "Are we going to continue with this? Does it seem to be helping at all? Or should we just—"

A door banged open behind us, and we turned to see Zoe, her hair wild, her clothing rumpled, her expression horrified. She could have been Poe's Madeleine Usher.

She looked around at all of us, and her eyes grew even wider when she saw Harry, looking mournful and clutching a cup of coffee.

"What the hell is going on here?" Zoe cried. "And where is Sasha?"

Six

"A good cop watches. A good cop listens. A good cop doesn't make a move until he knows the lay of the land..."

--from *Bound by Procedure,* by David Canfield, 2010.

"I think she might need to be sedated," Charlie murmured to a group of us as Gloria and Camilla comforted a tearful Zoe.

"Not until she tells us what happened last night," David said firmly. "Plus, we don't know what sedative she had before."

Charlie's expression said he saw the wisdom of this. "But she seems manic. Her behavior is probably due to extreme anxiety exacerbated by grief. All young people her age have anxiety, don't they?"

"She's only a few years younger than you are, wouldn't you say?" Oliver noted.

Charlie shook his head. "What is she, twenty-five? I'm thirty-eight. It's her demographic that has the most anxiety. They're all in therapy, they're all on meds. And it's worse since Covid."

Oliver huffed out a breath. "This feels like a horror novel."

David laughed grimly. "We're trapped in the wrong genre."

Half an hour later, Zoe was sitting against some pillows on the large couch, drinking a cup of tea. She said she felt able to talk now, though she wished that the police were present. "They need to get on this," she said, urgently. "There could be clues fading away or someone could be covering his tracks."

Gloria patted her shoulder again in a helpless gesture. Zoe said, "All that work. Sasha's work, my work. All her planning." She wiped at her eyes and then glared at the writers balefully. "And she did it for you! For all of you! She was always generous like that. For all her money and all her privilege, she just wanted to help other people." Zoe began to cry weakly, like an ailing baby, and I felt sick.

David cleared his throat. "Zoe. Charlie here is going to settle you with a sedative, to help you deal with all the stress of this. But first we need information from you. You're the one who was with her last, I would think. Did you see her after she visited Mondo downstairs?"

Zoe stared at him, her face bleary, and then she shook her head, visibly clearing the cobwebs. "Yeah. Yes. We were sitting at that dining room table at midnight, going through our agenda, double-checking the clues, and laying out the plastic wounds that I was going to affix to Harry over there. "

Harry nodded, still looking uncomfortable.

Gloria was straightening Zoe's messy hair, trying to relax her. "So how long were you there with her?"

Zoe sighed. "We were both really tired. We had some tea, and then Sasha said I could go to bed. But she said she was going to go over things one more time. So, I said I'd do it with her."

"Did you see anyone else during this time?" Camilla asked. "Anyone before midnight—or after?"

Zoe shook her head. "No, we didn't see them—but we did hear something."

"What?" asked several voices at once.

"We were at the table, and we heard a noise in the hallway, just outside the dining room. Sasha called out a hello, and we waited, but no one said anything."

We sat in silence, considering this. Zoe added, "Then, about ten minutes later, we heard a sound outside, and I jumped. Sasha said it was just Mondo, doing his evening rounds and checking the alarms."

"What time was that?" asked Mondo. His eyes were still red.

Zoe looked overwhelmed. "I don't—I lost track of time once we were in the kitchen having tea and working. I—maybe one in the morning?"

"I did make the rounds last night," Mondo said. "But closer to midnight. Maybe you have the time wrong."

"Maybe," Zoe said. "I don't know. It's all blurry now." She stared out at the snowy landscape. The sun had emerged, and it sparkled off the snow so intensely that it was almost impossible to look at the icy white ground.

"When did you go to bed?" David asked.

"I don't exactly know. It was after two, I think. I had been feeling tired, and then I suddenly felt like I might collapse if I didn't get to bed, like, right away. I told Sasha I had to turn in, and she said to go. That she would be turning in as well." Zoe's blue eyes flooded with tears. "She said, 'I'll be right behind you, kiddo."

"And you went straight up then?" Gloria asked.

"Yes. But I was so tired I was just—swaying on the stairs. I got to the top, and I lost my balance and banged against a door. It hurt—the doorknob got me right in a vulnerable spot."

She lifted her shirt slightly at the waist and checked her skin, which was indeed marred by a round, blackening bruise. "Ooh, that hurts."

I sat up straight. "I know exactly when Zoe came upstairs," I said. "I was awakened by the banging sound because it was my door she fell against. I looked at my clock, and it was three---"

Oliver went back to the whiteboard "So we know that Sasha was alive at three...," he said. "And Lena, what time did you let in Harry, here?"

I said, "It was before six. Maybe five forty-five?"

Harry nodded. "That sounds about right. I got here at five-thirty, and then it took me a while to find your number after no one answered the door or my texts."

Camilla looked at Zoe, her eyes sharp. "When you drank the tea with Sasha, dear, was it tea you made, or tea already in a pot?"

Zoe stared, surprised by the question. "It was already in a pot sitting on a cute little warmer."

The four writers immediately saw the significance of this, as did I. It meant anyone could have had access to the teapot earlier in the evening. Anyone could have drugged the tea, so that Zoe and Sasha could be put out of commission.

"Did Sasha feel tired, too? Extremely tired, as you did?"

Zoe smiled a little. "Yeah. She said that we should both consider another profession, one that didn't suck the life right out of us." She heard her own words then, and looked stricken. Then her expression changed again, to horror. "Wait, do you think someone drugged us?"

We looked at Charlie, who said, "You have clearly been drugged, Zoe. I would assume that Sasha had a similar dosage, if you drank the same amount of tea."

Zoe processed this, her eyes darting. "So—maybe she was asleep? Maybe she didn't feel pain?"

The room was silent again, heavy with sadness or dread.

Charlie said, "I would say she did not. If she was as unconscious as you were when we found you, then she would have been unaware of what was happening."

Zoe wiped her eyes and snuffled, and Oliver wrote more details on the whiteboard: the precise window of time that Sasha could have been killed, the fact that the two P.R. women had been drugged.

"Is the teapot still there, in the kitchen?" Oliver asked.

Gloria and Mondo were sent to summon the cook, who returned, looking mournful, and told us that she had washed and put away the teapot when she made breakfast.

Oliver winced slightly, as did David, but Gloria patted the woman's shoulder. "That's fine, then. We just wanted to double-check."

The cook started to say something, but then another woman walked into the room, and the silence suggested that everyone felt as dumbstruck as I did. I had never seen the woman before, and a quick glance around told me no one else had, either.

She looked about forty, with smooth blonde hair and an elegant outfit of heather blue sweater and tweed slacks.

"I wonder if I could speak to all of you," she said.

Seven

"The unexpected is a given, a reality, something we anticipate; and therefore, it is a paradox."

--from *Tripwire,* by Gloria Gale, 2014.

For a surreal moment, the room was silent. We stared at the stranger, unable to process thoughts to explain how she had come to be in the house. *Was she the murderer?* asked a vague voice in the back of my mind.

Then Oliver laughed. "Carla, right?"

The woman nodded, and Oliver said, "This is Carla, my limo driver. Remember how we rescued her from the blizzard? You all saw her last night."

Gloria said, "Oh, but you looked so different then!"

Carla the limo drive nodded. "I was pretty frozen and disheveled. Last night our hostess gave me clothes to wear today, and my room had cosmetics and a hair straightener and stuff. It was like being at a luxury hotel." She smiled briefly and then looked at her watch.

A palpable easing of tension brought smiles to most faces.

"Anyway," Carla said. "Much as I hate the thought of driving in the snow, I do need to get the limo back out on the road. I have other customers scheduled today." Her face grew sad. "I know that—something terrible has happened. But I wonder if you all thought it would be okay for me to go?"

"Of course, you can," said Gloria, waving her hand in a grand manner. "It's your job, and you don't want to upset your employer."

Carla nodded gracefully, but I found myself speaking. "I don't think Carla can go, actually. The detective in charge is on his way with the whole team, and he instructed that no one should leave the house. That includes people who weren't necessarily a part of the mystery weekend."

David nodded grimly. "Yeah, I think you'll need to call your boss and explain the situation. You're a potential witness at a crime scene, and the police are detaining you. Nothing he can say to that."

"Or she," Camilla added. David winked at her. What was it with these men and winking?

Carla looked uncertain, but also, I thought, relieved at the thought of staying off the road a bit longer. "Okay, well—I guess I'll go back downstairs and make a call."

"Aren't we also forbidding outside calls?" Gloria asked, with an apologetic look at Carla.

Carla hesitated, uncertain, until Oliver said, "Why don't you make the call right here? Then, group, I think we should all put our phones in Sasha's lovely basket, here." He grabbed a large white basket from a side table and dumped out its contents, which seemed to consist of potpourri.

The limo driver made her call, explaining about the snow. Her boss, whose voice was so loud that we could all hear every word he said, seemed reasonable enough. Carla also explained about the phones being out of commission, a fact which made him less pleased with the situation. Oliver offered to take the phone, and Carla handed it over. In his smooth, charismatic voice, Oliver introduced himself and explained that Carla was powerless in the face of an investigation. Before the call was over, Oliver had promised a signed copy of his latest book and a mention of the man's wife in his next one.

After her call, David walked around with the basket, and we all relinquished our phones. I was itching to text Sam, but the whole point was that we were not to contact anyone about what was happening in Sasha's house. Not surprisingly, Zoe and Bob were the most reluctant to part with their phones. For both of them, the cells were a big part of their profession, and must have felt like necessary appendages to their anatomy.

"We'll give them back," David said. "Just not right now. Not until we know what's going on here." He was standing in front of Bob, who stole one last glance at his screen before he dropped in the phone.

Zoe sighed, looking suddenly weary. "I guess there's nothing pressing now. All of my projects were planned with Sasha. Without her—" her eyes filled with tears, and she tossed her phone in the basket with a theatrical gesture. I felt suddenly worried for her. She didn't seem to be handling the trauma well, and of course the residual effect of drugs in her system could not have been helping matters. I knew all about the way that drugs could affect a person; I had gone through a dark time several months earlier, when a car crash had left me with my arm in a cast, and drugs had rendered me paranoid. But I had come out of it all right, and at the end of the dark time had come my engagement to Sam.

Sam. How I missed him. I spared one last glance for Zoe, whose hands were folded in her lap. Her eyes were downcast, as though she was studying the way she had wrapped her fingers around each other.

I met Camilla's wise gaze and saw that she, too, was concerned.

Carla the limo driver handed in her phone and said once again that she would return to the basement, where she and the cook had been playing card games.

Oliver's eyes were shrewd. "Two escorts, please," he said. "I can be one of them."

"I'll go with you," David said. "I'm going a little stir crazy." The two men got up and walked Carla out of the room.

Camilla sighed. "What's next? Shall we return to our whiteboard?"

"I can make a quick entry," I said. "I never met Sasha before yesterday, and I had absolutely no motive to kill her."

Charlie jumped up to write this on the board, and he said, "I'll put my name with Lena's. I have met Sasha before, but only briefly, at events Gloria attended. We have no shared past, and I have no motive, either." He jotted our names on the board and wrote, "No past, no motive."

Camilla said, "David and Oliver are conveniently out of the room, so let's move on to Gloria."

Gloria shrugged, flipped her lustrous hair behind her shoulders and stretched her arms toward the ceiling. I shot a glance at Charlie, who was just barely suppressing his drool. She was beautiful, I had to agree. If one had to guess her profession, they would think model or movie star, not writer. "I'm fine to go next. Sasha was my good friend, going way back. I've known her even longer than I've known Camilla. Sasha and I confided in one another. I knew I could trust her with my secrets, and she could trust me with hers."

"What secrets?" David asked, strolling back into the room. Oliver followed; he had snagged a tray of food somewhere, and he made the rounds, offering us cheese and crackers.

Gloria sent David an impatient look. "Nothing worth killing over, I assure you. Mostly we confided about men. Who we liked, who we loved, who we hated."

Camilla smiled at her friend. "I don't believe either of you are capable of hate."

Gloria studied the toes of her elegant boots. "Well, you know what I mean. Men who made us furious. We generally knew all the same men, so that made it easy."

"And did any of these men overlap with Charles or Mondo there?" Oliver asked.

Gloria seemed to absorb some of the ice from the outdoors. "I'm sorry?"

Oliver's eyes widened in apparent innocence. "I mean, were there any men who interested you while you were dating Charlie?"

She shot daggers into Oliver with her eyes and said, "No, Oliver. I love Charlie. In fact, you may as well know that he asked me to marry him, and I accepted."

Charlie didn't seem upset that the news had come out in this way. His expression was something between smug and besotted, and he stood clutching his whiteboard marker as though it were a holy candle.

"I must be mistaken, then," Oliver said. He was up to something, and based on the "mischief" Camilla had exposed the previous evening, I assumed he was doing it for his own entertainment. "Don't be mad, Glor."

Gloria's rod-straight posture suggested that she was indeed angry, and she didn't meet Oliver's eyes. "Returning to the topic at hand, I had no grudge against Sasha. She was my friend. She had nothing that I wanted."

"Except those secretes you spoke of?" David said. "Could that be a strong enough motive?"

Gloria whirled to look at him, her blue eyes flashing. It made her even more stunning. "No, David. I would not kill Sasha for any reason. I would not kill anyone. I doubt I could bring myself to even strike someone." Her gaze slid to Oliver, as though she was considering trying out the theory on him.

Camilla said, "Thinking over Sasha's confidences to you, can you think of anything that might be significant now?"

Gloria squinted, looking inward. "I would have to

think," she said vaguely. "Everyone loved Sasha, you know that."

Camilla nodded, but said nothing.

Zoe, her face white, said, "Not everyone. Sometimes she got mean letters from some of her clients. And once she got a phone call that made her gasp out loud. I asked her what it was about, and she just shook her head. She had hung up the phone quickly, like it had burned her hand."

The silence in the room conveyed our shock and surprise over this detail.

"Did you ever find out?" Oliver asked. "Who was on the phone?"

Zoe looked at the floor. "I did go to the phone—it was that big landline she has in her office—and I checked the caller id. It just said 'unknown caller.'"

I looked around the room, gauging reactions to this information. Gloria seemed more concerned about catching Charlie's eye. Camilla looked thoughtful, her gaze on the mounds of snow outside. Oliver had narrowed his eyes again—an expression that made him look particularly sinister—and sat studying Zoe's face. David stood up and paced to the window, staring out at the white expanse of lawn. Bob had looked as though he was going through withdrawal ever since he had parted with his phone, and even now he seemed to be twitching with the desire to send messages or take pictures. Poor Mondo wore a melancholy expression. How could he help but think of the lover who lay in the room we all ignored, the chill room with its ghastly occupant? My thoughts skittered away from this terrible image, and I focused once again on the people around me.

I wondered what fans were thinking. Sasha, Bob and Zoe had been posting regularly on the blog, and now it had been hours since anything had appeared. Were people beginning to wonder? To worry? To complain?

Finally, David shrugged. "That call could have been anything. Some old boyfriend or nasty client or angry family member."

"Does she have any family members left?" Gloria asked, her face sad.

"She's got some distant relations," Oliver murmured. "An uncle and an aunt, I think. Maybe some others."

"We need to find them," said Zoe urgently. "We need to notify them!"

Camilla smiled at her. "We will, dear. But nothing will happen until the police come and give some directives. That's their job, not ours."

Zoe seemed to be coming back to herself and thinking along the same lines I was. "We haven't posted in forever. Can I just go online in front of all of you and say that there's been an unexpected incident, and the game is on hold?"

"On hold until when?" Gloria asked rather coldly. "The game is cancelled, is what you mean. It's not like we're going to do some lighthearted publicity stunt in light of poor Sasha's death."

Zoe conceded this fact with a nod. "So can I at least go online and say it's cancelled?"

"With what explanation? The police will not want this information shared with the public," I said.

Zoe looked as though she was about to explode, and David took pity on her. "Why don't we just let Zoe go on her page, right here on this laptop," he said, gesturing to a sleek thing that sat on a nearby desk, "and she can thank everyone and say that a tragic event has occurred and that she was forced to shut down the event. No further information until the event is fully investigated. That's giving some information, but nothing anyone can turn into a story or a news clip."

Everyone pondered this idea, then agreed to allow Zoe access to the laptop. We watched over her shoulder as she logged into the site that had been created just for this event. It was called Murder Mystery Weekend, and a disturbing graphic in the form of a bloody knife appeared beside the title. Then, a line of publicity photos of the four writers. Camilla was striking in hers; she wore a lavender sweater, and the morning light had been on her face when Adam snapped the picture, highlighting her purple eyes.

Zoe was tap-tapping away, and we read as she typed:

Hello, mystery fans! We are thrilled that you came to visit the site and support your favorite mystery writer. Unfortunately, due to a tragic event that has occurred here at Green Glass Manor, we must cancel the event until a thorough investigation has been conducted. This has been a traumatic time for everyone involved, so please keep us all in your thoughts and prayers.

Charlie commented first. "Suitably vague," he said. "Although it does seem to invite speculation."

"At least that gives them something to do. They all

invested energy and excitement in this event, so let them continue that excitement in another form. They can remain intrigued until the news emerges."

"They'll probably think one of the four of us has suffered a tragedy," David mused.

"They'll know differently soon enough," said Camilla. "I think it looks fine, Zoe, dear."

Zoe looked around, making sure she had everyone's approval before she clicked "publish."

"Okay, shut it now," David said. "No more social media."

Oliver touched his toes and flexed some muscles. "Let's hope they come soon, before we all go nuts. I feel bad for the people who just happened to be here. The cook, and the driver, and this poor fool—" He turned to look at Harry, who had been silent for the entire conversation.

There was good reason for his silence: the seat by the fireplace was empty, and a quick glance around the room revealed that Harry was simply gone.

And not one of us had noticed his departure.

Eight

"Dexter had tracked people in every weather, and he always found his quarry. But he had never tracked anyone in snow this deep."

--from *Hunted,* by Oliver Lord, 2009.

The room seemed to grow darker as the possible implications of Harry's absence dawned upon us. David dove for the basket of phones. "Was he here when we collected these?"

Oliver sprang into action. "I'll check the bathrooms. Charlie, come with me." The two men ran out of the room, but they returned five minutes later, shaking their heads. "Nowhere in sight," Charlie said. "And all of the facilities are empty."

"Could he be in the basement with some of the others?" Camilla asked. The men disappeared again, then returned to say that no, only some staff and the driver were in the lower apartments.

Mondo stood up, looking suddenly dangerous. "I'll check outside," he said.

"I'll go with you," I practically shouted. The room had become horribly oppressive, and I was having trouble keeping my eyes away from that dreadful shut door. The hours of tension had given me a headache, and I longed for fresh air. No one objected to my volunteering to be Mondo's companion, so I donned my boots and coat and followed him out the front door.

Mondo was in tracking mode. He pointed left and right. "He didn't leave this way. No footprints. Let's check the side and back."

He led me around the house; it was rough going because of the high drifts, although Mondo had made an attempt to shovel the evening before. We found the prints behind the house, heading directly into the forest that backed the property. "He went through the kitchen, the little rat," Mondo said through gritted teeth.

"He might have just wanted to leave. It doesn't mean he had anything to do with—"

"It's suspicious behavior. And now the police will want to know why. I know I do." His mouth, a straight grim line, told me of his determination to find Harry and make him explain.

A movement to my left caught my eye. Something jumping in the snow, something bright and reddish-brown. "Oh, I think it's a fox!" I said, surprised. I had never seen a fox in the wild.

Mondo shook his head. "Stray dog," he said. "The family moved away."

I stared at him. "They moved away and just left their dog?

He shrugged. "It fends for itself."

Horrified, I said, "I'm going to see if it's all right." I

stomped away from him and marched toward the dog, which was jumping as best it could through a large snow drift. The dog and I made it to the slightly less snowy road at the same time. I saw that it was a fairly small creature and that it did have foxlike coloring and a very fluffy tail. But the face was all dog—sweet and soulful eyes framed by droopy ears of reddish brown, but with a white stripe across the snout. The dog was lifting its feet, one at a time, as if to keep them out of the cold.

I knelt down. "Are you okay?" I asked softly, not wanting to make it run away. "Are you hurt?"

To my vast surprise, the dog ran, not away, but straight to me, and leaped into my lap, where it cuddled against me. "Oh, you are precious. And you are frozen!" I felt a mix of anger and protectiveness. "You're coming home with me, you poor thing."

I lifted the dog and marched back toward the house. Mondo had disappeared, apparently in quest of his quarry. I didn't care about Harry anymore. I had more pressing things on my mind, like saving a creature from freezing to death.

I reached the front door and kicked it with my foot. David opened it and said, "What--?"

"This little dog is half frozen," I said. "Help me get her warm."

This mobilized everyone. Zoe disappeared and returned a moment later with a large blue towel, which we wrapped around the dog. Oliver turned up the flames on the gas fireplace, and I set the pup on the carpet in front of the fire. Charlie stepped forward to examine the animal, at Gloria's urging, and he studied its little paws.

"I don't think she has frostbite, at least not something that goes deep into the tissue. But her paws are sore from exposure. I think I have some cream that I can put on them. He touched the dog gently on its face, its neck, its little tummy. "She doesn't seem to be in pain, aside from the snow-chapped paws."

"Well, that's a good prognosis, right, girl?" I said, petting her ears.

The little dog wagged her tail so hard that it made a breeze that cooled my face. I scratched her ears and watched as she relaxed, noticeably, in front of the fire. Who knew how long she had been struggling in the snow? Now, around friendly people and in a warm room, her eyelids were growing heavy. I finished drying her fur with the towel and let her snuggle into the rug. She curled into a ball and wrapped her foxlike tail around her face.

I turned to the group. "Mondo said she was owned by a family, but they moved away and left her here. Who does that? To such a precious little animal?"

Camilla looked angry. "Not someone I would like to meet. Lena, if you don't adopt her, I will."

I smiled gratefully at Camilla. She never disappointed me. "Oh, she's definitely going home with us."

"It is odd," said Oliver, who had come to sit near the dog. "She doesn't seem like an animal who was left on a chain in the yard. She looks domesticated and previously pampered. Why would they go from taking care of her to leaving her behind?"

It was a good distraction for us all, pondering the

callousness that would make someone leave a defenseless creature to her own devices. A distraction, that is, until we realized it was just another form of human cruelty, like the one that allowed someone to plunge a knife into Sasha's back.

Bob cleared his throat. "We were listing our possible motives for—hurting Sasha. I'll go next and say that I've worked with Sasha as a photographer and media specialist for almost ten years. We had a great professional relationship, and I'd like to think we were friends. She was a very generous employer, and I had absolutely no reason to want to hurt her. I am—I still can't believe this, truly."

Charlie went back to the board and jotted Bob's name, then bullet-pointed his links to Sasha. "Any questions for Bob?" he asked.

"Were you ever lovers?" Gloria asked.

Bob looked surprised, then shook his head. "I'm happily married. Sasha is—was in a relationship. We thought of each other as colleagues."

Camilla said, "I think two notable people haven't shared yet." She looked at Oliver, and then at David, with an expectant smile.

David grinned. "You are so right, Cammy. Fine, I'll go. I met Sasha way back when, at a Chicago conference called Lost in the MYST, or something like that. She and I were joking about the lame title. We hit it off. Not long after, I hired her as my personal publicist."

"You were married to Elaine at the time, weren't you?" Oliver asked, plucking at the fringe on an expensive-looking carpet. The dog snored slightly beside his hand.

David's face grew taut. "Yes, as you know. And also, as you know, Sasha and I had a brief fling. After a few months, it was over. I kept her a bit longer as my publicist, but that ended a couple of years later. We remained friends, against all odds."

Charlie labored at the white board, trying to break all of these facts down into digestible bits.

Camilla said, "As I recall, you and Oliver eventually got into an argument about Sasha, did you not?"

David smiled thinly. "Yes. Oliver found out that I had been with Sasha. He took the liberty of telling my wife, good friend that he is, and that was the beginning of the end for Elaine and me."

Oliver held up a hand. "First of all, I did not tell your wife. She asked me, and I didn't want to lie to her. She also confided in me that she felt neglected by you. So, it wasn't only your affair that made her feel distressed."

"Well, how noble of you, Oliver! Because God knows you are the model for treating women with respect."

The two men glared at each other, and I shifted uncomfortably in my seat near the fireplace.

"Let's not go down this road," Oliver said, looking back at the carpet.

"What road?" David was fully riled up now. "The one where you painted me as a world-class jerk to my wife? Maybe we should ask Rebecca how your second marriage ended!"

Oliver's compelling eyes lifted then, and there was fire in them. "I'm sorry? What would you know about my second marriage?"

David smirked. "You think you're the only one who can ruin a marriage? The only one who can nobly tell a man's wife that he is fooling around?"

Oliver stood up. "What did you say to Rebecca?" His tone was quiet and terrifying.

David stood, as well. "Nothing but the truth. That you slept with some twenty-something publicist at that Dallas convention, and that she was in your room when Rebecca called to say goodnight."

Oliver's fists clenched. "That's a lie."

"Do you remember the girl's name? It was Judy. And she told me as much, a day later, when you left the conference early without a word to her. She was quite distressed."

Now Oliver's voice was as sharp as a knife and seemed to suggest something as lethal. "I didn't sleep with her, you interfering idiot. She wanted writing advice. We had a beer in my room. That was all. Believe it or not, I was devoted to my wife."

"Which one?" David said.

Oliver lunged forward and threw a punch at David's jaw. David stepped aside quickly, but Oliver still made contact, with a sickening sound, and then the men were grappling, punching, gasping, until they fell to the floor, still attempting to kill one another while the rest of us cried out in protest.

I got up and ran to the door, thinking that I would blast them with cold air until they came to their senses. I grabbed the gold doorknob, twisted it, and wrenched it forward, letting in a burst of cold and a slight sprinkling of snow.

And on the stoop was the best sight I had ever seen: Doug Heller and Cliff Blake, snow-suited and official, ready to take this horrible burden from our shoulders.

I turned toward the room and called to the writhing, punching men. “David and Oliver! Get up. It’s the police.”

Nine

"By the time the police arrived, she realized, it would be too late. It was already much too late."
--from *The Lost Child,* by Camilla Graham, 1972.

Both Doug and Cliff seemed to understand that they should remain professional rather than display their friendship with Camilla and me. They stepped into the room, and Doug said, "I'm Detective Doug Heller with the Blue Lake PD. This is Detective Clifford Blake." His eyes went to the men who had risen from the floor with newly-bruised faces. "What's going on here?" Doug asked.

Oliver summoned some of his charm and offered a rueful smile. "Just a private war, Detective, uh—"

"Heller."

"Detective Heller. David and I will resolve it some other time." He didn't look at David when he said that, but his expression suggested that their fight was not over.

Doug nodded, eyes narrowed, and Cliff said, "Where is the body?"

Now both men looked shamefaced. They had

forgotten, in their fury, why we were all here, why we were reviewing our relationships, why poor Sasha was not able to take part. They had lost sight of the horror, and what lay in the other room.

"I'll show you the door," Zoe said. "I'm Zoe. I'm—I was—Sasha's P.A." She walked stiffly down the hall to the dining room door. The men followed her. We heard the door open, and then there was silence.

A moment later Doug and Cliff returned, their faces blank and professional. To my vast relief, they were all business. Doug said, "The crime techs will be here within the half hour. We cannot go near the scene, and in fact it would be better if none of us was here." His phone buzzed, and he turned away to take the call.

Cliff said, "Don't look so eager to leave. You can't be here, but you still have to be in the area so that we can interview. We've done a bit of research and found there is a bed and breakfast at the end of this street. We will ask that you all move down the road, with a police escort, and check in there. I believe your event was going to last another day, so I'm sure you won't mind using that day to help us determine what happened to your friend."

Camilla raised a hand. "Detective Blake, there are two people missing. One, a man named Harry, slipped out at some point. He was supposed to play the part of the dead body in Sasha's mystery."

Cliff noted this with a terse nod. "And the other?"

"The other is named Albert Mondragan. Sasha called him Mondo. He was her security officer, but they also had a personal relationship," Camilla said.

"He's an ex-Navy Seal," David added, as though this were significant.

"And why did Mondragan leave?" Cliff asked. Doug had returned and was listening, trying to catch up.

"He went hunting for Harry, and I went with him, because we were going everywhere in twos," I said. "But then I was distracted by a stray dog," I pointed at the creature curled by the fire, "and I had to get her somewhere warm."

Cliff clearly wanted to roll his eyes; his girlfriend Isabelle had a similar ability to attract strays, and they now lived in a small apartment with two cats and a St. Bernard named Barkley. He couldn't blame Isabelle for the cats, though. Sam and Cliff had found those together. "How long ago?"

"Not even half an hour," Charlie offered. "I'm sure Mondo is just trying to track him. He feels—the need to do something. He was Sasha's protection, and he feels that he failed."

I hadn't thought of this, and I spared a moment of sympathy for Mondo. He had loved her, the poor man.

Doug said, "I think Detective Blake has filled you in on the plan. If you'd all like to go to your rooms and pack a few things—just the necessities—you'll be moving down the road within fifteen minutes. Please do not contact anyone while—"

David held up the basket. "We collected phones," he said.

Doug nodded approvingly. "Good. We'll return them when our interviews are finished."

Cliff pointed to the whiteboard. "I assume you kept copies of all your notes?"

Charlie said, "I took pictures on my phone. But I didn't make any calls."

"Good. Okay, go pack, everyone. We'll see you down here in fifteen."

When the others left, Camilla and I got big, comforting hugs from our friends. "You okay?" Doug asked us.

We nodded. Camilla said, "There are more people in the basement. Some staff, a cook, and a limo driver."

"I'll check it out. Where's the basement?" Cliff asked.

Camilla led him out of the room, and I said, "How did you guys get here in this crazy snow?"

Doug grinned. "We had a crazy vehicle. And a good driver. You should meet him." He nudged me toward the door. "But grab a coat."

My coat lay nearby, cast on the floor when I brought in the dog. I threw it on and marched back outside in my boots. At the foot of the driveway sat a giant SUV with ridiculously huge tires. It seemed almost like a bus. I moved swiftly toward it, and the driver got out and grinned at me. "Sam!" I shouted. I bounded a few more steps, and then I was in his arms.

"I was so worried about you," he said in my ear. "I made a deal with Doug. I'd find a way to get them here if I could come along. Totally against regulations, but Doug was just grateful for the vehicle."

I was still squeezing him, but I studied the car over his shoulder. "And just where did you get this behemoth? We don't own it now, do we?"

He disentangled me enough that he could see my face. "I like the fact that you said we. Makes us sound married."

"We essentially are," I said, beaming at his handsome face, and soaking up the beauty of his blue eyes. "Which means everything that's yours is mine."

He laughed. "But not vice versa?"

I grinned. "I don't have a lot, but if you want Lestrade, I will share him."

"God, it's good to see you." He kissed me, and I clung to him for a moment, wanting his warmth. Eventually he pulled away, his expression at least one-fourth smug. "And now, about the vehicle. You know Ken Schuler, of the Blue Lake Schulers?"

The Schulers had a long history in Blue Lake, and their descendants dotted the landscape for many diametrical miles. "Yes, I've heard of him."

"Well, he has a car dealership. And he has a twenty-year-old son who loves monster trucks, and who kitted out an SUV to be able to drive through any weather that nature could throw its way."

"And you had to pay—what? For the use of this monster?"

He shrugged. "I would have paid anything. Seeing you safe is worth the price."

"Oh, I have a confession. You and I have become adoptive parents again."

His eyes widened. Lord, he was an attractive man. "What? Another cat?'

I shook my head. "A very sweet little dog, actually.

Her owners moved and just left her out in the cold."

Sam's face turned grim. "That's a mighty horrible thing to do."

"I know. Listen, come inside. I have to pack."

He shook his head. "Doug doesn't want me linked with them in front of the suspects. Someone will complain and cry improper procedure. I am to be a driver only, and will ferry people down to the B and B a few at a time. Then of course I'll stay there. But from this point, I am Sam the driver. Tell Camilla."

"Okay, Sam the driver. I fear the B and B might be overloaded. I might have to share my room."

His lip twitched. "What you do on holiday is your own business."

"Exactly." I touched his nose. "Here I go." I turned and plowed through the snow in a much happier frame of mind. I still felt sad about Sasha and suspicious of the people in the house, but the terrible row between David and Oliver had utterly slipped my mind.

For the time being, anyway.

***

Because of the giant vehicle, Sam only had to make three trips down the road to ferry a total of fifteen people away from Green Glass Manor. The relief of departing was so great I felt a general unclenching of my muscles as we drove through the white world to another destination. I had not wanted to witness the crime scene people in their clinical white garments, to look on as they carried a stretcher with its grim and painful burden. Poor Sasha. She had been so happy, so vibrant, so excited about her big adventure, perhaps the biggest promotion she had ever created.

I sighed as I walked up the steps of the Bed and Breakfast, named Dark Woods Lodge, with Camilla and Gloria at my side. Some of the men were handling the luggage, and we were supposed to check in.

Zoe sounded resentful and tired. "Who's supposed to pay for this? I don't normally stay in upscale vacation rentals, and my funds are limited." Two of the "basement people," the cook and the driver, stood near her, and they nodded their agreement.

Oliver appeared behind them, holding some bags. "The rent is covered," he said. "Your stay is free, all of you. David and I have already made arrangements with Michael there, so he knows to send your bill to us."

Zoe and the other women murmured their thanks, and people began to drift out of the darkly-paneled room. Doug said, "Get settled in your rooms, and we'll meet in the Forest View Room in half an hour."

I heard Doug and Cliff murmuring to the innkeeper, Michael, about turning off the phones in the rooms. I understood the reason for this, but suddenly the darkness of the place, and the oppressive feeling of confinement, sent my mood plummeting again.

Camilla appeared at my elbow and said, "I feel I've been smuggled back to England. Dark Woods sounds a bit Gothic for an American Bed and Breakfast."

"It feels Gothic, too. Do you feel it? Or is it just me?"

"I do feel it, but it's not only the place. It's everything." We moved toward the counter.

I murmured, "I suppose you and I can pay for our own rooms."

Camilla lifted her chin. "No. I intend to let Oliver and David pay. It's the least they can do after that dreadful display."

"Yeah, what was that all about? And did you—incite things a bit?"

She smiled sadly. "I did. But only because I was tired of them lying to each other. The rest of us knew how they had sabotaged one another. It's a shame, Lena. They have always been good friends. Perhaps they will remain so. I don't know."

We checked in with Michael and accepted our room keys, then made our way up a dark wood staircase that curved into an upper landing. My mind was on the other people who had climbed these stairs, who had climbed Sasha's stairs, as well. Someone had climbed down, when we were all asleep, to commit an act of murder. Could it really have been one of Sasha's friends? Or did Harry's unsanctioned departure mean that he had done it? If he had killed Sasha, why would he have returned at six in the morning?

Mondo, who had returned just as we were leaving Green Glass Manor, told Cliff and Doug that he believed Harry had made it to the main road and been picked up by someone.

"We'll get him," Cliff had reiterated, and then he and Mondo talked a bit about Mondo's time in the Navy before Cliff dismissed him and went on with his police business.

We tromped into the lobby, to the surprise and delight of Michael Davis, the trim innkeeper who stood behind the Dark Woods counter, assessing the large size of our party. He had probably assumed the snow would cancel all business. Yes, he had rooms for everyone, he assured us, and he was solicitude itself when he heard of the traumatic event. "For those of you who need to relax, we have a sauna, and a tiny solarium with padded chairs. The sun is a great healer," he said in a soothing tone.

He was also quite amenable to the dog's presence, as long as we paid the pet fee. I held her in my arms, and she curled against my chest contentedly, watching the world from her new and improved vantage point.

Soon I had been settled into a small but pretty room with a peacock-toned coverlet on the bed and a compelling woodland scene on the wall. The dog was curled on the bed, watching me closely as I moved around, putting my few things in a dresser drawer and a tall wardrobe. "Don't worry, Sweetheart, I'm not going to put you out in the snow."

A knock sounded on my door, and I opened to find Camilla, looking thoughtful. "It's a bit unclear what we should do next," she said. "We still have thirty minutes before the police briefing."

I pointed at the little bathroom in one corner. "This room is small, but surprisingly, it has a full bathtub. I'm thinking I'll give that pup a good cleaning."

Camilla brightened. "I'll help! She will be so much easier to bathe than my two brutes." She looked fond as she mentioned her dogs.

I laughed, and we went into the small bathroom to fill the tub with warm water. I feared I would have to wrestle with the dog to get her in the tub, but she surprised both of us by trotting into the room and leaping in.

"Apparently she has bathed before," I said, as I wiped droplets of water from my face.

Camilla did the same, laughing. "She really is quite pretty."

"I know! Okay, I'll be shampoo girl, and you be rinse girl."

Dutiful, Camilla lifted the sprayer and tested the temperature on her wrist. Together we washed the little dog and enjoyed her changing expressions and little doggie sounds.

Camilla turned to me, suddenly beaming. "Oh, Lena. I will have such fun when you have babies. I so want to be there at their bath time, watching them sail boats, and standing ready with a towel and a grandma hug."

My expression must have been strange, because her brows went up. "I thought you told me that you and Sam want children."

"Oh, yes, we do," I assured her. "But—it will all be so real soon, Camilla. Sam will be my husband, and you and Tabitha will be proud Grandmas."

"Honorary ones, but as devoted as blood," she said, smiling.

I sighed. I had finished shampooing, and the dog's coat was emerging as an appealing mix of copper and white. "I suppose this lady could use a name."

"Indeed. What does she look like? Or should you call her snowflake because you found her in the snow?"

I thought about this, and an idea bloomed. "Camilla, what's that surreal Scandinavian novel about the woman who sensed snow and ice?"

Camilla was like an encyclopedia, especially for mysteries. "Smilla's Sense of Snow. That was a beautiful book, wasn't it? But sad."

"Well, it's Scandinavian."

She grinned. "Who was the author? Peter Something. Peter Hoeg! Yes, a great novel. So." She looked at the pretty dog that I was lifting out of the water. We both went to work with towels, rubbing her fur. "You think Smilla suits her?"

The dog looked up at her, its face bright. "Oh, look at that. She knows her name. And she did have a sense of snow, because she survived in it."

"Smilla rhymes with Camilla," she said, playing with Smilla's whiskers.

"Then it was meant to be."

We laughed as we tidied the room and treated Smilla to bowls of food and water that Michael brought up at our request. He continued to look radiantly happy at the thought of the day's custom.

We left Smilla to her food and her post-bath nap, and we headed downstairs to the Forest View room, a large porch-like area with windows on three sides that allowed one to feel utterly lost in the woods. It was both beautiful and mildly discomfiting. We sat down on a small couch that was part of a large conversational grouping. My eyes were drawn to the wildlife. I saw several squirrels, and two chipmunks that looked like

Sam's little friend Eager, and birds that flashed past in a series of bright colors. At one point a hedgehog ambled past, unhurried and unafraid of the humans behind the glass.

Doug cleared his throat, and I turned to see that everyone was present, including two "downstairs" people from Sasha's house, young men who had unknown job descriptions. They sat near Mondo, who mostly stared at the floor. Zoe was once again chatting to the cook, who had finally been introduced as Evelyn Barnard, and Carla the driver sat close behind them. Gloria and Charlie sat on another loveseat, and David and Oliver sat in single chairs. Bob looked pale, probably going through camera withdrawal.

"Thank you for coming down. I understand that this has been a terrible shock," Doug said. "Sasha was close to almost all of you, and even if you only worked on her staff, you were probably fond of her." People nodded, some wiping their eyes. "But we are faced with an inescapable fact: someone killed Sasha last night, quite brutally, and that someone is most likely someone in this room."

"What about Harry? Or whatever that guy's name was?" Mondo said, his chin jutting out. "Slipping away while we weren't paying attention? What could be more suspicious than that?"

Doug nodded. "Definitely suspicious, but obviously we need to interrogate him. He could be a murderer, or he could be someone who simply felt uncomfortable, or who had another job to do. We'll find out."

Cliff, who had been on the phone, moved to Doug's side. "We found him. Some officers have detained him and will be bringing him here in short order."

Mondo looked gratified. He nodded.

Doug looked around at the group. "Let's not assume that Harry is the guilty party. Someone had a motive for killing Sasha, and someone thought it would be a smart idea to kill her when lots of people were wandering around, hoping they could slip into the crowd and escape detection. But you know what they say—every contact leaves a trace."

Cliff nodded his agreement. "What we'd like to do is interview all of you. Doug will be at the end of the hall in the conference room, and I will be in the solarium." He pointed in the appropriate direction as he mentioned the rooms. "After all the interviews are complete, we'll let you eat some dinner. If it seems prudent, we'll return your phones. If it doesn't, we'll hold on to them for a bit longer. We may ask to speak with some of you more than once. This won't necessarily mean we think you're a murderer. You all saw things from individual and distinct perspectives. Some of you might have evidence without realizing that you do. Finding that evidence will take time."

Once again, there were murmurs of assent. The group looked fairly docile at this point. I wondered how they would look after a few hours of interrogation.

Doug was speaking again. "Before we begin individual interviews, I have some questions I'd like to ask of the whole group. Perhaps we can put some puzzle pieces together. First, when did everyone last see Sasha?"

We went down the line, each person describing their final encounter with her. No one had seen her after midnight except Zoe.

Doug looked at Zoe. "And you and Sasha both drank this tea, which had been sitting in a pot in the kitchen?"

Zoe nodded. "We had kept it on hand if anybody wanted it. It sat on a warmer, so it was a drinkable temperature."

"And anyone could have accessed the pot—for how long?"

Zoe shrugged. "About—four or five hours? I think Mrs. Barnard made a pot at about seven or eight for people to drink with dessert."

Doug looked at Evelyn Barnard, who nodded assent. His expression was quizzical. "And yet no one could have known that you and Sasha would stay up late, or that you would drink tea."

Zoe shrugged at this, unable to add more information. Charlie lifted a hand and said, "We did know, actually. Sasha said something about it before we all left. Someone asked if she would be following her own curfew, and she laughed."

Oliver sat up straight. "That's right! She said she would probably be up until the wee hours, drinking tea and making plans, or something like that."

"How many people heard her say this?" Doug asked, his face alert. Then he shook his head. "Let me put that another way. Raise your hand if you heard Sasha make that comment about the tea."

After a moment, most of those assembled raised their hands. Evelyn, Carla, the two young men, and Mondo kept their hands down.

Cliff and Doug glanced at each other, their faces inscrutable, and Doug made some notes on his phone.

Cliff said, "Lena told us that she heard Zoe fall against her door at three in the morning. Did anyone else hear that sound?"

David held up his hands. "I sleep like I'm hibernating. I heard nothing."

A few other voices chimed in, suggesting that they too were heavy sleepers. Camilla, who had been observing everything with her usual thoughtful expression, said "I may have heard it. I know I had a dream about a brick wall falling inward, trapping people below it."

This small detail seemed to cast a pall over the group. She had only been describing a dream, but something about the idea of being trapped under a giant wall raised unpleasant associations, at least for me. I thought of Poe's *The Cask of Amontillado*, and the ghastly jingling of a jester's bells….

"Lena, after that sound, did you hear anything else?"

I shook my head. "No. I listened for a while, thinking it might be part of the game, but then I fell back asleep. I didn't wake up until Harry called my phone."

At the mention of Harry, we all looked at Cliff, who looked at his watch. "He'll be here in about ten minutes. Then he can join us in answering questions." Cliff's jaw looked hard, unyielding.

Doug asked, "Did Sasha talk to any of you about

feeling nervous, or out of sorts? Did she express any anxiety?"

Gloria spoke. "She was anxious about the event. She had a lot riding on it, in terms of her reputation. She wanted everything to go well, but she admitted that you can't account for everything. You can miss small details, and one little thing could bring it all crashing down."

Again, I thought of the brick wall, falling with inevitable weight.

"And was she worried about a small detail she might have missed?" Doug persisted.

Gloria shook her head. "Not that she mentioned. Mainly she was just excited, and glad to see us. Us four," she clarified, pointing at the competitors. "We were all friends, going way back."

No one else seemed to notice her use of the past tense, but I wondered if in fact some of their friendships were now in question.

Camilla was still deep in thought, but she raised a finger as she thought of something. "I spoke with her before I went upstairs. I thanked her for the invitation, and I said that I had found some intriguing clues. Her eyes grew bright at that. She loved a good mystery." Camilla's eyes were bright, too, but with unshed tears. "She asked what clues I thought I had found—because of course we didn't even know what the crime would be—and I told her some of the things that had caught my notice: a calendar with a large red X on several dates. A lamp with a torn shade—very unlike Sasha, to let that go unrepaired—and some family photographs that seemed out of place. Sasha nodded at these details, but she also looked slightly troubled, as though one or more of them had not been as she expected."

Doug tapped away at his phone. "Helpful. Thank you, Camilla." He and Cliff murmured to each other for a moment, and then Doug said, "Now. Please think back and tell me which other people you saw that evening, after Sasha set you free to look for clues. Think also about anything that seemed strange or out of place."

"Or any people who seemed out of place," Cliff added.

We all sat and thought. And as we attempted to surface memories from the previous night, the mood in the room seemed to change, and the light outside grew suddenly dim. A palpable misery sat upon us. Mondo sat up. "I did my evening rounds at about midnight. Just before, I guess, because some of the guests were still moving around." He pointed at David. "I saw him coming out of Sasha's office."

David looked unperturbed. "Indeed. I went into every room on the main floor, trolling for clues. I felt paranoid that Camilla knew something I didn't." His final comment was meant to be a joke, but somehow it fell flat.

Mondo said, "I also saw her," he pointed at Zoe, "and that guy," he indicated Charlie with a lift of his chin. "They were talking, looking kind of intense."

All eyes turned to the two young people. Charlie shrugged. "Zoe and I were both concerned about Sasha. I had noted a sort of manic quality in her behavior, and

I asked if she was getting enough sleep. Zoe said no, that Sasha had been working too hard and sleeping too little."

"I think she might have been taking some pills, you know. Like caffeine pills, or whatever is in those energy pills. Like uppers, I guess."

Doug's eyes lasered in on her. "Are you sure she was taking pills?"

Zoe shook her head. "No. I just—had the sense that she was on something. Not, like, illegal drugs. Sasha didn't do that stuff. Just some sort of stimulant. But I never asked her."

"We'll know after the autopsy," Doug said. "And that's all you were talking about? Just Sasha's demeanor?"

Charlie glanced briefly at Gloria. "I think I asked something about Gloria's, uh—previous relationships."

Zoe's face was eager. "Oh, right!! You asked me if she had ever dated Mondo, or David or Oliver."

Charlie's face reddened, and Gloria looked at him, surprised. "Charles, what--?"

The door opened, and Harry appeared, his face a mixture of embarrassment and defiance. His escort, a uniformed officer in a puffy coat, waved at Cliff. "Thanks very much." Cliff called, waving back. "We'll take it from here."

The officer disappeared, and Doug invited Harry to take one of the few empty seats. Harry plopped in a chair.

Doug said, "Your full name, please?"

"Harry Pratt. And before you ask my occupation, I am a trainer at Pumped, the Health Club in downtown Daleville. Sasha worked out there, and we always chatted."

"And that's how she came to ask you for help in her P.R. event?"

"Yeah. I thought it sounded hilarious, and she was offering me a bundle of cash. It was perfect timing, because I wanted to get my girlfriend something nice for Valentine's Day."

When Sam and I would marry. I looked around, hoping to spot him, but he was lying low as the "driver."

"Did you have a key to Sasha's house?" Cliff asked.

Harry sighed. "Obviously not, or I wouldn't have frozen my private parts off waiting for someone to answer the door."

"And how exactly did you get my number?" I asked.

He looked up. "I couldn't get Sasha or Zoe to answer the phone, so I went to the event link that Sasha had sent me and scrolled through the names. I didn't think the big-name writers would be listed, so I decided to go through the names of the minor players. No offense," he said, shooting an apologetic glance to me.

I nodded. I thought of myself that way, too, especially in contrast to Camilla. She had earned her greatness. Time would tell whether I had her staying power.

"Anyway, thank God Miss London's number was listed. I was starting to worry I would ruin the whole event by being late, or in the wrong spot, or something."

"And why did you leave Green Glass Manor before the police arrived?"

He scratched his head, a nervous gesture. "Frankly, no one was paying any attention to me at all, and I felt like I wasn't really necessary to their whole dialogue they were having about motives and clues and stuff. Like they thought they were in a detective novel." He paused, perhaps assuming we would all shout at him, but the room was silent. He said, "Everyone was going in and out of the kitchen to get some food. I remembered that when Sasha gave me the word, I was supposed to quietly disappear, and she said she would leave my payment inside a black box on the kitchen counter. I went in there and found an envelope with my name. I know I didn't do the job, but I did show up at the crack of dawn, and it was no longer possible to do what I'd been paid to do. I took the money and walked out the kitchen door."

Cliff and Doug nodded at each other. Doug made some notes, and Cliff said, "Did you have a romantic relationship with Sasha Hardwick?"

Harry looked surprised. "No. I told you I have a girlfriend. And no offense, but Sasha is way older than me."

Than I, corrected my grammar brain. A devotion to correct grammar and usage was another thing I had in common with Camilla.

"Age doesn't matter," Charlie said. "Sasha was a beautiful woman. Who cares how many years she had lived?" Gloria looked almost amused at these words, but she was clearly gratified, and she sent Charlie a smoldering look.

Harry shrugged. "Yeah, she was pretty, but we were never involved that way. And I was really upset and sorry to hear that someone had—that she—was dead."

Zoe wiped at her eyes, and Evelyn Barnard slung a

motherly arm around her. Carla leaned forward and whispered something in her ear, and Zoe nodded.

At this point, Doug seemed to realize that we needed a change of scene. "All right. We'll start our interviews now. If you could all wait in the main lounge, you'll find some food and drink out there so you can have some dinner and relax while we get your individual statements."

I wondered where Doug had procured food in the middle of a snowstorm, but it turned out that "Sam the driver" had gone out in his monster vehicle with the edict that he should find any kind of food-making establishment that had dared to stay open despite the giant drifts.

When we entered the lounge, we found that Sam had come through with some fragrant pizza, stacked in a tower of boxes that would feed far more than fifteen people. The group fell on the food hungrily, supplied with plates and napkins by a beaming Michael. We all drifted to seats in the main lounge, except for David, who was sent to Cliff's interview room, and Gloria, who was sent to Doug's. They told us that we would be questioned in random order, but I wondered if there were any pattern to the way that they wanted to question us. Camilla and I ate our food and looked out the lounge window at the last visible lines of orange on the horizon. Dusk had fallen quickly, and darkness would be upon us in minutes. The coming of the dark seemed to weigh heavily upon us. While the sun had shone and the snow had sparkled, we had been able to distract ourselves with a mystery, with a disappearing man, with a half-frozen animal, with a move down the wooded lane to another residence.

Now, in the dark paneled lounge, there was a weary sadness on the faces in the shadowed room. Now, in the snowy silence, we had nothing to divert us from the truth. Camilla and I sat without talking, comforted by one another but thinking our own thoughts. For some reason I was recalling Sasha's perfume, a sweet scent that was also sophisticated—something that implied both fresh air and glamour. I recalled the way her fall of hair had swooped forward when she bent to greet us. She had been so capable, so strong. It was hard to imagine anyone overpowering her or out-thinking her.

The sun was gone. David and Gloria were back, both looking rather shaken. Charles and I were the next to be summoned—he to Cliff and I to Doug. As we left the room, he gave me a weak smile. "Quite a day, huh?"

I nodded. "A horrible day. I want to wake up tomorrow and find it was a nightmare."

"You and me both. No offense to Indiana, but I don't think I'll be returning in this lifetime."

His final word silenced both of us. We had been reminded that a lifetime could be very short, indeed.

We parted in the hallway to travel to our different rooms. Charlie waved, and I moved down the dark hall, disturbed by a new and unwelcome thought: had that been a trace of Sasha's perfume that I had inhaled as he waved farewell?

Ten

"The sound of the shot comes after the impact, after the first glimmer of pain. To the wounded man, reality travels faster than a bullet."

--from *Officer Down*, by David Canfield, 1997.

Doug was sitting at a desk in one corner, texting. He looked up at me and set down his phone. "Belinda says to hurry home. But she said not to worry because she, Allison and Isabelle are taking care of some little wedding details."

"Oh, the wedding." I waved my hand. "It seems like a world away from here."

Doug put on his sage face. "This too shall pass. Cliff and I are on it. When have we ever let you down?"

"Never," I admitted. "But this seems impossible. These are real people, Camilla's friends and other nice people just doing their jobs, going about their day. No one could possibly have a motive to do a brutal thing."

"Anyone can kill, Lena," His voice was soft. "We're all capable of it."

"Well, that's heartening."

He laughed and lifted his phone. "Okay, I'm going to take notes. You start with your arrival at Green Glass Manor. Tell me everything, but think back to things that were strange or out of place."

"I mean, I wouldn't know, because I've never been there before. Camilla would know, maybe." I saw his expression and said, "But okay, here we go. We arrived and dealt with some reporters. Camilla spoke to them, being all adorable and smart. Then David appeared out of nowhere and lifted Camilla right in the air; I thought it was rude, but Camilla laughed. She looked like a twenty-something the minute she reunited with her old friends."

Doug nodded, tapping at his keys.

"Then we went in and met Zoe, who seemed very organized and busy, and I happened to glance at David, and he had this angry look on his face. I didn't know if he was angry with one of us, or he remembered something, but it made me uncomfortable. A moment later he seemed fine."

"And you didn't ask him anything about it, curious cat that you are?"

"No. I—didn't like him at first. He seemed ready to hit on me, so I mentioned Sam or Camilla did, and then he backed off."

"Did he seem—predatory?"

"Not really. But he and Oliver both—they seemed to have this mindset that just because they were at this event, they were on a hunt for women. I don't know if that's just who they are, or if they were trying to maintain some façade of being—I don't know, virile and sexual."

Doug thought about this as he typed. Perhaps he saw a motive in the idea of a man whose sexual advances had been rejected. But how would that result in a knife in the back? It didn't seem likely to me.

"Go on."

"Okay. We met Sasha, and then Gloria and Charles, and we sat down for some refreshments. Sasha was excited and glowing and in total hostess mode. I liked her." I paused. My body felt heavy, and warm. I imagined going outside and flinging myself into the snow. "She showed us our rooms, and I spent time looking around. The house is amazing, and there really is green glass everywhere. My room had this little hall with a wide window and just tons of green glass objects. I wouldn't have thought green was such an amazing color, but it was magical—like being under the sea, or in Coleridge's land of ice."

Doug pursed his lips. "As always, I don't get your reference. Save the literary stuff for Camilla."

I sighed. "Samuel Taylor Coleridge? The Romantic. He wrote 'The Rime of the Ancient Mariner.'"

Doug brightened. "The guy with the albatross."

"Yes. And he goes on this voyage, and before they know it, the ship is surrounded by walls of ice. Like glaciers, or fjords, or something. But the ice is higher than the ship, and it's green. Other-worldly and enchanting, I always thought, that image."

"Yeah."

"So that's how it felt. Kind of magical. I thought it

was beautiful that Mr. Hardwick was smitten with his wife Selena to the extent that when she said once that she loved green, he just showered her with green. Camilla said she wore a giant emerald, too. Their lives sounded idyllic, but their children suffered terrible fates."

Doug sat straighter. "What do you mean, children?"

"Oh, Sasha told me she had a brother, but he died young. Back in the late nineties. He was just a kid, essentially. He had cool collections, including Teddy Bears. There was one in my room, and that's what got us talking."

"Died how?"

"In a car accident. She said it was a long time ago, but I could see that it still hurt to think of him."

He typed for a while. "Then what?"

"Then . . . I texted Sam and we chatted for about an hour. Eventually we went down for dinner, and I met Oliver. He's very charismatic, have you noticed? I was sort of under his spell, and Sasha had seated us next to each other, so we were talking a lot."

"About what?"

"I don't really remember." I didn't. It seemed like a year ago.

"He flirted with you?"

"Yes, I suppose. Like I said, he's very charming, and he has this kind of forcefield around him."

"Thinking of canceling the wedding?" Doug said, his blond head lowered so he wouldn't have to see my face.

"Haha. He's got nothing on Sam. Besides which, he acted like a child. I was in my room later while we were all supposed to be gathering clues. But Charlie and I had been told we couldn't collaborate with our partners, so I kind of gave up on the mystery part. I felt pretty confident that Camilla would win. Anyway, I was in my room and someone knocked and shoved a note under the door. By the time I went over there and flung the door open, the hall was empty. The note said something about how I shouldn't trust Oliver Lord."

Doug's brows rose. "Did that frighten you?"

"No, because Camilla came, and I asked if she got a note. She hadn't, but she looked at mine and then marched straight down to Oliver and made him admit he wrote it. Like I said, childish."

Doug frowned. "But for what purpose? Even if he wanted to seduce you, why would a note telling you not to trust him help with that endeavor?"

I shrugged. "I have no idea. But later, when he and David got in a fist fight in front of all of us, I realized that they were not the kind of men I had thought they were. Camilla was disgusted, too."

"And the fight was about their respective wives?"

"Yes. Apparently, they both had affairs, or David thought Oliver had an affair, or vice versa, and they told each other's wives, supposedly out of respect for those women."

Doug wrote. Then he said, "Whose behavior seemed the oddest to you, out of everyone?"

"Gosh, I don't know. Everyone looks weird in retrospect. Harry showing up at that crazy time, and then leaving. Zoe being drugged. Charlie being so infatuated with Gloria. Mondo with his Navy Seal energy. Then there was that weird "Manor House" feeling of the people who were downstairs and the ones who were upstairs. I mean, every floor was luxurious, but it felt odd, sending "the help" downstairs. Even Mondo's apartment was down there, I think."

Doug was typing rapidly now, deep in thought.

"It was also strange that David and Oliver kind of became the authorities when we found Sasha's body. I don't know if they were making the sexist assumption that as "the men" they should automatically be in charge, or if it was something else. Even Mondo pointed out that he was the security officer, and he should be in charge. But I think he was too devastated about what happened. I think he really cared."

"She was quite rich, correct? Her own business, and then family money?"

"Yes, that's what Camilla said."

"And no one to inherit now?"

"I think Camilla said there was a cousin or two. One of them runs a children's charity. Maybe some of the money will go to that."

"Hmmm. Anything else you can think of?"

"No. Just that I realized several people are out of work now. The cook, and those young men who work at the house, and the little waitresses who came from down the street. And the poor limo driver had to call her boss and explain that she couldn't come back until she was released."

Doug scowled. "What waitresses?"

***

I went back to my room, drained, at about eight o'clock. Camilla had given me a warm hug and said she would retire for the evening, and I felt happy to do the same. I opened the door to find Sam lounging on my bed, Smilla tucked against him. He was absently petting her ears while he watched some hockey game on television. Smilla's little snout rested on his thigh, and it looked as though they had been loyal companions forever.

"Isn't that just predictable. I rescue her, nurture her, bathe her, feed her—and she falls in love with you." I walked into the room and perched on the edge of the bed.

He grinned. "All the ladies in this room are in love with me."

"Egotist." I lifted my legs onto the bed and scooted up beside him letting my head drop on the plump pillow.

"Tough night?"

"Yes. Doug is a thorough interrogator. But I can't complain, no one can, because look what poor Sasha went through. What she lost."

He stroked my hair with his free hand. "We'll go home soon."

"Thank God. I feel bad for Camilla, too. This was supposed to be so fun. And it was going to be such great publicity for her—a way to get lots of new young fans."

Sam smoothed my eyebrows with a gentle finger. "I think social media has already taken care of that. People are chatting away as though the event had really happened. I went to the site, and the conversation has become huge. That interview with Camilla that they did in front of the house? Millions of views. It's a great clip."

"Well, that's good. That means book sales, of course." I closed my eyes. "We are due for talks on a new one. We've almost finished *Danger at Debenham Station,* and Camilla has already sent in her memoir. She wrote it in a matter of weeks. Her editor loves it."

"Always working, you two. So, what do I call my little companion here?"

"I named her Smilla. From Smilla's Sense of Snow."

"I read that," Sam said, pleased to know the reference.

I opened one eye. "Yeah? Do you know 'The Rime of the Ancient Mariner'?"

Sam said, "That's a great poem!" To my surprise, he adopted a sonorous voice and recited:

The many men, so beautiful!
And they all dead did lie:
And a thousand thousand slimy things
Lived on; and so did I.

"Oooh. You picked a very creepy part. I'm so impressed, though! Doug didn't even recognize the name."

Sam nodded gravely. "Because he is a philistine."

I laughed. "He remembered eventually. But you win." I turned to look at him. "For many reasons."

"Why don't we put Smilla on the floor?" he asked, his voice low and sexy.

"Yes. But let me get ready for bed first." I forced myself out of my comfortable position and dragged over to the bathroom, where I changed into pajamas, washed my face, and brushed my teeth. These ablutions had a revitalizing effect, and I went back to Sam feeling brighter. "Let me find some extra blankets, and I can make her a little nest by the heater. Oh, but I should probably take her out for a nighttime wee," I said. I could hear the reluctance in my own voice.

Sam laughed. "I already did, my pajama princess. She's ready to doss down for the night."

"Perfect. Okay, Smilla, let's get you set up." I found a very cushy comforter in the closet and folded it into a pillowy shape. Smilla slid off the bed and came over to investigate. She stood briefly by the heater, which was currently blowing hot air, then sniffed me, then put a tentative paw on the silky coverlet. "Go ahead, sweetie," I encouraged her.

She jumped in. She seemed to appreciate the softness for a moment. As we might have expected, she made several intense doggie-circles before settling into a spot with a tiny "hmmph" sound.

"That was surprisingly easy," Sam said. "Unless she jumps back the minute I have you in my clutches."

"How very villainous that sounds. I think she'll stay. Her eyes are already closed." Sure enough, when I was safely cuddled against Sam, Smilla stayed where she was, snoring delicately.

Sam had begun to investigate my neck and shoulder with his mouth, as though he were searching for some invisible treasure that could only be detected through touch. "That's very sexy," I said.

He was not deterred, but he murmured, "Practicing for the honeymoon."

I giggled, and felt myself melting, relaxing, letting everything go.

***

It was still dark when I woke. I slid my hand across the sheet to find that Sam was gone. I sat up and peered toward the bathroom, which seemed dark. "Sam?" I called in a hushed voice.

My eyes moved downward, and I saw that Smilla was missing, too. Ah—so she had wakened him in the night and he had decided to take her outside. I waited a while, then slipped out of bed to look out the window. Naturally, I saw only the outlines of trees in the dark. A flash of light almost blinded me, but then went out. I heard a dog bark, and a voice shouting. Was it Sam's? Butterflies began to flutter in my mid-section, and something cold crept up my spine. Wrong, something was wrong.

I ran to the closet, donned my coat and boots, and made my way into the dark hall. I had no idea where I might find a light switch, so I had to feel my way toward the stairs. The hallway smelled slightly musty, like an attic in an old house, and I longed suddenly for Graham House, or Sam House, where I felt comfortable and at home. My hand found a banister, and I toed my way tentatively to the top stair, making my way down in gloom and silence. I reminded myself of the layout when

I reached the bottom step: a lounge to the right, a hallway before me leading to the front door.

Swiftly, on little cat feet, I moved to the door, found the lock with hurried fingers, and unlatched it, letting myself out into the crisp, cold night. There were woods in every direction, though straight ahead was the woodland road from which we had come. My window had looked out to the back of the building, so I turned right and moved around the house, my feet crunching through snow that glowed slightly in the dark.

A figure came hurtling around the corner and almost knocked me down. A face came close to mine, and two hands steadied me. "Who is that—Lena? Did you hear a shot?"

"A shot?" My dull brain could not process what he meant. I thought of whiskey shots and a shot put. It was as if my brain purposely avoided the obvious connotation.

"A gunshot. I heard something, and a shout, and—"

Before he could say more, a sound tore through the darkness, an exploding sound with an echoing effect that shivered away into the night.

"Shit," said Oliver. He turned back and began to run toward the woods. I followed him, still strangely muddled in my thoughts, with the cotton-wool feeling that shock sometimes brings. There was a mini flashlight in my pocket, the one that I used when I walked Smilla. I fumbled for it now and shone it on the path, and Oliver turned. "Good. Good. I've been wishing for my phone light. I need to see." His voice was urgent, yet distracted.

Oliver's fear ignited my fear. "What is happening?" I demanded. "Where is Sam?"

"Who?" Oliver asked in a soft voice. He had paused, panting slightly, and was listening for a sound, any sound.

"Sam?" I called. "Where are you?"

"Shh," Oliver warned with an angry look at me. "We don't know who's out there!"

I knew Sam was in those woods, but I took his point. We didn't know who was lurking nearby with a gun.

We approached a small clearing, and Oliver shot out an iron hand, stopping me in my tracks. "Wait," he breathed. "Look."

I peered into the murky clearing and could just make out a figure lying in the snow. It seemed to be a man, flat and unmoving.

"No," I whispered. "No." And then I ran. How I made it through the giant drifts as quickly as I did, I had no idea, but I was there in mere seconds, falling to my knees next to the supine body in the snow. The man's eyes were open, and he looked at me. It was David.

Relief flowed through me like warm water; I almost tipped over. Now that my eyes had adjusted to the light, I saw what I had not seen before—blood. The snow had turned red near David's side, and he was clutching his left arm with his right hand.

"Are you alright?" I asked, feeling inept.

"Shot," he managed. "Losing blood."

Oliver reached us and began to examine the wound. "Why were you out here, you fool?" he asked, but his voice was gentle, and he had thrown off his coat and removed his shirt to make a tourniquet. It was impressive, how quickly and deftly he moved.

David managed the ghost of a smile. "Thought I saw something. Figured we were in the real mystery now. Couldn't resist."

We heard footsteps coming toward us, the gentle squeaking of boots in the snow. I held up my light to behold Sam, moving toward us with Smilla at his side. He lifted a hand in greeting, just as we heard another rifle shot, ripping its way into the quiet air, reverberating, filling me with terror.

And with that sound, Sam fell.

Eleven

"It dawned on me, in that moment, that we were surrounded. And then I understood the meaning of helplessness."

--from *One of Us is Guilty,* by Gloria Gale, 2014.

"Sam!" My scream was pitched so high it barely made sound at all. I stumbled to my feet and ran, fears tumbling over each other in my head. We were about to get married! We were supposed to be happy. This was meant to be the year of good things for Sam, after several years of suffering. How could the universe do this to him? To us? No, no, no, no, went the refrain as I ran.

He wasn't dead. By the time I threw myself on the ground beside him he had struggled to a sitting position. I was patting him all over. "Are you hurt? Are you shot?"

Sam nodded. "Yeah, I think so. But I'm not gushing blood; I think it's a graze. Who's the lunatic out here with a shotgun?"

Feet ran toward us, and Doug and Cliff knelt to examine Sam.

"Where have you been?" I asked, feeling angry, but sounding near tears.

"We've been stalking a killer," Doug said. "And not finding him."

"David's shot," I said.

"I know. Oliver has him. We all need to get out of the open, before he picks us off one by one."

"Why?" I asked. "What did we do? Is this person just insane?"

Cliff had been checking out Sam's injury. "It's a nasty graze on the top of your shoulder. It's going to hurt like hell for a few weeks, but you were mightily lucky."

Doug looked thoughtful. "Get his coat, and let's go. Run!"

We all ran, keeping low and clustered together. We made it to the trees, and waited for Oliver to join us, supporting David under his good arm. A minute later we heard sirens.

"Hold on, buddy," Oliver said. He was worried; how much blood had David lost?

"Do my best," David muttered. He seemed close to losing consciousness. I bent and scooped a handful of snow, then dabbed some on David's cheeks. His eyes widened, and he nodded. "Thanks, Lena."

We plodded through the snow; I clutched Sam's hand in an iron grip, not willing to let him go. Smilla stayed close to him, moving silently at his feet.

For a surreal moment we all stopped, listening. Aside from the sirens, the forest was silent, and yet we had all sensed something, nearby and sinister.

"Hold still," Doug ordered in a whisper.

A figure burst out of the trees in front of us,

breathing raggedly, just as we heard another rifle shot. The figure screamed; it was Zoe, and as she moved closer, we saw that her face was covered in blood.

***

"Get him, get him!" Zoe cried, obviously close to hysteria. "He attacked me."

"Who attacked you?" Doug asked as Cliff moved forward to examine her wound.

"I don't know." She took a deep breath. I thought she was trying not to cry.

"Why are you out here?" Doug asked.

She shuddered. "I couldn't sleep, and I went downstairs to see if there were any more of the snacks. Then I saw Mr. West with his dog. They went outside. I thought maybe I'd go with them, get some fresh air. So, a minute later, I followed them."

"How did you know his name?" My voice sounded cold, suspicious, even to me.

She tried to roll her eyes, but it obviously hurt. "Probably everyone knows. And plus, Sasha and I kept up with the whole saga of him and his wife, and then him and you. It's not some big secret."

Doug persisted. "So, you went outside, and what?"

We had started moving again, toward the waiting ambulance. "And I couldn't find him. I thought I heard the dog barking a couple times, so I followed the sound. Then I got kind of lost because it's so flipping dark out here."

"So, you never caught up with him."

"No." Again, she sounded near tears. "And I was

starting to think I was lost out here and would die of hypothermia, and then this person just appeared on the path in front of me, holding some big long stick, or—"

"Rifle," Cliff said, almost cheerfully.

"Oh, God. I started to say something, and they just lunged forward and jammed it into my face. It hurt like crazy." She touched her face and winced. "And I fell down. I didn't even make a sound. I was so shocked, and scared, I just lay there, and they went running away."

"Man or woman?" Doug asked.

She shrugged. "Sorry. They had a hood on, and it was all dark in there. I couldn't tell. They never said a word."

We had reached the house, and the ambulance attendants summoned by Cliff and Doug ran around the side wall moments later, stretcher at the ready. They did a quick check of David and then loaded him onto the stretcher.

I heard Oliver talking to them. "One rifle shot. Might be through the arm and a partial wound on the chest. Bleeding heavily for the last, maybe ten or fifteen minutes."

The stretcher was whisked away. The EMTs seemed to want to take in Sam and Zoe, as well, but they both resisted.

Mondo appeared then, from the rear exit, stalking into the back yard, looking rumpled and half-unconscious. "What's happening?" he demanded.

Oliver went to him and spoke in a low voice for quite some time.

Mondo pointed at Sam and Zoe. "I have EMT

training; I can take care of these two. I have a first aid kit in the house."

Why? I wondered, my eyes meeting Doug's. He had the same question, I imagined, as well as where Mondo, the trained Navy Seal, had been all this time.

The ambulance left with David, and the red lights receded into the darkness. The rest of us moved into the warm house, where our host, Michael, stood in the entrance, wearing a quilted robe and looking worried.

"It's okay," Doug said. "We're all safe in here, but I am putting us on a hard lockdown until the shooter is apprehended."

"That's what I'm concerned about," Michael said. "My rifle is missing."

Twelve

"The white world exploded with the sound of guns, and Evan knew, as he hurled himself behind a frozen rock, that it meant death."

--from *Snow Hunger,* by Oliver Lord, 2015.

"So, we have a person who is out in the woods. David apparently sees something suspicious and goes to investigate," Cliff said, starting off our debrief session. Mondo had taken Sam and Zoe to another room to treat their wounds. I had followed, but Sam sent me back, saying he would be fine.

"In the woods, in the middle of the night," Camilla said angrily. "Really, I have to agree with Oliver. He was foolish to do that, to take such a risk." Her violet eyes brimmed with tears. She had joined us in the lounge the moment we returned. She had been watching for us through the glass-walled room, hoping for a glimpse of someone.

Cliff went on, concentrating on his timeline. "Then someone shoots David. Oliver hears it—right?" he turned to Oliver, who nodded.

Oliver Lord looked gray around the edges, perhaps

due to shock or worry. "It was loud. I thought everyone would be in the hall. I went running out there, looking for I don't know what, and then I ran back, thinking I should alert someone. I ran into Lena, and we both heard another shot."

Cliff looked at me, and I nodded. "And I was looking for Sam. He had gone out with Smilla, but he was taking a long time, and I was worried. I saw a light from my bedroom window, a really bright light. Was that you?" I asked Oliver.

He shook his head. "No, I had no light. I didn't think to bring anything."

Doug studied him for a moment. "So, Lena was looking for Sam, and you were looking for whomever fired the rifle."

"Yes." Lord looked thoughtful. "I don't know why; I just felt the urgency of it. Then Lena and I found David. The shooter got him in the clearing, which is also where he got Sam."

My face felt suddenly cold and bloodless. A shooter. A murderer. Picking off people in the dark as they walked through the woods. Why?

"What did David say? Anything about what he saw?"

"He saw nothing," Oliver said. "He was walking, and then he was on the ground."

"Will you be going back to search for this person?" Camilla asked.

Doug shook his head. "Not in the dark. Cliff and I don't have the equipment to take on someone who has, I'm fairly sure, night-vision capabilities."

I gasped. "But that's—pre-meditated. How could they have known anyone would be in the woods? Why were THEY in the woods?"

Doug nodded. "Great questions. We'll be looking to answer them."

Sam returned, his shirt open to reveal his naked chest. A large bandage had been wrapped under one arm and over his shoulder, securely and professionally. "All cleaned up," he said. "And not too bad a graze."

"Did Mondo say that?" I asked with narrowed eyes.

Sam shrugged, which meant no. I opened my mouth, but Cliff said, "What did you see out there?"

Sam shrugged again. "Nothing. I was walking that little lady," he pointed at Smilla, who sat in my lap, "and the next thing I knew there was a bright light, like lightning. I turned to see where it had come from, but it blinded me for a second. Then I got turned around. When I found the clearing again, I saw Lena, and the two guys, and I was just starting to greet them when something hit me and I went down. I heard the shot a second later."

Doug shook his head. "This doesn't make sense. I don't like it. We're missing some crucial pieces."

"We all need to sleep on it," Cliff said. "No one can come up with answers when they're exhausted. Doug and I will process the scene, with reinforcements, in the morning."

We agreed that this was the best plan, and I returned to my room with Sam and Smilla. The little dog went directly back to her nest and cuddled down. Sam and I did the same. Once I was nestled against him, I said, "It would be nice if you stopped trying to get killed right before our wedding."

He laughed, surprised by my ridiculous accusation, and said, "If one were to do a comparison, they would find that you try to get killed more often than I do."

"Let's just agree that neither of us will get killed."

Sam made a faux grave face. "I think that would be best."

I swallowed the lump in my throat. "When I saw you fall—"

He clutched me more tightly. "It's over. Don't think about it." He kissed my hair, and I closed my eyes. But I knew I would see it for the rest of my life: Sam's smiling face just before he dropped soundlessly into the snow, and the wrenching fear that he was dead. Even in that moment of terror, I knew that if I lost Sam, my heart would grow hard, and all lightness would disappear from my life.

***

In the morning Sam came through with egg sandwiches and bakery rolls, telling us that the roads were a bit better after a night of plowing.

Camilla sat in front of an untouched cinnamon roll, sipping tea and looking indignant. "How did I sleep through all of this? I think just about everyone was out there taking part in this horrible drama except for me."

"You're better off," I murmured. I had told her of the traumatic experience of encountering three bloody people and not knowing what the anonymous shooter was trying to prove.

"Let's think about that," she said thoughtfully, pulling off a piece of her roll. "My first thought, based on the drama of the whole thing, was that it was meant as a distraction. But if that is the case, a distraction from what?"

"Oh. That is a really good point. It does seem over the top, doesn't it? Like there was no real target. But why be out there with a gun at all? Are you saying that something else could have been going on while it happened?"

Camilla's face was at its loveliest when she was thinking. I admired it for a while, letting her apply her intelligence to the problem while I drank tea and ate some reviving chocolate in the form of frosting on my own donut. Finally, she said, "A possible distraction—from something going on in the house. But there are other possibilities. Let's say one of the three victims was the real target, but the shooter wanted to confuse the police by making it seem random."

This was also an excellent point. "You should have been a cop, Camilla."

She sipped her tea. "Oh, my dear, I would never have consented to wear the uniform."

I laughed. "I can think of a third scenario."

"Yes?" She looked at me with bright eyes.

"Well, a couple of them. First, let's say the shooter was out there for some other reason. I don't know what that could be that would require night vision and a rifle. Maybe they just wanted to leave, and the rifle was simply an insurance policy. And then they ended up having to use it, more than once, to make sure no one witnessed their departure."

Camilla tore off another bite. "This is good," she said. "If that theory were true, someone would be missing this morning, yes?"

We looked around the room. Right now, the only people in the lobby with us were Mondo, Evelyn Barnard, and Charlie. Mrs. Barnard was having an animated conversation with Michael, our proprietor, and I thought I even detected a bit of flirtation on both sides. Interesting. "I guess we'll have to wait until all are assembled."

"And what was your fourth theory?" she asked.

"Let's say the shooter was targeting David. They managed to lure him outside and get a shot in, but perhaps Sam passed too close to him or her, made them feel exposed, so they wanted to eliminate Sam, too. And then Zoe just appeared in the wrong place at the wrong time."

Camilla thought about this. "Here's what makes it seem odd to me. They had night vision glasses and a rifle. Yet they were unable to mortally wound any of their targets. Maybe because they never intended to do so?"

I leaned forward. "Which seems to support your distraction theory. It also bothers me that there are so many types of attacks. Sasha is killed with a knife. Two men are shot with a rifle, and Zoe is hit with the butt of it. Why is the assailant so inconsistent, assuming the same person is responsible for all the attacks?"

Camilla's eyes widened. "Oh, I just had a thought,

and then it drifted away. It seemed important, too. Darn." She ate another piece of her roll.

"It will come back. Your brilliant mind is always working."

"Oh, Lena. I am starting to believe your compliments." She sent me a rueful smile.

"You should. Here's another thing: if the assailant ended up coming back to the manor here, might there have been a security camera?"

She shook her head. "Doug and Cliff checked that right away. There's nothing. And we all have keys that will let us in, so whoever it was could have returned quietly."

"But if they did that, they were risking detection. How were they to know whether or not the police were sitting there in the lobby, waiting to see who returned?"

"I think Doug and Cliff took turns doing just that. No one returned. They have an officer taking attendance as people come down, as you noticed."

"Yes. Sam is chatting with him right now, probably trying to get the scoop."

"He did a fine job with breakfast. What a good provider he is, your future husband."

I smiled.

Camilla said, "Where is our little Smilla today?"

"Stuck to Sam, as she has been since the moment she met him," I said, pretending to be angry.

"You can relate to that, can't you? I think that man fascinated you from the moment you locked eyes."

"You think right." I looked over my shoulder to peer

through the doorway, where I could just glimpse Sam, holding a smug-looking Smilla in his arms and talking easily with a young uniformed officer. Just then Charlie and Gloria walked down, both looking rather tired and reserved. They greeted Sam, checked in with the officer, and then came to the lobby and headed straight for the coffee machine.

"Trouble in paradise?" Camilla asked, looking concerned. "They look like a couple who talked all night."

"Or did something else all night."

"Perhaps." She seemed troubled. "Certainly, neither of them appeared last night, is that correct?"

"Yes. It was Mondo who administered first aid, although he appeared on the scene rather late. Assuming he's not the assailant, I would guess he took some kind of sleeping pill. He looked half asleep when he first appeared. But we seem to be dealing with a very good actor, whoever it may be."

We finished our sweet rolls in silence and then sat sipping our tea. Sam came to join us, holding an egg sandwich and a cup of coffee. Smilla stayed at his ankles. "Really, it offends me the way she just blatantly claimed you for herself," I said.

Sam sat beside me and kissed my ear. "There's enough of me to go around," he said. I rolled my eyes, and Camilla giggled.

While Sam ate, we shared our theories, and he said, "This is good. You need to tell Doug and Cliff."

"Yes," Camilla agreed. "But I wonder if we three can meet together privately first and make a little list."

“A list of motives, like we did at Sasha’s?” I asked.

Camilla shook her head. “A list of things that bother us.”

Thirteen

"What was that Frost poem about fire and ice suggesting that the world could end by either of the two extremes? It's true, in that fire is passion, and cold is hatred, and either can be a motive to kill."

--from *Sapphire Sea,* by Camilla Graham, 2000.

The day was cold, and tracings of ice formed a wintry lace on the window of Camilla's room in Dark Woods Lodge. Smilla lay like a princess in the center of Camilla's bed, her foxlike tail wrapped around her. Camilla sat on the edge of the bed, and Sam and I shared a large easy chair that we had pulled out of the corner.

Sam had volunteered to be the secretary, and "inspired by Doug Heller" he had opened a note-taking app on his phone. "Whatever we come up with, we can share it with Doug and Cliff. They're trying to be everywhere today: interviewing people, overseeing the search of the grounds, doing background checks---I've never seen them so busy."

"Yes, let's see if we can help them," Camilla said.

I played with the sleeve of Sam's sweater. "Why did you say 'things that bother us?' What bothers you?"

She concentrated, furrowing her brow. "Thinking back, the whole evening had the feel of a performance, before the actual performance was to begin. Do you know what I mean?"

I nodded slowly. "Yes, I think I do. But I can't pinpoint who was doing the acting."

"No. That's the difficult part. The four of us are used to being in the limelight, and have developed 'social faces' that we could have used to our advantage. And the others—we can't know how good their acting is."

Sam held up a finger. "So, let's do free association. Just say the first thing that pops into your mind when I say a word or phrase. Are you game?"

Camilla and I nodded.

Sam said, "Your arrival."

Camilla and I spoke at the same time. I said, "David's face," and she said "Sasha was worried."

Sam smiled. "Explain," he said. "Camilla, you go first."

Camilla looked out the window for a moment at the white laced trees. "Whenever Sasha was anxious, she went into overdrive. She became bright as a supernova, rushing around and smiling and laughing. The more she did it, the more I realized she was upset."

I thought of a psychiatrist as I looked at Sam's solemn face. He nodded at Camilla, encouraging her memories. "And this was how she seemed when you arrived? As though she were –overcompensating?"

"Yes. Yes, I believe so. I planned to ask her about it, but I wanted to let her finish all her plans. Obviously, I couldn't ask for a cozy chat while she was in the midst of a publicity event."

"Thanks, Camilla. A good start. Lena?" He turned to me. "What did you mean when you said 'David's face?'"

"I already told Doug this." Smilla had jumped off the bed and come to sit in my lap. I stroked her bath-soft fur and said, "We were being led into the house, and I was chatting with David, making sure he knew about you because he was flirting a bit."

"Thank you," said Sam.

"And I turned to follow the group, but I turned back for something—my coat, or purse? I can't remember, and I saw his face. His expression was angry, resentful. Not just a hint of it, but quite intense. It changed when I turned, but not quickly enough."

"So, who was he angry with?" Sam said.

Camilla looked thoughtful. "There were only a few people there—Lena, Zoe, and me."

"Zoe?" Sam said. "Could he have some grudge against her?"

I said, "Oliver made some comment about how he had a brief fling with Zoe at a conference once. Maybe David did, too? Or maybe David heard that Oliver had done so, and it made him angry to remember it? We all saw how they felt about each other's sexual escapades."

Sam typed for a moment and then said, "So, for number one, we'll recommend that Doug or Cliff look into Zoe's relationships with the two men, and how or why that might affect Sasha. Agreed?"

Camilla and I looked at each other and nodded.

"Now, back to word association," Sam said. I held up Smilla's ears, which were already pointing up, to make it look as though she was listening hard. "Strangest thing," Sam said.

We both pondered for a moment. Camilla said, "The drugging," just before I said, "Oliver's arrival."

Once again, Sam asked us to explain. Camilla said, "The drugging seems so unlikely. It wasn't a guarantee that Sasha would drink the tea, no matter what she said. That makes the whole plan seem predicated on chance rather than on premeditation. And I think this crime was premeditated."

"When we went to Zoe's room, I thought she was pretending. Then Charlie looked at her eyes and told us she was under some kind of sedation. So, the drugging is verified."

"By Charlie's word, and by Zoe's. We don't know yet if even Sasha herself was drugged," Camilla mused.

Sam frowned. "Why would Charlie and Zoe both lie?"

"I don't know that they did lie. But everything about the drugging is—anecdotal, shall we say."

I had a sudden thought. "And Mondo said that he saw Zoe and Charlie talking intensely to each other. They said it was about concern for Sasha—drugs again—and then some jealous interrogation by Charlie."

"But again, you have only their word for it.," Sam

said. He shifted in his chair and winced slightly. His wound was hurting him.

My jaw clenched, and anger rolled upward from my core.

Camilla, not noticing, said, "And then there's Mondo. The Navy Seal and security guard who somehow didn't protect Sasha, didn't hear the gunshots last night, showed up late to the scene twice. That's a bit suspicious."

Sam said, "He was alert when he did my bandage. And he did a really good job."

"I think he needs to check your bandage and give you some painkillers," I said.

Camilla broke out of her reverie. "Oh, of course. I'm sorry, Sam—I was lost in my ponderings."

Sam stood up and kissed her on the cheek. "I enjoyed our detective session. But not only should I check in with Mondo, I must also look into providing some lunch. I have become the unofficial food truck for this fruitless event."

Camilla nodded. "Yes, you and Lena go. Might I ask, though, for your phone? You can reclaim it before you go foraging. I need to check in with poor Adam."

Sam immediately took out his phone and handed it over. "God, yes. He's probably dying of worry and loneliness."

Camilla looked stricken, but she thanked Sam as he moved toward the door.

"We'll bring Smilla, too. That way you can speak to Adam without distractions," I said, approaching her and caressing her soft hair. "We'll see you soon."

She gave a distracted little smile; she had already tapped in a number, and as we left, we heard her say, "Adam? I know, darling, I'm so sorry! I assume that Doug told you the basics?"

We ducked out of the room. Sam said, "Quick, before she says something mushy."

"Mushy? That sounds like an old-timey word." I took his hand, and Smilla, the little traitor, attached herself to Sam's calf as we moved down the dark-paneled hall. There is a distinct smell in old houses; I don't mean a musty smell, or a mothball scent. I am referencing something that I had perceived in Camilla's house, in Green Glass Manor, and in this large vacation lodge. A scent redolent of the past, of nostalgia, of opportunities lost. A scent somehow both comforting and sad.

"By old-timey, do you mean that I am old? A man from another era?"

Sam was always worrying over our eight-year age difference, while I genuinely never thought about it. "Sort of," I joked. "But I have a thing for older men."

"Older *man*. No plurals allowed, fiancée."

I tucked my hand in his. "Is Doug reimbursing you for all this food you're buying?"

He shrugged. "I suppose. We haven't really discussed it. If not, I can underwrite it as a business expense."

I had been trying to distract him, but I saw that his eyes were starting to squint against the pain. "How bad is it?" I asked.

"Well, you're right about the painkillers. I think they're a necessity. I did take some when I got up, but they have officially worn off."

We reached the bottom of the stairs, and Smilla marched to the door. She was already adapting to the new space, and she knew where the exit was located. "In a minute, sweetie," I said. "Just let Sam get what he needs."

Mondo appeared, saw Sam, and ushered him into a back room somewhere. Ten minutes later, Sam emerged with a new bandage and a slightly less pained expression. "Mondo is really good," he said, echoing the sentiment he had shared with Camilla. I recalled that Cliff had liked Mondo, too, seeing in him a fellow authority figure.

"Good. Where should we pick up food?"

Michael the landlord left his post at the reception desk and came to join us. "I called around the likely restaurants to see who's open today. Stella's Subs has a fully plowed lot and they are open for business. Five minutes from here in good weather. There's also a Chinese place that's open, but it's more like twenty minutes."

"Stella's it is," Sam said. "Thaks for the information."

We put on our coats and went into the cold, snow-covered yard. Smilla trotted toward some trees to do her business, and Doug and Cliff came around the corner. They both looked grim.

"Anything?" Sam asked.

Cliff, clearly annoyed, said, "Tons of prints. The guy had to basically leap around through those giant drifts. I don't know how he moved so fast with a rifle and all that snow. Lots of prints, but no gun."

Doug shook his head in disbelief. "It boggles the

mind. Where did they go? Where did they put the gun? Even if the shooter doubled back and returned to Sasha's place, what would have been the plan? Zoe assures me that the only keys were Sasha's—which she surrendered to us when we arrived—and Mondo's. We questioned him, but I also checked him out last night, when he appeared so late in the game. He said he's been taking sleeping pills since Sasha died. I believed him, I think."

I picked up Smilla, who had run around for a moment and then returned to sniff at my shoes. "Couldn't he just have stuck it into one of those giant snow drifts? Then you wouldn't find it for days."

"Maybe," Doug said. "But we've got people combing those woods, and they would be looking for evidence of that. You're right, though—in snow this deep, people can miss things—but right now it's looking like the gun was not dropped in the woods."

Cliff stepped forward to pet the dog in my arms. "We've got footprints, up to a point. When they got as far as the plowed road, the prints taper off."

"So, they got a ride?" I asked.

Cliff shook his head. "No sign of a car, other than police vehicles."

"Could it be a ghost?" Sam joked.

His brother pretended to glare at him. "For a guy who got shot, you're awfully blasé about this whole thing."

Sam shrugged. "I know you two will find him, and then we'll all sleep snug in our beds." He turned to me. "Ready?"

Doug's face sharpened. "Where are you two going?"

"We're on another food quest. Michael recommended a sub sandwich place."

"You are doing noble work," Cliff said, approving of the idea. "Go, and the saints be with you. Make sure you get some with peppers on them."

Sam grinned. "You got it."

Our cop friends watched as we climbed (with help, in my case) into Sam's ridiculous vehicle and the tires crunched through the hard-packed snow on the drive.

"Escape," Sam said with a sigh, as he reached out with his right hand to touch my hair. "What an unexpected series of events."

I studied him, moving the top of Smilla's left ear from my nostril. "You are fond of understatement today."

"Yes. I feel inexplicably serene. I think it's because I know I will soon marry you, and every other fact of life is secondary."

Now I sighed. "You are something special," I murmured.

He smiled, pulling out of the wooded road and onto a local highway. "Michael said Exit 22. Don't let me pass it."

We saw the sign two minutes later, and Sam steered onto a ramp which deposited him neatly on Wolf Trail, the very street we were looking for. "Okay, that was easy," Sam said. "Now look for Stella's Subs."

We drove for half a block and I said, "There. On the right, with the blue awning."

We pulled into a well-plowed little lot, where some

other hungry souls had already parked. "Life persists, no matter what Nature throws at it." Sam really was a philosopher today.

"Hunger persists, you mean. But I guess that's the essence of life. We're all hungry for something, aren't we?" Now I was doing it.

Sam nodded. "You think the pup is okay in the car alone?"

I whispered in Smilla's ear, telling her that we were getting lunch, and that we would be back in five minutes. "And you can see us from this seat. See? You can look right in that window."

Smilla panted happily in my face. I took this as agreement, and Sam and I climbed out of the car. "We'll be right back, girl," I said. Smilla's face appeared in the passenger window, still smiling. "You are so cute," I said, and was rewarded with a frantically wagging tail.

I followed Sam into Stella's Subs, and we took our place in line. There were two people behind the counter, and three customers waiting. The man at the head of the queue told the room at large, "You heard about Sasha Hardwick? My friend with a police scanner said she got killed."

"What?" asked the older woman behind the counter. "Sasha? Why—how--?"

He shrugged. "I don't know. But she was like, our biggest celebrity in this town, aside from that writer, and the guy who killed his wife."

"He didn't kill his wife," said the younger woman behind the counter. "She's still alive. I followed the whole story." She was young, perhaps even a teenager, and she clearly had no patience for misinformation. "What do you want today, Len?"

The man leaned on the counter and gave his order. The older woman, who I thought might be Stella, looked pale and sad. She was waiting on an elderly man, and she kept having to bend forward to hear him.

The line advanced by one, and I turned to Sam and whispered, "Your reputation precedes you."

He shrugged. "Doesn't it always?"

I took his hand, and in moments we were in front of the older woman. "Hello," I said brightly. "Are you Stella?"

She nodded with a little smile. "Yeah, that's me. What can I do for you today?"

Sam had been skimming the menu on the board behind her. With a decisive nod, he ordered two six-foot subs and a couple of side dishes. I was always impressed with his ability to think and act quickly.

"Okay, you got it," Stella said. She began to make the food, going in the back and returning with two giant loaves of fragrant bread, which she expertly sliced and set on butcher's paper.

I said, "You seemed very distressed about Sasha Hardwick. Was she a friend of yours?"

She looked at me, surprised, and then wary. "Did you know her?"

"Yes," I said. "We came into town for Sasha's mystery event. We—it never happened."

Her eyes widened. "So—she's really dead?"

"Yes. I'm sorry. You were—a friend?"

She sniffed. "We were best friends in high school. Right here in Blue Lake. Still are friends, although I haven't seen her for years." She paused then, and her eyes grew wet. "Were friends, I mean."

Sam leaned in, sympathetic. "I'm sorry you had to hear the news this way."

She shook her head. "Not real. It's like when I heard that John Lennon died. I was a kid. I heard it on the radio. And that was my reaction: not real. The Beatles were, like, a solid thing, an unbreakable thing, even though they were all doing solo stuff. They were still the Beatles, you know? I feel that again. Sasha is my childhood friend. She's permanent. In my life until I die."

Or she does. The unspoken words hung in the air and Stella faced us bleakly, holding a piece of Swiss cheese. "Are they going to catch who did it? I want them caught, and punished."

"They've got their best people on the job," I assured her. "But I wonder, Stella, if I could ask you a couple of things?" I looked around at the people in line. One had left, but two more had come in, and they all looked curious. "Maybe after you're finished there, we could sit in Sam's car? My dog is out there and I don't want to leave her alone too long."

Sasha's eyes brightened, and she looked past me to the giant vehicle, where Smilla's head was just visible over the steering wheel. "I love dogs," she said, almost wistfully. "Yeah, let me finish up and get your sides, and then I'll come out."

Ten minutes later Sam paid the bill and helped Stella carry the containers out to the car. I had turned it on and restarted the heater so that it was fairly comfortable in the big vehicle.

"What is this, a Humvee?" she joked, hoisting herself up with Sam's help. "Geez, I feel like I'm getting into an eighteen-wheeler."

"I'm normally a bit more modest with my automobiles, but this one helped us get here in some pretty bad weather."

"Yeah." She settled herself in the back seat, and Smilla jumped immediately into her lap. She petted Smilla's head and then held her snout, studying her face. "I know this dog," she said.

"Oh? Did you know the family?"

"Isn't this Perry Johnson's dog? Perry and Vera. Are you pet-sitting?"

"No." There was some tension in my jaw as I shook my head. Had Mondo gotten it wrong? Had I stolen someone's dog? "We were told that the owners moved away and left her behind."

"What?" Her face turned red with what looked like anger. "I knew they were going to move. I didn't know they left already. And I didn't know they left—"

I held up a hand. "Don't tell me her name. I've already named her, and I don't want her old one floating around in my head."

Stella nodded. "Well, at least she's with caring people who will keep her warm and fed. Perry always was a jerk. A hot head. Maybe he got mad at the dog for some reason, or maybe he was mad at his wife and left the dog as a punishment."

"Neither of those is acceptable. It's abuse, one way or the other," Sam said, grim.

"If you ever find out their contact information, let me know. I'll contact his wife and say we're caring for the dog."

Stella petted the very happy Smilla, her face reflective. "She looks like a little fox, doesn't she? So pretty. I don't know her breed, but I think they actually paid money for her. It's some fancy breed I never heard of, from Denmark or Norway or something up there."

Sam was on his phone, searching. "Finland, maybe?"

Stella leaned in to let Smilla give her a kiss. "Yeah, that's it. A Finnish something or other."

"A Finnish Spitz," Sam said, holding out his phone. In the image he'd found was a dog who looked very much like Smilla.

"Wow, Smilla!" I said. "You're a very fancy dog."

Sam put his phone away. "Now, to a more difficult topic," he said.

"Yeah." Stella looked glum. "What can I tell you?"

I thought for a minute and said, "You said you hadn't seen her in five years or so. Had you talked to her, though? Or texted or something?"

Stella nodded. "Oh sure, we did the occasional phone call. She actually called me a couple weeks ago when she got to town. She said she was busy getting ready for this big event, but afterward we could get together and catch up." She understood the irony of these last words, and her eyes filled with tears. She wiped them away. "Anyway, at least I got to talk to her. She was in high spirits, like usual."

"Nothing bothering her?"

"Well—no, nothing obvious—but she was a little bit hyper. Sometimes with Sasha that meant she was covering."

"Covering?" I prodded.

"You know, like, refusing to think about something that bugged her by emphasizing the positives to the tenth power. I wondered a little at the time. She had made some comment about all her old friends coming in, and she said that she had a score to settle with one of them."

Sam and I both sat up straight. "A score to settle? Did she say who with?"

"No, just that she and this friend needed to have a long-overdue conversation. She sounded happy about it, but also really determined, you know."

This was crucial information. "Stella? Do you think your friend in there could cover for you long enough for us to introduce you to the detectives at Dark Woods Lodge? I think they really need to hear this."

"Sure. Let me call. I've got a couple people in the back room, too, so they should be fine." She pulled out her phone and dialed, then said, "Kimmy? Are you okay by yourself for about an hour? I have to make a statement to the police, about Sasha. Yeah. Okay, thanks, Kim-Kim. See you soon."

Sam put the car in drive and backed out of his space, then turned toward the exit. I looked at Stella and said,

"Thanks for doing this. Was there anything else that Sasha said that might be significant?"

Stella rubbed her nose. "I have to think back. I mean, Sasha talked a mile a minute, so even though it was a short call, she got a lot of information in." She smiled, then wiped at her eyes. "I know she said something about her family tree. Like, 'I've been looking into my family tree and finding some new leaves.' Or something like that."

"And was she happy about this?"

"Seemed to be. She was most happy because of a guy she was seeing. He worked security at her place, and they fell in love."

Poor Mondo. "And she was excited?" I asked.

"Yeah. She thought they might get engaged soon."

Sam turned to look at me. He understood what I was thinking. We too had high hopes about our wedding. But Sasha and Mondo hadn't been able to live out their dream.

Sam said, "Did she say anything about her staff? Anyone she had a disagreement with?"

Stella shook her head slowly. "Not that I recall. She said she was working poor Zoe to the bone, and she owed her. Her cook was another one she said was indispensable. She told me she was giving the cook a nice sum in her will."

"Sasha had a will?" I asked sharply.

"Sure. When you're that rich, it's just good business sense to make a will."

"Ah. Did she mention any other bequests?"

"She was generous," Stella said with a sigh. "She said even I was going to receive a little something. She said if she died first, when we were old, she'd leave me money to go on a joy ride with my rest home boyfriend." Stella smiled through her tears. "Other than that, I'm not sure. I didn't ask who the big stacks of money were going to, or the real estate. But I got the sense that her boyfriend would be her first choice. She was hung up on that guy."

Sam shot me a sideways glance. "That does make Mondo more of a suspect, doesn't it? Especially if he knew about a bequest."

"Yes." I wondered what Camilla would make of all this.

Stella said, "I mean, this could all mean nothing. It was just a quick little phone call. We mostly talked about the good old days, about her mom and dad and brother. I grew up with that whole family, because we were in and out of each other's houses. We had such a nice childhood," she said, sighing.

"What were her mom and dad like?" I asked.

"Oh, very nice and sweet. Kind of in their own world sometimes, you know, making eyes at each other. They were such a love match. Do you know how they met? They told me the stories a million times. He was a young businessman, and he traveled to some big convention in Florida. She happened to be there with a friend on vacation, and they were in the same hotel. In the evening, the hotel sponsored all sorts of night life things, and one of them was a dance contest. He was having a drink in the bar when the contest started, and people were just grabbing partners and running out there. He saw her sitting with her friend, and he said he didn't even think. He went up to her and said, "Will you be my partner?" And the funny thing was he had no idea how to dance. He'd never had one lesson."

She shook her head, smiling at the memory. "Her dad told the story in such a funny way. His wife, Selena, said yes, but then they got on the floor and she said, 'You can't dance, can you?' and he said, 'I can fake!' So, they did their fake dancing all night. They didn't win, but neither of them cared, because after looking into each other's faces for hours, they had a good sense of each other."

"That's a fun story. Is that what you reminisced about on the phone?" I asked.

"No. Just how sweet they were, and how good her brother was, what a great man he would have been in the world. I had such a crush on him." She sighed. "Life isn't fair. The Hardwicks were all good people, and now the whole family is gone."

"Do you know anything about a lawsuit that her father was involved in, after his son's death?"

Her brows went up. "Why do you ask that?"

I shrugged. "I read something online about a lawsuit, and how some sort of gag order was put on it, but Mr. Hardwick made some sort of comment about people trying to paint his son in a bad light, or something."

Stella frowned. "I remember Sasha being upset about it at the time. Women coming out of the woodwork to try to make a claim on her poor dead brother, meaning his fortune. Her father wasn't having that."

"No, of course not," I agreed in a soothing tone.

Smilla was almost asleep in Stella's lap, but we had reached the driveway for Dark Woods. "Here we are," Sam said brightly, pulling in. "And there are the men we want you to speak to, right there." He pulled the car into a plowed area and jumped out, then came around to help Stella and me make the mighty descent out of the car. Smilla waited, too, for someone's arms, and I said, "Come here, Finnish Spitz." She jumped into my embrace, and I carried her toward the door while Sam ushered Stella toward Cliff and Doug. I watched them as Sam made introductions. Camilla emerged from the building as I reached the door, and I touched her arm. "Camilla, that's Sasha's childhood friend. I want you to eavesdrop on their conversation so I can talk to you about it."

"Got it," Camilla said, with a wink at me. She crunched through the snow on her sturdy boots and stood near Doug's elbow, listening.

Sam went back to the car to retrieve the food, and I helped him carry it inside and set it up on the same table we had used for all of our meals. People seemed to sense the food, because they began filtering in, one and two at a time, and taking the plates that Sam handed them. "Help yourselves," Sam said. I took plates for Sam and me, as well, and filled them up before finding a little couch that we could sit on while we ate.

Sam sat beside me, studying his sandwich. "Looks pretty good," he said. "But imagine if we were trapped here with Carl Frailey. We'd be in food heaven."

I agreed with this assessment, since Belinda's brother

was a culinary genius, and said, "Carl reminds me of Wheat Grass, and Wheat Grass reminds me of Adam. I hope he's not too anxious now that Camilla spoke to him."

"I'm sure he's champing at the bit to get over here. I know I was."

"We're all magnetically linked." I smiled at him. I took a bite of my sandwich and said, "Ooh. This is good. Kudos to Stella." I peered at the front entrance. "Do you think they're still talking to her?"

"I hope so. She had a lot of information."

"I know! I hope Camilla is hearing it all. It's strange, that last stuff about Sasha's family."

"Why?"

I was poking my sandwich with a potato chip. "Hmm? Oh, just—how legendary they are, and how famous in Blue Lake—but also how crucial they seem to everything. To Sasha, to Stella, probably to a lot of Blue Lakers from that time. I don't know, I just have the sense that they're important. Maybe that lawsuit. Or lawsuits? Stella mentioned 'women.' And why only women? Wouldn't men be after money, too? Or is she saying that the women were accusing the brother of sexual indiscretions?"

Sam's mouth was full now, so he only shrugged.

Camilla appeared in the doorway, and I was glad to see that there was a spark in her eyes. She had found it interesting, all right. She made a beeline to us, and I held up my plate so that she could share the food. Sam pulled over a chair for her so that we could sit in a conspiratorial triangle.

"Stella was a good find," she said. "And that is some very interesting information. What a nice woman," she said.

Sam slapped his legs. "I need to drive her back."

Camilla held up a hand. "Cliff has already done so. Doug is going to follow up some of Stella's leads. But I made a request of him, on behalf of us three."

"Oh? What is that?" I asked, noting that Doug was coming toward us with a determined expression.

Camilla said, "To go back to Green Glass Manor. I'll let Doug explain." She patted his arm and smiled at him as he sat down beside her. Doug gave her a quick one-armed hug, then turned to us. "What was the question?"

"Why are we going back to Green Glass Manor?" I asked.

Doug cleared his throat and took a sip out of his travel mug of coffee. "Based on what Stella said, I think it's very important that we get back into Sasha's house. Keep in mind that my forensic team consisted of two people, and we were lucky to get that number in this weather, in Blue Lake. We are considered the far side of nowhere by the crime scene techs."

"So, you're on your own?" Sam asked. Smilla trotted up, finishing a tour of the manor's first floor, and sat begging for Sam's food.

Doug sighed. "They've given me the all-clear, but they are not going to crawl through that giant house looking for clues. That's going to be my job." He looked around at us and said, "But also our job. They haven't found a will, and Cliff and I want to make that a priority.

Beyond that, we're not sure what to look for. Sasha's friends, however, especially those who share a history with her, might be able to point us in the right direction. When Cliff gets back, I'd like you three to join us in Sam's house on wheels so we can get back to work."

Camilla looked thoughtful. "I think that's a good instinct, Doug. Something in Sasha's personal life was not quite right. It was making her tense. She was planning to confront one of us four visiting friends, and she was 'looking into her family tree.' The crime scene techs might not even know a clue if they saw one. Only people who knew Sasha might be able to see something crucial that objective eyes missed."

"So—"

"So, we need to find the evidence at the source," Camilla said. "And that evidence, I believe—and I think you and Cliff agree—is in Green Glass Manor."

Fourteen

"Danger waited until night before emerging from its silent cave, and no one saw it coming because they could not see in the dark."

--from *Bereft*, by Camilla Graham, 2015.

Green Glass Manor looked much the same as it had the first time I had pulled into its majestic driveway, except that first time a magical snow had begun to fall, and this time that snow lay in giant heaps, burying everything but the trees tall enough to loom over the drifts. Even from the first glimpse of the house I could see green glass glinting in the late afternoon sun. A lovely place to grow up, and an enchanting act of devotion. I tried to picture what Sam would do if I suddenly professed a fascination for the color silver. Would he drape his house in tinsel and white lights?

We had all bundled into the large car to make the short trip down the road to the Hardwick place; the road was still bad enough that the car had been a necessity. I had sat listening to the conversation and thinking my own thoughts about Sam, and tinsel, and love.

I smiled at the image, watching Sam surreptitiously

where he sat next to me, in the spacious back seat, chatting with Camilla. Since I had met him a year and a half earlier, he had only grown better looking. He was healthier now, both physically and emotionally, and that glow of health merely enhanced his attractiveness. His thick brown hair, always enticingly messy, had been recently styled into a semblance of order, although the messiness was creeping back in as his hair grew out. His skin had lost some of its summer tan, but he had retained some color and a hardy appearance overall. One of his hands sat casually on my knee, and I studied it—the long, tapered fingers, the strong wrist that disappeared into his winter jacket.

He noticed me then. He leaned over and spoke into my ear again, because he knew it aroused me: "Are you checking me out?"

I giggled. "Yes. I'm full-on stalking you."

Cliff turned around from the front seat. "That's an arrestable offense, young lady."

"Lock me up then, because I can't stop obsessing over this guy."

Sam sat back with a smug expression and said, "Make sure we put that in the vows."

Doug rustled restlessly behind the wheel. "Okay, lovebirds. Let's make a plan of action. Cliff and I are going to go through the papers in her study. I asked Zoe to join us there—" he held up his right hand— "I know, I know, she's a suspect, but she's also the only one who knows administrative details about Sasha. Mondo, maybe, but I'm guessing Zoe knows more. So, we'll keep her on hand to answer our questions, not to let her in on our investigation. Camilla, you and Lena can look at any bedrooms you want. They've already been through them."

Camilla nodded. "There's also that little reading room near the main entrance—it looked as though she had lots of personal possessions in there. I think she had a good view of the property from that vantage point, so it probably became a favorite spot."

Cliff consulted his notes. "That room is fine. It's been cleared."

Sam said, "Do you want me to look at Mondo's room, some of the other basement areas, before he shows up again?"

"I do," Doug said. "We'll all keep in touch via text. Message me if anything looks suspicious and I'll come down to see."

Cliff dug around in a rucksack he had with him, pulling out Camilla's phone. "Here you go, dear lady," he said. He plunged his hand into the bag again and retrieved my phone, tossing it to me. "Everyone's getting them back now," he said.

"I have sorely missed this piece of technology," I said, running my hand along my phone's smooth, rubbery yellow case. "Probably more than I should have. But it is a new phone, after all, and a gift from Sam."

Sam nodded. "Sometimes, when a madman destroys the phones of everyone you know, it just seems right to splurge a little on something special."

A collective shiver ran through the car as we recalled

the madman in question: a man who had shot Belinda, set a building on fire and stalked Doug through the smoky air, and who had been about to murder me when Doug caught up with him.

"I don't really want to earn my presents that way." I sent Sam a meaningful look, and he nodded.

Doug had parked the car in front of Sasha's house, and we all climbed out. The snow had created a magical wonderland of Sasha's property—all lacy trees and snow-capped fence-posts along the forest perimeter. Sam held Smilla against him, and she nuzzled into his chest. I wondered if she recalled the scents of this place, and her terrible ordeal in the woods before she and I discovered each other.

Doug unlocked the door as we ascended the grand steps together. Just two days ago I had come to this same spot while the snow bucketed down and Camilla smiled sweetly at reporters and told them she would win.

Two short days. Now Sam had a bandage on his shoulder, David was in the hospital, and Sasha was dead. Had these crimes been planned, all of them? Had only Sasha's murder been premeditated? Or had every act of violence been an impulsive decision, made by a person who felt cornered? If so, cornered by whom?

No, I decided. It hadn't been a spontaneous act. Camilla and I had decided that the drugging had made pre-meditation clear. Yet, back in Sasha's house, all of our contentions seemed impossible.

The rooms were eerie now with the unreality of death. A sweetish chemical scent dominated our senses, and Doug opened a window to air out the main room.

Sam kissed my cheek and walked away, bound for the basement door. Doug and Cliff disappeared into Sasha's study, where a file cabinet and a desk full of papers awaited them.

Numbly, I followed Camilla up the stairs we had so recently climbed with Sasha, chattering away and wafting that alluring scent, flipping her silky hair, emanating excitement.

"Life is cruel," I said softly. "Or death is, I guess."

Camilla turned on the landing and shook her head. "No, *people* are cruel. Someone did this to her, and tried to hurt the others, and neither life nor death conspired in the matter."

Profundities like that flowed out of Camilla, impressing me, always, with their wisdom. I nodded, slowly. A thought, unexpected, suddenly demanded explanation. "Camilla, when I woke you up to tell you about Sasha, you asked me if something had happened to Adam."

"Yes?" she said.

"Is he—I mean—do you have any reason to think that he--?"

She shook her head, placing an arm around my shoulders. "No, Adam is healthy. We both are. But we're realistic about the fact that we are in our seventies. We might be lucky enough to reach an advanced old age and have another twenty years together." She looked at me with those wise purple eyes. "And we might not. I suppose that was the first thing I thought of. I knew you were safe, and you and Adam are the people I most want to hold onto. I've become rather fond of you two," she joked lightly.

I put my arm around her waist and pulled her even more closely against my side. "I am relieved to know that you are both healthy. Let's count on at least twenty years."

She nodded. "It's a plan. Now—which side of the hall would you like?" She pointed left. "Those rooms were David's, Zoe's, Gloria's. And then on our side it was you, then me, then Oliver."

"I guess I'll take the other side," I said. "Aren't everyone's possessions gone, though?"

"Doug told them to take a small bag to Dark Woods. I think people had much more extensive luggage than that."

We parted at the first set of doors. I went into David's room, and Camilla went down to Oliver's. David's chamber, too, was a large and airy space, just as my room had been, but it had a more masculine feel. I had no doubt that Sasha selected rooms based on traditionally gendered decorating. The floor was polished hardwood, and in front of a small fireplace was a striking navy-and-green wool rug. The bedspread, too, was navy blue, with small green squares around the edging. Green throw pillows sat against the headboard, and one of Aaron Hardwick's collectible Teddy Bears sat nestled into the pillows. A large green suncatcher hung in a square window, catching the last rays of evening sun.

The green light cast an eerie glow in the room, creating an almost mythological tableau, worthy of Atlantis or the Palace of Poseidon, where murky, irridescent light would be the norm. Nervous now, I moved toward a large suitcase that sat on a chair in one corner. It wasn't zipped—we had left quickly—and I flipped it open, feeling rebellious, almost criminal, as I carefully examined the contents. Shirts, pants, ties. A small container with cuff links and earbuds. An inner pocket held an airline ticket and a travel itinerary, along with the original invitation sent by Sasha. I lifted it out, recalling the day Camilla had received the same invitation—how happy she had been to find it in her mail pile.

The stiff, expensive card was made of creamy paper and embossed with coffee-colored letters, inviting the recipient to the Great American Mystery Challenge!

Sasha had scrawled a note at the bottom, as she had done on Camilla's: *You must take part, Cammy! It wouldn't be a contest without you." XXXX Sasha*

David's note took a moment to decipher. It seemed as though Sasha had written it hastily. *Come and play, Davey. We can have it out before the others come, and after that it will be like old times.*

Have it out? What did she mean? Was David the person that Sasha had intended to confront? It certainly seemed that way, and David had, in fact, been the first of the four to arrive. Had they "had it out?" I remembered David's look of dislike. Had it been aimed at Sasha? Had their conversation not gone well? Did he hate her so much he wanted to kill her?

It seemed hard to believe. It was Oliver that David had seemed to hate, evidenced by their ridiculous wrestling match. On the other hand, someone had shot

David, and Oliver had been quite worried about him. He had called him a fool, but his voice had been concerned, almost tender. How were Doug and Cliff supposed to navigate this contradictory terrain? I was reminded of a line from *Macbeth* that Camilla and I had quoted in *Death on the Danube:* "Nothing is, but what is not."

That about summed it up. I used my camera to take a picture of the invitation, and then I put it back in David's suitcase. I texted the picture to Doug and Cliff, then moved around the rest of the room, scanning for anything that the police team might not have seen, unlikely as that was. David had only been planning to stay for one or two nights, so it wasn't as though he had possessions scattered around the place. I opened a corner closet and peered inside, but it was empty.

I shrugged at the blank space, shut the closet door, and moved out of the room. Smilla, who had been investigating the halls of Green Glass Manor on quiet little feet, suddenly appeared beside me and smiled up at me. What a sweet dog. I picked her up on some maternal impulse and snuggled her against me. She rested her little chin on my shoulder and sighed with apparent contentment.

I grinned, and we walked into Zoe's room. Setting Smilla down, I noted that this room had a bit more to investigate, although Zoe had removed all the items from her dresser and her side tables. Clearly, she didn't want investigators touching her things. Gone were the brush and comb, the framed pictures, the little alarm clock. I opened some drawers, feeling guilty, and saw that most of the contents of her dresser were still there. Zoe lived here, after all. She had to assume that she'd be returning at some point, perhaps even continuing to live here until Sasha's affairs had been sorted. I thought about that for a moment, riffling absently through Zoe's clothes. In her bottom drawer were only a pair of jeans and a sweatshirt that said Blue Lake. It was pretty, and I wondered where I could get one. My eyes caught on the neat patterned paper that lined the bottom of the drawer. One corner had been torn off, but something was visible beneath. I lifted the paper and found a little pile of news clippings.

I pulled them out with care, my heart beating slightly faster. Was this something? Nothing? I feared Zoe might arrive at any moment, and I did not want her to find me rooting in her drawer. Surreptitiously, I snapped for Smilla and we exited the room in a stealthy fashion. We traveled across the hall to my room, where I sat on the bed with the stack of articles, laying them out in a row. There were five of them in all; the first was a copy of the story I had seen online, the one about the lawsuit that Hardwick had kept closed. Someone, perhaps Zoe, had highlighted certain lines that seemed to show Hardwick in a prejudicial light, like "Hardwick declined to answer reporters' questions," and "The Hardwicks have long had an acrimonious relationship with the press." Had Zoe marked these lines? Or someone else?

The next article was just a tiny clipping about students graduating with honors from Blue Lake High school. The date of the article was May 20, 1987. One of the names, I saw at once, was Aaron Hardwick. The others, which I read with less attention, were Thomas Myers, Patricia Morsen, Angela Hall, Oscar Olivier, Marquis Washington, and Angel Rodriguez.

I set the tiny article with the first one and looked at a more recent article, this one printed out from a computer site. The headline read, "The Mysterious Mr. Hardwick." The article had featured a picture of Hardwick looking like a Carnegie or a Rockefeller in his expensive suit. He stood with a confident air in front of Green Glass Manor. I skimmed the date—it had been written ten years earlier—and scanned the contents for a gist. The article seemed to be about the house, and Selena, and the romantic story of its building, but it also suggested that Hardwick's fortune was rather a mystery. Apparently, Hardwick didn't talk much about his family finances. He had used them liberally for improvements in Blue Lake, and gave generously to Blue Lake charities, the article asserted, so the tone was not particularly hard-hitting. The implication was that the reporter had gone into the interview with some real questions and concerns, but Hardwick had charmed him enough that it took the piece out of expose range and kept it within an "eccentric millionaire' personality profile.

Had Zoe saved these for herself? Or had she, perhaps, been hiding them from Sasha, fearing they would upset her? If the latter option was true, then why wouldn't she throw the articles away?

The fourth clipping was about Aaron Hardwick's car accident. According to the police report, young Hardwick had been driving in unincorporated Blue Lake on Farm Fields Road, which was bounded by corn crops on both sides. Aaron had been speeding, but only slightly, and he did not see the opening in the corn that was a vehicle transport road. A tractor came suddenly out of the dirt road, and Aaron swerved to avoid it, then overcorrected and flipped his car. He was airlifted to Rush Hospital in Chicago with serious internal injuries, and he died the following day.

A wave of sadness engulfed me. Poor Aaron. And the poor farmer, who had to negotiate a blind opening and who had said, "I never heard a car." How guilty he must have felt. And how terrible for the Hardwicks, to lose their only son. Poor Sasha, as well. Her brother, and her only sibling. I thought of Sam, who had lost his little sister, Wendy, to the same plane crash that had killed his parents.

Why, though, was this article under the paper in Zoe's dresser? Then again, how long had Zoe been Sasha's assistant? Not more than a few years, I thought. Perhaps these articles had been placed here by a former occupant of the room. Who could I ask, I wondered, for that information? Perhaps only Sasha would have been able to tell me.

The metallic chunk of a car door shutting sounded distantly. I barely noted, but then I heard the crystalline tinkling of Sasha's door chimes. Zoe had arrived, I was guessing. Moments later I heard her voice, and then Doug's. Zoe's voice grew louder. "I'll be right there," she called. "I just want to get something from my room." Her footfalls were on the stairs, ascending.

Quickly I went to the dresser and put four of the

articles back under the paper. The fifth one, which I hadn't had a chance to read, I slipped into my pocket. I had just shut the dresser drawer and taken a few steps toward the door when Zoe came bursting in, then stopped short at the sight of me.

"What are you doing in my room?" she asked, more confused than suspicious.

There seemed no harm in telling the truth. "Camilla and I were helping Detective Heller. Just glancing through all the bedrooms for anything unusual."

Her brows drew together. "Why would he have you help him? You're not the police." Then she paused. "Oh, but those cases you solved, about Sam West and stuff. You worked with him, didn't you? You're *friends* with him."

"Yes."

"That doesn't seem fair, or, like—legal."

I smiled at her. "The crime scene techs have already been here. We're just helping him do a final sweep. It's a big house."

"But you're in my room. You don't think that I would *hurt* Sasha? I mean, what did you think you would find? A bloody knife?" She grew pale at her own words. She looked sick, in fact.

"No. Just glancing around."

"Well, this is my private room, and I still have to live here until I make other arrangements, and I would appreciate it if people stayed out of my space." Her eyes darted toward her closet and then back to me. I had already searched the closet, but now I wondered if I should have looked more closely.

"Sure," I said. "I was wondering. Do you know who had this room in the past? Who lived here?"

Zoe shrugged. "I think Sasha used it as a general guest room for a long time. When her brother was alive, she told me it was called "the guitar room," because her brother was obsessed with guitars, and he had a collection. He would come in here and play. She said he was really good." Zoe's face looked wistful, as though she wished she could have heard that long-ago music. "When Aaron died, the family auctioned off the guitars for charity. They couldn't bear to look at them. They gave the money to Aaron's particular favorite foundations."

"That's nice," I said. The information had not been helpful in terms of the articles' origins. It seemed likely still that Zoe herself had stowed them there. "Did you know the Hardwick family before you got a job with Sasha?" I asked, keeping my voice casual.

"What?" Zoe looked distracted. "Uh—no. I mean, I knew of them. I grew up in Blue Lake, after all. Although I went to high school in Blueville. We're closer to there, anyway—right on the border, you know?"

She seemed to be attempting to lead the conversation away from my question, and that was interesting.

"Oh, okay. So, you obviously knew the Hardwick name. Did you know who Sasha was when she posted your job?"

Zoe's white face grew defensive. "Yeah, okay, but that's not why I applied. I happened to be extremely qualified. My degree—"

"I'm not questioning your competence," I said,

holding up my hands. "You're obviously very good. And you and Sasha clearly worked well together."

Zoe's eyes filled with tears. "Yes," she said thickly. "Excuse me, I want to grab my sweater. It's cold in this house."

She said the final words in a sad, weary way, as though the heat source for the building had been Sasha herself. Zoe yanked open a drawer and dug around until she found a blue sweater, warm looking and covered with little fabric pills. It was obviously a much-loved garment. Zoe put it on and snuggled into it for a moment, as though receiving an imaginary hug. Then she said, "Okay, well, I have to go help them sort through Sasha's papers."

"Sure. I'll leave, too. I have to talk with Camilla."

She nodded, and we walked out together. Zoe made her way back down the stairs, and I heard Cliff's voice this time, murmuring quietly to her.

I turned and saw Camilla at the end of the hall. "Want to talk?" I asked.

She moved toward me. "Are you finished?"

"No. I haven't gone into Gloria and Charlie's room."

She reached my side. "We can do that one together. Meanwhile, let's compare notes in my room." We walked into Camilla's room and sat at a small table near the window. I told her about David's invitation. She frowned.

"We'll have it out," she said. "And she wanted to "confront" one of us. Is this the same thing, or were there two people she needed to sort things with?" She looked at me, her violet eyes wide. “I’m beginning to think I am the only member of our little group who had no secrets. Around whom there was no intrigue.”

“Do you wish to be more intriguing?” I joked.

“A bit,” she said with a smile.

“I have more for you.” I told her about the articles, detailing the four I had read. “And then Zoe came in, and we had a rather stilted exchange. She seems—emotionally unpredictable.”

Camilla nodded. “I’m a bit worried about that girl. She has secrets, too, but there’s something else—something like remorse—but I don’t necessarily suspect her. Remember, she was one of the people attacked last night.”

“Yes.” I told her about Zoe’s evasive conversation, about her longing look at the closet, about her reluctant admission that she knew the Hardwicks.

“Hmmm,” Camilla said. “And now I must complicate matters more.”

I stiffened. “Oliver, too?”

“Yes. His room seemed essentially empty, aside from a nondescript suitcase. So, I searched, and I left. But then something popped into my head. You know Oliver’s main character?”

“Logan Winter,” I said. “I have a crush on that character.”

“Do you remember where he hides the things that he doesn’t want people to find?”

I thought for a moment, then practically shouted, “Under the base of his heavy lamp!”

"Yes." She looked thoughtful, her expression a mixture of amusement and disappointment. "So, I went back in and tilted up his bedside lamp, and found this." She handed me a little slip of paper that said, "Ollie, I didn't tell anyone. I told Sasha, you know that, but no one else. Tell him to calm down. And don't be mad at me."

I read it twice, then looked at Camilla. "So, Oliver is Ollie. Do we assume the other "him" is David?"

"I think so."

"So—what secret did David have that Oliver knew and confided to someone else—Gloria? Zoe? —and told that person to keep it secret? And if that person told Sasha—"

"Is it a secret that someone would kill for?" Camilla finished, and we stared at each other. "You recall that Oliver admitted to a brief affair with Zoe, young as she is. So, my suspicion is that Zoe wrote the note. I've never heard Gloria refer to him as "Ollie.""

"On the other hand, if Gloria and Oliver had a secret thing going, well—people call each other more intimate names during pillow talk."

Camilla smiled a little smile. Then she straightened and said, "So what do we have here? One: Sasha told David that they needed to "have it out." This could explain his angry expression."

"Or he could have been looking at Zoe, if she knew his secret and told it to Sasha."

"Agreed. Two: Zoe seems to have saved all sorts of articles about the Hardwick family, including one about the death of Aaron Hardwick. Three: Oliver Lord received a note, probably from Zoe, saying that she didn't tell 'his' secret to anyone but Sasha. She implied that the mysterious 'he' was angry."

"Not much of a secret, is it, if David, Oliver, Zoe and Sasha all know it?"

"Three may keep a secret, if two of them are dead," Camilla quoted solemnly.

"If only Ben Franklin were here to help us through this little puzzle."

Camilla sighed. "Well, we came here to solve a puzzle. So, let's use the wits that we packed for a different adventure."

"Could this note be related to the reason David went outside in the night? Did Sasha get killed for this secret? Did David almost get killed because of it? And remember, Oliver and Zoe were out there, too."

"It always comes back to the same people, doesn't it? David, Oliver, and Zoe," she noted, thoughtful.

"But if we are looking at Zoe, we also have to look at Charlie, don't we? Did you believe that story about why they were talking intensely together?"

Camilla frowned. "No. But I told myself that young people make everything intense. I remember when you and Sam first fell for each other—those were some dramatic scenes."

"We're still intense," I said, my face hot, and Camilla smiled. "Anyway, Gloria seemed surprised, too, by something Charlie said about her and other men, and it didn't ring true, maybe even to her. Something's off there."

"The problem is that something is off everywhere. Everything is off kilter."

While we sat pondering, Smilla came trotting back in the room, smiling at us and looking very much like a little red fox.

"Be our good luck charm, Smilla. Help us figure this out." I reached down to pet her, and heard a crinkling sound. "Oh! I grabbed the final article when I heard Zoe coming, and I never read it." I took the little clipping out of my pocket and read the headline: Did Aaron Hardwick Have an Illegitimate Child?

I gasped and handed it to Camilla, who said, "Who—"

And then Zoe was standing in the open door, staring at us with a strange expression on her face.

Fifteen

"Suspicion is born in the gut. And when suspicion rises to the surface, a situation can become very dangerous, very fast."
--from *Midnight Showdown,* by David Canfield, 2011.

"Hello, dear," Camilla said, covering the little clipping with one smooth movement, pretending that she was studying her nails. I had seen, though, that Zoe had spied the article and seemed to recognize it. Her face was stony.

"What are you guys doing? Doug said you should come down."

"Oh, but we haven't quite finished up here. Does he need us urgently?"

Zoe took a step closer to us. "No, but he said soon."

"Thanks," I offered, hoping she would go away.

"What are you guys doing?" she repeated.

"We're talking about the very dramatic and horrible events of the last two days," Camilla said, giving Zoe a frank, direct look. "It helps to talk it out sometimes. Truths emerge through dialogue. Would you like to join us?"

Zoe sat on a little wooden chair against the wall, a few feet from us. "In what respect? I mean, what are you dialoguing about?"

Camilla and I hesitated, and Zoe said, "That article, maybe? The one you took out of my drawer?"

She was suddenly bolder, leaning forward, waiting for a response.

I said, "What were the articles doing in your drawer? And why were they hidden under shelf-liner paper?"

Zoe shrugged. "Sasha always got upset about stuff like that. I tried to catch them before she saw them—"

"Except that some of the articles were written when you were a teenager," I said. "So, Sasha didn't just 'encounter' it. Someone looked up those articles, or dug in old files, or had them since the day they were published."

Still going for casual, Zoe said, "Well, whatever reason, I saw them in Sasha's office and I decided to hide them. You have to understand, she never got over Aaron's death. He was her little brother, her only sibling, and she—he was still important to her. Literally, to her dying day."

I didn't believe the first part of her story, and I could tell Camilla didn't, either. The second part seemed merely a distraction from the question we had asked.

Camilla held up the article now. "What was her interest in this one? Was she angry about the speculation, or was she happy to think she had a nephew or niece out there somewhere?"

Zoe paused and licked her lips. They did look quite

dry, as though she was dehydrated. "She said that when her parents were alive, she abided by their wishes. People tried to suggest that Aaron had gotten a girl pregnant—probably his girlfriend from high school, Sasha thought—but after they died, she had no family left, and she said she liked the idea of having someone out there, someone who could be her family." Zoe's eyes filled with tears once again. She was grieving, and there was no faking that. The wound on her forehead, though scabbed over now, still looked fresh and painful.

Camilla nodded. "There was an article about Aaron that I read earlier today. Lena, can you find it on your phone? The headline was Hardwick Heir Dies in Crash."

I took up my phone and searched, then clicked on the headline. For a moment I simply stared. Beneath the header were three pictures of Aaron Hardwick—one as a baby in his mother's arms, one as a teen, and one as a young man at a charity event. The teenage picture looked familiar. And then it came to me, and I knew the truth. I handed the phone to Camilla. "A very handsome boy," she said, her face regretful.

"You know what's strange, though? "I asked. "How much Aaron looks like your brother, Zoe."

She stared at me, her face as featureless as a pancake. "What?"

"The picture of your brother that you had on your dresser yesterday. It was so very similar to this one." I paused. "How long ago did Aaron die? Was it twenty-seven years ago?"

"Twenty-eight," Zoe said tonelessly. "1996."

"And how old are you, Zoe?"

"I'm twenty-seven," she said hoarsely.

The room was very quiet. Outside the sun was setting, and some last warm rays of light settled in the room like wisps of memory.

Smilla went to Zoe and sniffed her knee. Zoe petted her absently.

"Did Sasha know you were her niece?" I asked. "Because that was a picture of your father on your dresser, wasn't it? Was that your only picture of him?"

Tears rolled down Zoe's face, and she nodded.

We waited while she wiped her eyes. Then she said, "Sasha didn't know, but I was going to tell her after this weekend. I wanted—I wanted us to be family."

Camilla's face was sympathetic, but I could see in her eyes that her mind was working over this new detail. "Haven't you worked for Sasha for several years? Why didn't you tell her much earlier?"

Zoe shrugged. "There was a chance that she would—take it badly. Think I was a poser, or a gold-digger, or someone who had taken the job under false pretenses." She dug in her pocket and pulled out a crumpled Kleenex which she straightened to blow her nose. "I did know I was related to Sasha when I took the job, but I wasn't trying to pull anything over on her. I just wanted to meet her, to be around her. And yes, I wanted to see what it was like to be a Hardwick, at least by association. When my grandparents were alive, they refused to acknowledge that I existed, as though it was some shameful claim. So, they deprived themselves of a grandchild, and deprived me of grandparents."

She was looking a bit healthier, as though letting go of this secret was healing her from within. "And now I will never get to tell Sasha that she was my family, and I loved her." Her expression was so mournful that I felt answering tears in my own eyes.

"Did your lawyer consider a DNA test?" Camilla asked.

Zoe nodded. "Yes, we offered that, but the Hardwicks refused to consider it. No one could force them to submit a sample. It was their prerogative to refuse."

"Yes." Camilla's eyes were distant, and I knew that she was sifting through facts.

"You know we have to go downstairs and tell the detectives this information, don't you?"

She sighed. "Yes, fine. Can we do it now? I want to go back to Dark Woods and lie down."

We agreed. As we left the room, I said, "Camilla, I never looked in Gloria's room. You two start down and I'll take a quick peek."

Camilla agreed. She put an arm around Zoe and the two of them headed for the shadowy staircase. I walked down the darkening hall to Gloria's room. It was another enticing space, with a large suitcase sitting on a chair beside the bed, and a scattering of make-up and perfume on the small dresser. I peered into the bathroom and saw a negligee hanging on a hook behind the door. It was very sexy—a blue and black teddy that would look amazing with Gloria's torrent of hair—and I wondered if I should buy some extra special lingerie for my honeymoon. I already had some nice pieces, but still . . .

On the bathroom counter were a few of Charlie's items—a shaving kit and a rolled-up tie. A tiny date book, small enough to fit in a shirt pocket, was filled with what seemed to be medical appointments or the occasional date with Gloria. One notation, listed on a day in February yet to come, said simply "2400 dollars and R.J. will keep quiet."

I took a picture of the notation and finished flipping through the book. Nothing else as intriguing as that little nugget of information. Was this referring to yet another secret? Zoe had just revealed one, but there was still the secret that she and Oliver and Sasha and David had concealed, and then there was whatever "R.J." needed to keep quiet about.

I realized with a flood of homesickness that I just wanted to be in Graham House, playing with Lestrade and the dogs, introducing them to Smilla, or napping on my bed at the top of Camilla's stairs, or sitting in my purple chair across from my partner in crime, or at least in mystery writing. I missed sipping tea and pondering settings and suspicions with Camilla—but the fictional kind, the kind that were fun to write.

I would be equally happy to be at Sam House, cuddled up with Sam in front of his fireplace and watching the antics of his cats, Geronimo and Arabella. Or reading one of Camilla's books out loud to Sam (he had gotten as far as number ten, and we decided to read it together), savoring her excellent writing while Sam played with my hair. Or making some gourmet dinner in Sam's designer kitchen, chopping peppers or onions while he regaled me with some silly story about Eager the chipmunk or the deer that kept taking shelter under his back awning and staring in the window with mild curiosity. Or turning off the lights and climbing the stairs to Sam's large bedroom, to his comfortable bed, where we liked to lie twined together while we talked about our plans or ponderings.

Here we were, at the outer edge of Blue Lake, and yet my Blue Lake, the Blue Lake I had called home for almost two years, felt very far away.

Distantly I heard Sasha's front door chimes and wondered who it could be this time. Weren't we all here? I left Gloria's room and trotted along the hall, Smilla at my heels. We moved quickly down the stairs and reached the bottom in time to see a man hanging up his coat. Was it Mondo, or—he turned around—it was David, looking pale and somehow thinner. He was bandaged, and moving slowly, but he spared me a thin smile.

"Why aren't you in the hospital?" I asked, shocked.

"You know how it is. They fix you, then they kick you out. They gave me some pills and said 'Farewell, Sir' and started changing the sheets on the bed." He moved forward gingerly.

"Everyone is staying at Dark Woods—"

"A place I would prefer to never see again," he said wryly. "And also, your police friends sent a message that I should stop by. Where will I find them?"

"Well, there's a whole party of us," I said with a tentative smile. "Follow me."

We walked toward the hall that led to Sasha's study,

passing the closed door of the dining room and crime scene. I saw David's grim glance in that direction as we moved past.

In the office, Doug and Cliff seemed to be finishing some last sorting, and Cliff was holding a stack of files and winding a scarf around his neck. "I'll head back to Dark Woods, then, and check on the troops."

"Do take Zoe with you," said Camilla with concern. Zoe was indeed looking peaky.

Cliff smiled down at the drooping girl. "Yes, Zoe and I will have a little chat, and then she can rest." Cliff and Doug exchanged some quiet words in the corner of Sasha's office, and then Cliff nodded and said, "I'm off! Come on, Zoe."

The two of them left the room, and moments later we heard them leaving the house, making the chimes tinkle merrily.

"David, good to see you," said Doug. "I was just on my way to the second floor. Zoe gave me one last idea about where to search for the will. Can you handle the stairs? We can talk on the way."

David nodded and followed Doug, but I noticed his face was white with pain. Camilla and I ascended behind him, keeping a watchful eye on his progress. Doug led us to a room at the end of the hall, which turned out to be another spacious office. David moved to a straight-backed chair and sat down with a relieved expression. Doug went to a large desk and began riffling through a drawer. I texted Sam to let him know where we were.

"Amazing that you're back already," Doug said.

David shrugged, then winced. "I complained a lot. I'd like to go home, but apparently, I am not to fly for a while."

"You must stay with me," Camilla said. "I have plenty of room, and my house is much more cheerful than that house of horrors down the street."

David shuddered slightly. "You know, as a writer of cop stories, I always tried to imagine what getting shot was like. Now I know." He managed a weak grin. "I think I was happier just imagining it."

Sam appeared in the doorway and looked around. "The cast has changed," he said, coming to sit by me on a little couch near the window. Camilla was in a chair near the desk, studying the blotter on the smooth wood surface.

Doug waved at Sam, then turned back to David. "I've got some questions for you that I couldn't ask last night."

David said, "Shoot. No pun intended."

Doug looked tired, and he wasted no words. "Why were you outside in the middle of the night?"

David was looking at his knees. "Believe it or not, I don't exactly know. I got a note under my door that said, 'I got the message you sent at dinner. I know you think I did it, but you're wrong, and I can prove it. Meet me tonight at twelve behind the manor. I'll only tell you because I'd be in danger if I told the police.' Something like that. And before you yell at me, yes, I can see NOW that it sounds like a set-up. At the time I was intrigued by the mention of something I said at dinner. My brain told me that this was a person who wanted to join forces with me, to solve a real crime. I was still aching with the pain of Sasha, and—I guess I wanted to be the guy who solved it."

Doug stared at him, and David glowered. "I know!" he repeated. "And then when I got out there, I didn't see anything at first. Then this really bright light was shining in the woods, and I figured the person was letting me know where they were. I was in that little clearing—you know the one—and the next thing I knew, I was looking at the sky, and snow was seeping into my clothes. I don't remember hearing the shot. I heard running, though. Footsteps. More than one person. Then Oliver's face was there, and Lena was there." He pointed at me. "I thought she was an angel. But Oliver was there, so I wasn't sure if it was heaven or hell." He managed a smile at his own weak joke, and I looked at Sam. It was the kind of thing he and Doug and Cliff always said to each other. The insults of men that became a safe form of affection.

"You never saw the shooter? No one started talking to you, pretending to be the innocent from the dinner table?"

He shook his head. "No, nothing. And I've been scouring my brain, trying to figure out what the heck I said at dinner. Did I say something controversial? Something that implicated someone? I genuinely can't remember."

I, too, was having trouble remembering the dinner, the happy little exchange before all the tragedy occurred. That meal, it seemed, had been one thousand years ago.

Sam slung an arm around me and kissed my hair. I must have looked slightly traumatized after David's story.

Doug pointed at David. "So, I have three questions. Why did someone shoot you? Why did someone shoot at Sam? And why did someone hurt Zoe? What's the motive for all this?"

"Misdirection?" I asked.

Doug nodded. "Cliff and I have been wondering that, as well. But misdirection from what? It's not like there was a big jewelry heist in the house while we all ran through the snow."

"No," I said.

Doug scratched his head. His blond hair was looking very messy indeed after a day of raking a hand through it. He turned to Sam. "Anything of interest downstairs?"

Sam sat up straighter. "I sent you the pictures. First, Mondo had a ring down there. Seems like he was going to propose to Sasha. He had a little pad with notes on it, considering various ways to pop the question. It was painful to read."

Sam shot me a warm glance, and I knew that, like me, he was remembering his own proposal, romantic and firelit, glimmering in the darkness on a bluff overlooking Blue Lake. I squeezed his hand. He turned back to Doug and said, "Really nothing in the rooms the ladies were staying in. Mrs. Barnard has a tidy room with framed paintings of drawings by her grandkids. A large wall-mounted TV, an easy chair. No apparent boxes of papers or mysterious keys. Lots of tops with sequins on them that hinted at her nightlife."

Doug grinned. "And who else? The chauffeur didn't know she was staying, so, nothing, right?"

"No, aside from a pair of shoes that I think were replaced by a loaner pair of boots. And a book on the bed that I think she borrowed off a communal shelf down there. The basement is amazing. It's like another house, well-furnished and full of guest rooms."

I kind of wanted to go down and see it, but I remained, pressed against Sam. Smilla, who had been patrolling the hall, now came in, looking tired. She jumped onto Sam's lap and I made a wry face at him. "Your girlfriend," I murmured.

Sam touched my nose, then turned back to Doug. "The two young men, whose names are Rick and Trevor and who alternately function as busboys, mechanics, computer wranglers, errand runners, and butlers, both have small rooms down there, very nice, also with some impressive electronics. Pretty sweet job, considering the free room and board at the fanciest house in town, and a salary from Sasha to boot. But they're general "dogsbodies". Nothing distinctive in the rooms except that Rick had a BB gun, and Trevor had some Playboys."

I sent Sam a disapproving look, as though he had published the magazines himself.

He grinned and scratched Smilla's pointy ears.

Camilla rustled in her chair. "So how do the police resolve something like this, Doug? How do you take all of this disparate information and somehow turn it into a solution?"

Doug slumped slightly in his chair. "I need a nice, strong coffee."

"We can head back to Dark Woods and discuss this there. The landlord has been very forthcoming with beverages, even if he has no food," Sam said.

"Yeah. I think we're mainly done here for the day." Doug stood up and stretched. "Sam's right. A change of scenery will do us good."

"Just one more thing," Camilla said. She turned to look at David. "What's the secret that you were so desperate for people not to tell? Apparently, Sasha knew it and told it to Zoe, who then passed it on to Oliver when they had a brief dalliance at a conference last year. I got the impression you were quite angry about the fact that the secret had not stayed with just one person."

David did look angry all of a sudden, and he glowered at Camilla, who stared blandly back at him, her posture relaxed.

"If I wanted to tell people my secrets," David began, his body stiff with indignation, "I would—"

A sound reached us then—surprising as a whisper in the dark house—a glimmering, shimmering sound, like tinkling of chimes in the wind. The door chime, I realized, was wafting toward us in the quiet room, lit now with only one corner lamp.

Sixteen

"It's not a good feeling, being terrified. But the reality is that fear is essential. Fear is the thing that keeps us alive when we can't see danger coming."

--from *The Blue Door*, by Gloria Gale, *2009.*

Doug held up a hand and left the room, his other hand already resting lightly on his gun. We sat, still and vigilant, listening.

A bullying fear pushed past my shock and complacency. There really was a monster out there. An unknown person who had shot the two men in the room with me, who had killed Sasha. Now, feeling the bones of Green Glass Manor settling around me, I shivered.

Sam put Smilla gently on the floor. "I should go—"

I gripped his arm. "No, you should not. You've already been shot once. Doug is trained and armed."

Sam acknowledged this with a dip of his head. He seemed to sense my rising worry, and therefore chose not to do anything to exacerbate my fears.

We sat, looking almost guiltily at one another, a certain misery pervading the room. I thought of one of

Camilla's favorite Dorothy Parker quotes: "What fresh hell is this?"

Then Doug was back. "False alarm. It's really windy out there, and Cliff, but more likely Zoe, didn't latch the door all the way. It blew open and set off the bells."

We relaxed, and I let out a huge sigh of relief that made Sam laugh. Smilla was looking uncomfortable on the carpet beneath us, pacing around and looking pointedly at the door. "I should take her out," Sam said. "Just right in front of the house," he added as he saw the protest forming on my lips. "She hasn't been out for ages, has she?"

I admitted that she had not. Sam got up and said, "Here, girl." Smilla didn't even glance back at us. She trotted after Sam as if he were the answer to all of her doggie dreams.

Doug looked at me, his face wry. "Are you jealous of the dog?"

I forced a smile. "Yes; she loves him." I shifted in my chair, uncomfortable. "Is anyone else bothered by the fact that last night he took the dog out in the dark and someone shot him?" I stood up. "I'm going out there."

"No, you're not," Doug said firmly.

David stood up. "We can see the front yard from this window, can't we? I'll watch the two of them."

Doug nodded his approval. "But that doesn't get you out of answering questions, I'm afraid."

David stood at the window, looking pale in the lamplight. "You have until Sam comes back, at which point I will be in search of my pain pills."

"Duly noted," Doug said. "Regarding the secret. It won't leave this room, David, but I need to know what it was in case it got Sasha killed."

A sigh escaped the man at the window. "Do you know, I've gotten rather tired of writing mysteries? Especially now that I realize how miserable it all is—the intrigue, the violence, the fear." He looked out, peering down to check on Sam, then gave me a thumbs-up. "Anyway, two years ago I told my agent I wanted to take a short break and try a new genre. She was all for it. But, stupid as it is, I felt embarrassed enough by the possible reaction to it that I published under a pseudonym: Charity Vine."

I sat up straight. "You're Charity Vine? You wrote *The Rising Blue*?"

David nodded. "I don't look like much of a romance writer, do I? But I had an idea, and I thought it would sell best as romance rather than fiction. And Charity, ironically, knocked David off the bestseller list."

"So, you told Sasha," Camilla said.

"Yes. I swore her to secrecy, but I wanted to get some PR wisdom from her. Apparently, she couldn't resist telling her little assistant—"

"Zoe," I said. "Who then told Oliver when they had their little fling at a conference last year."

"Yes." David looked indignant still. "You see how well that secret lasted. Oliver made some comment about it to me, and I shouted at him and ended the call. I suppose he then shouted at Zoe." He turned to look at Doug. "I cannot imagine how any of that would lead to stabbing Sasha in the back. I was upset with her, but she and I talked it out when I got here. I arrived early for that express purpose. Eventually, she convinced me that it had not been an intentional betrayal. She had received a promotional copy of Charity's book, and she took it out of the envelope and said, 'Oh, it's gorgeous! I have to call David.' And of course, the ubiquitous Zoe was at her side, asking, 'Why would you call David?'"

"And Zoe had made no such promise about keeping a secret," Camilla noted. "Although I assume Sasha warned her to keep mum."

My eyes wandered to the window, and to David. "Can you see them?"

He nodded. "She's been playing, but I think she's getting down to business now."

I looked at Doug. "I think Zoe might be tired of keeping secrets. I mean, she held on to the one about her father for twenty-some years."

David flicked a glance toward me. "Who is her father?"

"Sasha's brother," Doug said. "Not even Sasha knew."

David whistled. "That seems a lot more likely to be at the root of some of this," he said.

Doug turned sharply. "In what respect?"

David looked surprised. "Well, if Zoe has a link to the Hardwick family—and God, all the Hardwicks are dead now—doesn't that mean Zoe could inherit?"

I shook my head. "But if she were concerned about inheriting, why wouldn't she make her connection to Sasha clear while she was alive? Assuming that Zoe wanted to kill her, which, frankly, I have trouble imagining, she'd need people to know that she was a relative. And Sasha would be likely to put her in the will. She won't be there now, except as an assistant. Right?"

With a shrug, Doug said, "I don't know. There was no will here in the office. Zoe gave us the name of her law firm, and we'll be contacting them tomorrow. I'd like to lock down our gunman first." Doug's face, like David's, looked drawn and pale, making me think of vampires.

David said, "Zoe is so close to all of Sasha's affairs, though. There had to be a hidden angle. Zoe did all the grunt work, which meant she knew all the behind-the-scenes stuff. She was the one who sent us our plane tickets, and itineraries. She was the one who helped Sasha put this whole thing together—a gargantuan task for the two of them—and it gave her full access to Sasha and all things Hardwick. Doesn't that seem fishy?"

We thought about this in silence. Then Camilla said, "If you're making the assumption that Zoe had some sort of grudge against Sasha, it doesn't quite fit. The girl is devastated."

Doug stood up and stretched. "The one who would really have a grudge would be her mother. Who is her mother, anyway?"

Silence again. Slowly, an idea came to me, rising like a sickness from my gut to my brain, and I pointed at David with a shaking hand. "Did you say that Zoe arranged for Oliver's limo?"

David looked at me, his bleary eyes suddenly sharp. "Yes. She did. And Oliver told me—"

A creaking sound in the hallway, and then a rifle floated through the doorway, by itself, it seemed, until the woman at the other end of it appeared, her face bright with malice. "What did he tell you? That I asked if he thought I might be able to stay the night because I was so *very* afraid of driving in the snow?"

Carla, the soft-spoken limo driver, had been a mirage, and the woman who stood before us now was utterly real.

The danger was real, as well.

Seventeen

"Memory can be deceptive. Reality itself can fool us, make us question the basics. When we get to the point that we're second-guessing everything that used to be obvious, we lose the ability to protect ourselves."

--from *It Came from the Woods,* by Oliver Lord, 2004.

She let out some hard laughter. Her rifle seemed huge in the small room, seemingly aiming at all of us simultaneously. Doug's hand moved slightly and she turned the mouth of her weapon toward him. "Kick your gun over here."

We all knew she wasn't bluffing. She'd shot at all of us the night before, and she had meant business.

David seemed to be on the same line of thought. "Why did you shoot me? What could I possibly have—?"

She looked surprised. Doug had kicked his gun over to her, and she, in turn, kicked it into the hall behind her, never taking her eyes off of us. "Because of what you said at dinner. About how you knew people's secrets. And you winked at me."

"I was joking," David said. "You could have killed me. Over nothing."

My throat was dry, but I wanted to push out words, to make her talk rather than shoot. "Why did you shoot Sam?"

She sighed, glancing at her watch and then looking back at us. "I needed a distraction. A couple men down seemed to do the trick."

"A distraction from what?" Doug asked, his face calm.

"I had to get back here and return my rifle to the trunk of the limo. I didn't think anyone would be chasing me down the street until they made sure their precious friends were okay." Her face settled into lines of bitterness that seemed to have been carved over many years.

Camilla folded her hands, perhaps to keep them from shaking. "Who are you?" she asked. "I doubt your name is Carla."

Carla shrugged. "I'm nobody. That's what the Hardwicks thought. After Aaron died, and I lost the love of my life and the father of my baby, I went to them for help. You know what they did? They kicked me out. Threatened to sue me, to have me arrested for trespassing. Guess who wins when one party has money and the other has nothing?" She looked around at us like a parody of a teacher awaiting a student response. "I'll tell you. Money wins. It wins every time, and in the last twenty-seven years I could have used some of their buckets of money for a lot of things—my daughter's education, for starters—but that was not to be. Never mind that Aaron returned my feelings, never mind that my blood was mingled with his—they looked at me and saw trash. You get it? Or are you guys all rich, too? Rich people can only see each other. The rest of us are invisible."

"Put the gun down," Doug said. "What do you plan to do, kill all of us, and then somehow get away? There are cops all over the place. I think it will be pretty obvious that you're missing, and you won't get far in this snow."

She grinned. "I'll do fine. Zoe's stepfather was an army man. Taught me everything he knew. How to shoot, how to track, how to hide."

I took a stab in the dark. "Is your name Angela?"

Her face changed for a moment, as though a monster mask had fallen off to reveal her real, vulnerable features. Those seconds without pretense told me I was right. "You went to high school with Aaron, right?"

"Yeah, okay. And we kept dating all through his college. I didn't go. My folks didn't have the money. See, money again. The root of all evil."

"Clearly," said David in a cold voice. "Since you killed my friend to get your hands on some."

She shook her head, an almost condescending gesture. Obviously, David didn't get it. "If she had once, *once* reached out to me. She knew what we had was real. She'd seen us together, knew that he still dated me, on and off, and—"

"On and off?" David said. "Then it's not surprising they didn't think your baby was his."

She swung on him, her rifle veering in a terrifying

way. "One DNA test would have proved it. I was ready. I had a little lock of Zoe's hair. It was very pretty hair, golden, like Aaron's." There were angry tears in her eyes. "I offered it to the Hardwicks. I said, 'Don't you want the part of your son that survives?' They turned me away. They said I was a liar." She wiped her eyes, her face furious. "Twenty-seven years with nothing. Aaron would have lavished us with gifts, the way his father did for his mother. Right? She got this place," again, she gestured with her gun and a small gasp escaped from Camilla, "and fancy jewels and clothes, and I got a studio apartment and a lifetime of worry that I couldn't pay my bills."

Pity came in an unexpected rush, I knew not from where. Her tears, her anger, her frustration, had led her to this, and now there was no going back.

"Dear," Camilla said, almost conversationally. "Why don't you put the gun down, and we can help you work out what happens next. You don't want to make things worse for yourself or your daughter."

The look she gave Camilla was fierce. "My daughter knew nothing about this. She knew I was coming, and she knew that I was going to tell Sasha the truth—that's what I told her—but I had other plans. Poor Zoe is unhappy about it, but—I was boiling over. Just *boiling*. There's not enough snow out there to cool this anger, you know? But that's fine. Because Zoe will get what's coming to her. She's the rightful heir, and she didn't know what was happening."

"Is that why you bloodied her face with a rifle?"

Her eyes went blank. If I didn't know better, I would have said it was real shock. "What?"

"She was covered in blood last night. Another one of your victims." Doug didn't seem tempted toward pity. His look was flinty.

"I didn't touch Zoe. She must have fallen, or—"

"Or done it herself," David said. "I would, too, if I feared that I would be associated with the madwoman shooting everyone. Poor Zoe wanted to be one of the victims. My guess is, she bashed her face into a tree."

I thought about Zoe's injury and realized he was probably right.

"Angela," Camilla said again, in her sweetest, most grandmotherly voice, "Put the gun down and let's try to salvage this situation as best we can. Doug will have to arrest you, but you can call a lawyer, and—"

She laughed. "Who can afford a lawyer?"

"You can," I said. "If, as you said, your daughter will inherit the Hardwick fortune. They'll be lining up to defend you."

Something flickered in her eyes. A fearful hesitation looked out at us for one moment, then was gone. She shook her head. "You know what else my army husband taught me before he took off? That if you end up in a situation like this, you got more than one way out, as long as you have your weapon."

Doug was about to lose control, to shout and lunge. Camilla spied this and held up a delicate hand.

"Angela, you have a daughter who needs you. Her father's entire family is dead. Would you really deprive her of yourself? She would rather visit you in jail than at the cemetery."

Angela was crying again, her face furious as a frustrated child's. "No. I won't listen. Who's a likely suspect here?" She looked around, then pointed to David. "You. Something went wrong with your medicine, and it made you violent. You found the rifle from last night, and you shot everyone."

"A pointless addition to your sentence," Doug said. "Be rational."

I knew that was the wrong thing to say, and her face told me that she had experienced her share of male condescension. She lifted her rifle and aimed it at Doug Heller's head. Her hands did not shake.

"No," I said, and then a blur of motion hurtled into her back, knocking her forward at force. Somehow, she didn't lose her hold on the rifle. Doug lunged forward and sat on her back, struggling with her for possession of the gun. Sam, winded from the fall, looked up at us and said, "Run."

A moment hung suspended while we stared at him. David appeared in front of us and began to tug on Camilla's hands. "Cammy, now," he said, and she got up and followed him, pulling at the sleeve of my sweater. I went, and Smilla was right behind me. I swooped her up and yelled, "Sam, come with me!"

Sam didn't want to leave Doug. He moved toward the struggling people just as Angela, with a desperate spin that brought her from prone to supine, caught Doug unawares with a punch to the jaw and a knee to the groin. Doug tipped sideways, the breath knocked out of him, and Angela swung her rifle toward Sam.

"Now I'll run," he said, and we were out the door before she could get her bearings or scramble to her feet. David and Camilla had started down the stairs, and Sam and I raced after them, saying, "Go faster, faster! She's on the loose."

We made it outside, only to realize that none of us had coats, and it was freezing. A light snow was falling. We dove toward the driveway, where Sam's jumbo vehicle sat waiting for us, but Sam put out an arm to stop me. "Doug has the key," he said. "If we get in, we'll be sitting ducks unless he comes out first."

I remembered the force of the impact to Doug's private parts, and I didn't think he'd be out first. *Don't let her shoot him, God, please don't let her shoot him.* My teeth chattered as I followed Sam and David, who headed for a large shed that was just visible at the end of the giant east lawn. Still clutching the dog, I put my free arm around Camilla, and together we struggled through the high drifts, walking in the footsteps made by the men.

"It's like King Wenceslas," Camilla whispered, and I realized that fear made her talkative.

We reached the shed, and Sam held a finger to his lips. "I heard the door close," he barely whispered. "Don't make a sound."

Smilla, to my vast relief, seemed to understand our prey behavior, and she snuggled against me. David's hand moved, very slowly, toward the latch on the shed, and then he swore under his breath. "Locked," he told us in another barely-there whisper.

"We'll freeze to death before she finds us," said Camilla. She looked suddenly quite frail in her cardigan and turtleneck. Ice crystals glinted in her soft gray hair. I freed one hand from holding Smilla and pulled Camilla against me, the dog in between us creating a little ball of warmth.

We clung to each other, unsure of our next move, and the snow danced lightly down in a mockery of our peril.

Then we saw her, tall, wild-haired, and angry in the dim glow of the landscaping lights. She lifted her rifle and aimed it at the front right tire of Sam's vehicle. She was going to strand us here and make her escape in the limo. Well, good luck to her, my brain thought dully. At least she would be gone.

Before she could pull the trigger, a limping but very angry Doug Heller appeared behind her, then took an impossible flying leap (David couldn't restrain an impressed "wow" at the athleticism of it) which ended in him sitting, once again, on our assailant's back while she screamed and swore in the bitter snow. Sam and David, limping slightly themselves, moved swiftly toward Doug to help him contain his prisoner. Sam offered his belt, which Doug affixed none too gently around Angela's wrists. Moments later he was on the phone to Cliff.

Camilla and I had moved back more slowly, and now stood again in a circle around our fireplace of a dog. Doug was murmuring Angela's rights in between her furious screams, but he looked up and saw that we were freezing. "Lena, take this key. Get in the car and put the heater on. When Cliff gets here, we can find everyone's winter gear."

I handed Smilla to my shivering companion and went to retrieve the key from Doug. Angela had gone silent, her eyes vacant and staring in the direction of the woods.

I experienced another rush of sympathy. She had been an outcast for too long; she had spent decades brooding over her loss—of Aaron and of the luxurious life she might have enjoyed with him—and she couldn't let it go. Her face, now, reminded me of Smilla's bleak expression when she was alone in the snow, trying to keep her little feet from freezing in the drifts. To be so alone, so without help . . . and, in Angela's case, to be disbelieved. Who knew how years and years of that could twist a person's thoughts?

And yet, she had stabbed Sasha in the back. She hadn't tried to talk, hadn't attempted to work things out, but had drugged Sasha and her own daughter and then committed murder. It was hard to maintain sympathy in light of Sasha's death. I remembered, too, the terrible blow, like the cutting of all my muscles, when I thought that Sam might be dead, as well. How Angela had stalked through the winter woods with, Doug surmised, night-vision glasses, and shot people as they came out of the lodge.

No, I thought sadly, looking at the woman on the ground. Angela had made choice after terrible choice, and now she was going to have to face the consequences of her actions. I only hoped that Zoe had really had nothing to do with it, and that she could prove it to the police.

Angela's eyes slid to me, but her expression remained vacant.

I went to the metallic behemoth of a car and unlocked it, then took three tries to climb into the immense driver's seat and fumble with the controls.

David helped Camilla into the back seat, tucking the dog beside her, and then he got in himself, emitting a gasp of pain. I considered his forced run down the stairs, his rapid walk to the shed, none of which could have helped his injuries. I hoped his stitches were still intact.

"Are you alright?" I asked him.

"I will be. With the magic of pharmaceuticals." He sent me a weak smile and leaned his head back on the seat. Smilla licked his hand, and he rubbed her ears, his eyes closed.

I had the heater going now, the fan on full blast, and Camilla said, "Thank God for the heat. I don't know that I've ever been so cold."

David, who seemed half unconscious now that relief had begun to set in, said, "That would be a good first line, wouldn't it? Starting with a cop in peril, and saying, *I didn't think I'd ever been so cold.*"

Camilla gave a half-hearted chuckle. Smilla, who had nudged her way into Camilla's lap, curled up and closed her eyes. I wanted to do that, too—to curl up with Sam and assure him that he and I would never end up in a situation like this again. We would move somewhere far away—the Swiss Alps or the Mohave Desert—and we would never interact with human beings again because they simply could not be trusted.

Cliff's face appeared in my window, and I jumped. Opening the glass by only a crack, I said, "You scared me."

Cliff's sharp eyes took in our expressions and the limpness of our bodies and said, "Are you alright?"

I nodded. "We—put it all together just before she came bounding in. She's been nurturing her anger for almost thirty years. It was inevitable that she would explode somewhere, sometime. Poor Sasha."

Cliff said, "Give us five minutes, and I'll get all of you home. Doug will take my car."

"Is Doug okay?" I asked, craning my neck for a view of him past the other uniformed officials.

Cliff smiled slightly. "He's okay. But he is one *angry* policeman."

***

Sam sat beside me in the passenger seat, and Cliff drove in what, for him, was a restrained and dignified silence. He knew how to read a crowd, and he knew we were beyond the ability to do anything, including laugh at any jokes he might tell.

We drove, thawing and recovering, back to Dark Woods Lodge. Oliver and Mondo met us at the car door. Mondo took one look at David and said, "Let's have a look at those bandages. And then I'm guessing you'll want some pain pills."

David actually hugged him, and Mondo laughed a little, despite his obvious sadness. He pointed at Sam.

"I'm in Room 112. If your injury needs attention, come down."

Sam nodded. He and Cliff escorted Camilla and me into the lodge. Oliver had followed David, looking concerned. Our innkeeper was there in the lobby with some hot chocolate, and I didn't think I had ever tasted something so delicious.

Our escorts followed us upstairs and to the very doors of our rooms. Camilla gave Cliff a hug and thanked him for his help. Oliver appeared behind Cliff, hovering over Camilla and looking worried. "I'm fine, Ollie, really. How is David?"

Oliver shrugged. "Mondo sent me away. Said to come back in ten minutes. I need to know what happened," he said, almost plaintively.

She touched his cheek. "You and I will have a nice early breakfast, and I'll tell you every last thing. But right now, I need to call my husband and go to sleep.'

Oliver hugged her again, waved at Sam and me, and disappeared into his own room.

Sam, who was now the one holding an essentially comatose Smilla, smiled down at her as I unlocked the door. "Our baby overexerted herself."

"Didn't we all."

Sam followed me in and set Smilla carefully in her little blanket bed. She stretched out slightly, snored once, and remained asleep.

"What can I get you?" Sam asked.

"I will get *you* a fresh bandage so we can see what's under there." My stern tone didn't conceal the quaver of emotion. "Then I will take a quick, very hot shower, and then I will go to sleep, preferably for about twelve hours, and definitely with my arms wrapped around you."

Sam was taking off his shirt with careful, delicate precision. "Your plan is both detailed and well-organized, General. I will follow your orders to the letter."

"Don't make fun of me." I wasn't angry, just feeble with exhaustion.

"I never would. I think you are both brilliant and beautiful."

I leaned forward to peer under his bandage. "Amazing. It's intact."

"Fine. We'll put the new one on in the morning."

I didn't argue. I dragged myself to the bathroom, did an abbreviated nighttime routine and thawed my bones in a hot shower. Eventually I came out feeling refreshed, ready to collapse into slumber.

Sam was already in bed, and he patted the place by his side. "Come, Sleeping Beauty. I'll wake you tomorrow with a kiss."

I fell onto the mattress, pulled up the covers, and, for the first time in my life, was asleep before my head touched the pillow.

Eighteen

"She was safe now, warm and safe. So why did she still tremble? And why did she jump at every shadow?"

--from *The Salzburg Train,* by Camilla Graham and Lena London, *2016.*

Morning brought stern reality and a dip in temperature, and a glance through the windows of Dark Woods Lodge showed us a frozen world. The snow-covered tree limbs were now encased in clear, hard, icy, bejeweled fingers. The branches clicked and clacked against the walls in the frigid wind and made me feel nervous.

It was Cliff, this morning, who had provided breakfast, and Michael milled around the parlor, offering coffee and tea. We found Camilla and Oliver deep in conversation at a table by the window. Camilla had promised explanations over the morning meal, and she was obviously following through. I noticed that Oliver's face expressed shock over and over again, with each new revelation. David approached their table, walking gingerly, and was warmly welcomed by Camilla and

Oliver, and they helped him settle into another chair at the table. Gloria and Charlie were at a nearby table, and Gloria got up to give David a kiss and to chat briefly with everyone else. Sam and I stayed on the periphery, drinking coffee, looking alternately at the weather and each other. We had learned, not long into our relationship, that we could sit in silence and still communicate, and we did so now, in relative peace. Cliff joined us briefly, bringing us a plate of sweet rolls, and telling us that he and Doug had been up until the wee hours, processing Angela's arrest.

I looked at him with concern. "But you can both sleep soon, right? It's not safe for you to drive when you're tired."

He patted my hand. "Yes, pretty soon. Are you two doing okay? Sam, how's the injury?"

Sam nodded. "Fine. Only hurts when I laugh, or make sudden movements."

Cliff smirked. "You know, if this is some kind of competition, you and I taking turns getting shot—"

Sam held up his hands. "You win. I have no desire to ever be shot again."

"Me, neither. I've got sacred duties to attend to." He sent me a wily glance. "Best Man type duties."

I narrowed my eyes at him. "Sam has no interest in strippers or bawdy behavior, he told me so."

Cliff snorted. "I wouldn't expect my little bro to indulge in tawdry shenanigans. But *some* shenanigans are called for. What are the bachelorettes doing?"

I shrugged. "We're going out for dinner, maybe dancing. Just me and my three bridesmaids, Camilla, and maybe Tabitha, if she's in town."

"That's your step-mom, right?"

"Yup. She and Camilla have been working together with a lot of behind-the-scenes stuff. They're thick as thieves these days."

"That's funny. I wonder if—" Cliff paused, looking at the doorway. I turned to see Doug, leading in a fragile-looking Zoe. She was pale as the snow outside; her hands trembled slightly, and her face had been ravaged by tears. Her hair was uncombed, and her facial injuries had begun to morph from scratches into bruises. Doug looked down at her and said something we couldn't hear, his eyes on hers. She nodded, listening.

Then they came toward us, and Cliff stood up. "How are you holding up, young lady?"

Zoe shrugged. Doug settled her into Cliff's chair and said, "Let's get some hot coffee into you, and some breakfast."

"I can't eat," Zoe said, her voice slightly hoarse.

"Try, at least," I said. "You have to keep your strength up."

Zoe rubbed at her eyes and then looked up at me, her gaze uncertain. "Does everyone hate me?" she whispered.

I reached out and touched her hand. "No one hates you, Zoe. You didn't know, right?"

She shook her head, and a tear rolled down one cheek. Doug appeared and set some coffee in front of her. He turned to us. "Whenever you two want to leave, you can go home in Sam's car. I can take Camilla home in your car when she's finished with her friends."

"What about Zoe?" I asked.

"Zoe is going to stay here for the time being. A couple of Sasha's cousins are coming out in a day or two to debrief with her. One of them is Terry Wentworth, who is the CEO of an organization called Childheart. Cliff spoke to her at length and she was quite sympathetic, to everyone involved. Sasha, Zoe—and Angela," he said gently, a hand on Zoe's shoulder.

Zoe sighed and took a sip of coffee. Doug said, "Terry was very concerned about Zoe, and about Angela's defense team. And though she is very sad about her cousin, whom she loved, she wants to do the right thing by the family she has left."

Another tear ran down Zoe's face.

I looked at Sam, then at Doug. "I think Zoe might want to—talk to someone. A professional."

"We're on it," Doug said.

I pushed a sweet roll toward Zoe, and she poked the edge of it with her finger. I doubted she was aware of what she was doing.

"Zoe, maybe you'd like to lie down," I said.

She shrugged. Doug put a comforting hand on her arm and said, "I'll be right back."

He walked away. I turned back to see Sam looking at Zoe with compassion. "Zoe. We understand what a difficult spot you were in. No one thinks you wanted to hurt Sasha."

Another tear rolled down her face, and my heart hurt for her. "I loved her," she whispered. "I admired her so much. I wanted to be just like her." She let out a ragged breath and pushed her hair behind her shoulders. "Mom said she wanted to get the truth out there. Tell her that I was the child they'd rejected all those years ago. That I was a Hardwick, and what was Sasha going to do about it?'"

She broke off a piece of the Danish, but didn't eat it. "I figured I may as well let her get it out in the open. I hadn't summoned the courage to tell Sasha the truth in three years, and my mom was obsessed with the idea of confronting her. She said I had to get her to a face-to-face meeting." Her sigh was reminiscent of the guilty Lady Macbeth's own sad exhalations. "I had mentioned the event Sasha and I were planning, and she said 'Why not then? I'll show up with all those witnesses and tell them who you are. She won't be able to cause a scene or throw us out in the cold."

"Did you think it was a good idea?"

"No." She smiled a sad smile. "But it was like a dam about to burst. I knew it had to happen, so I arranged things so that Mom could drive Oliver's limo. She really did work for that company."

"Didn't you think Sasha would recognize her?"

Zoe shook her head. "My mom was a teenager when Sasha saw her last. A dark-haired girl with a short haircut. Now it's dyed blonde and much longer, and her face has aged. She's been angry—for a long time. It makes you old, anger." There was regret in her face, and a kind of exhaustion.

"So, the night that it happened," I said. "You knew your mother was going to drug Sasha?"

Zoe's eyes were wide as saucers. "No! God, no. We

were going to sit down together, after everyone went to bed, and just tell Sasha the truth. But I started feeling woozy, and really tired. My mom said, "Just have a quick lie-down, and I'll wait for you."

The tears had stopped, and some anger had crept into her expression. "She lied to me, but by then I couldn't think too well. I barely made it to my room, as you know. I was too drugged to even realize I'd been drugged. I just thought, 'Wow, I've never been this tired.' I thought it was the stress of the event."

Sam looked as somber as I felt. The betrayal that lay behind Angela's lie to her only child was enormous. Zoe had woken to a nightmare world: the event ruined, the suspects gathered downstairs, and Sasha, lying dead in the dining room.

"I'm so sorry, Zoe," I said.

"It's not you who should apologize," she said. "She took Sasha away from me, and now she'll be taken away, too. And my dad died before I ever met him."

There was nothing to say to that. She was right, and it would be painful, probably for a long time. Sam pointed to her injured head and asked, "How did that happen?"

She let out a sort of miserable chuckle. "Well, once I realized that dear old Mom had gone Rambo with her rifle in the snow—" the anger was back now, with a good deal of resentment and shame— "I figured I would be sure I was aligned with the victims. I was one, after all, wasn't I? I figured I'd let her take the responsibility for practically killing people that I liked, that were my friends." Her voice cracked on the last syllable, and Oliver appeared suddenly beside her. "Come here, Zoe," he said, opening his arms. She stood and walked into his hug, then began to sob.

He patted her hair. "You'll get through this, kid, and we'll all help you. Okay? All of us old mystery writers that you and Sasha helped so much."

"She was my aunt," Zoe said. "And I never got to tell her!"

Oliver held her tightly, patting her between her shoulder blades as though trying to burp her like an infant. "I'm going to tell you something that might be hard to hear, okay?"

She leaned away from him, tears like stars in her eyes. "What?"

Everyone was listening now; Camilla and David had come closer, too, and stood behind Oliver, listening. Gloria rushed to them, looking concerned.

"Oll, is this the right time?" she asked.

He nodded. "The kid's in pieces because she'll never be able to tell Sasha the truth."

Oliver looked at Gloria. "You're the one who told me this. Now you can tell it to Zoe."

Zoe turned to Gloria, who blushed slightly. She looked into Zoe's face and said, "She knew, Hon."

"What?" Zoe asked blearily. "Knew what?"

"She knew you were her niece."

"What?" Zoe's face was flushed with some emotion. "What do you mean? How do you know?"

Gloria bit her lip. "We were talking once, maybe a

year ago, and I said it was a shame she and I had never had children. She told me I still could—that having a baby at forty-nine wasn't unheard of." Gloria smiled wryly at the memory. "I told her it was too late. Then she said, 'I may not be a mother, but I am an aunt'. I asked what she meant, and she said, 'Have you ever looked closely at Zoe? She's the spit of my brother when he was in his twenties. And there's a resemblance to me, too.' She said she had guessed soon after your first interview, when you apparently said something about having a special reason for wanting the job."

Zoe's mouth hung open, and she snapped it shut. Then she asked, "Why didn't she tell me? If she knew, why—"

Gloria's voice was gentle. "She said that you obviously had your reasons for keeping it secret. And she felt quite guilty for the way her family had treated Aaron's girlfriend, who had gotten pregnant and said the baby was a Hardwick heir."

"Why didn't she just tell my mom that she believed her?"

Gloria paused, choosing her words with care. "She—didn't necessarily believe her. She said that Aaron had dated around in his early twenties, and he wasn't committed to one person. He told her that all the young women were aware of that; he hadn't kept it a secret or misled them. He wasn't ready to settle down. She had said that he should be careful not to produce a little Hardwick before he was ready, and he assured her he was very careful about birth control." Gloria stopped, a look of guilt creeping over her pretty face. Charlie came forward and put his arm around her. "Sasha said that his old high school girlfriend—Angela—was a kind of grasping person. He didn't like that, but he did like her, and he found it hard to cut her out of his life entirely. He had feelings for her to the end."

Zoe thought about this. "So, I don't get it. Why didn't she just tell me?"

Gloria hesitated again, and Charlie said, "Because she thought there was a reason you hadn't told her, and that she wanted to let you reveal the truth in your own good time. She believed, by then, that Angela had told the truth, but she was too ashamed to admit that to Angela, or to you."

Zoe's face was suddenly furious. "God, if everyone had just told the truth!!! No one would be dead, no one would be hurt! Except maybe my dad." She buried her face in Oliver's chest again, and he gave her some more paternal pats.

David edged forward. He was still pale, but he seemed a bit more himself today, and now his expression was firm. "Zoe. None of us blame you, okay? And I'll tell you another thing. Your mom shot me, and really for no good reason." Zoe groaned, and Oliver shot David a look that seemed to say, "*Where are you going with this?*"

David was undeterred. "But I still find myself wanting to help her. Okay? And I know several really good defense attorneys that I interviewed for my novels. Any one of them would be thrilled to take this case, I know it. It's complex, and there's a great deal of pathos involved. Let me help you find her a lawyer, okay?"

Zoe looked at him, her eyes solemn. Then she nodded.

"Good," David said. "If everyone will excuse me, I'm going to my room to rest. We'll talk later, right, Zoe?"

She nodded again. I realized that she was just about out of energy. She turned to Oliver. "I don't know what I'm supposed to do next. Or where I'm supposed to go." Her expression was so bereft that tears spiked my eyes.

Then Mondo was there beside her. I had not seen him approaching, and I didn't think anyone else had, either. That must have been the Navy Seal training.

He said, "Zoe, Kiddo, you won't believe this."

She stood up straighter and stepped away from Oliver, giving him a grateful smile. "What's up?" she asked. Her voice was weak; I doubted she could stand one more revelation.

Still, Mondo was about to utter one. "I had a video call this morning with Sasha's lawyer. He called me," he said quickly, looking around at everyone. "I have no interest in any of Sasha's worldly goods."

"So why did they call you?"

He cleared his throat. "Because she left me this house."

Zoe brightened. "Oh, Mondo!! That's so great." She looked genuinely happy for him, and a feeling of real affection seemed to pass between them.

"Well, this is what I want to say." He cleared his throat. "Sasha and I had talked about getting married. And that would have made me your uncle."

Zoe's tears were back again.

Mondo persisted, red-faced. I doubted he had ever had such an intimate conversation with anyone, except perhaps Sasha. "And I know I don't want to live in this place alone. I'd really love it if my niece would live with me. We can renovate so it isn't full of ghosts and memories. Maybe we can turn part of it into some kind of public service center. God knows we could live in only half the house and still have a mansion—"

Zoe threw herself into his arms. For the first time, I realized how truly healing an embrace could be. Between Oliver's arms and Mondo's, Zoe had lost a good deal of her pallor. "Yes," she whispered. "Yes, please."

Mondo looked both relieved and happy, and then the military man kicked back in. "Meanwhile, you're about to drop from exhaustion. Come down to my apartment where it's super quiet. You can conk out down there, and I'll wake you when the police or whoever needs you again."

She nodded, too tired to object. She managed to say a weary thank-you to everyone assembled, and then she moved away with Mondo, who had a protective hand on her shoulder.

"I didn't see that coming," Charlie said, with a quick smile at me.

Gloria touched his face with a loving hand and said, "I'm going to start packing."

"Be right there," he said, and she walked gracefully away.

He turned to me. "You suspected me for a while, didn't you? You and your partner both." He pointed his chin at Camilla, who was now back at her table with Oliver, deep in conversation.

"Yes, we did," I said. "But we suspected everyone, briefly. We were using process of elimination. But we realized that we had only your word that Zoe had been drugged. And the two of you were seen speaking intensely. We thought maybe you had dreamed up a plot together."

He shrugged. "It makes no sense, but I can see how you might go there."

"So, what were you talking about?"

Half of his mouth twitched into a smile. "I'm a jealous idiot when it comes to Gloria. I was asking Zoe if any of the guys had been in a relationship with her. Like I said earlier."

"And I'm guessing they had not."

"No, nothing to speak of. Zoe told me that Gloria didn't stay long in relationships, and that I was an exception."

"Well, that should tell you something." I smiled.

"It did, but I was afraid she would say no when I proposed."

"Oh, Charlie!"

He held up a hand. "We can't get married now. Not while she's in pain. But in a month or so, when we're far away from here, I'll see if she wants to elope."

"Well, in any case, congratulations on your engagement."

He grinned. "I'm sure Gloria will let Camilla know when it happens." He turned to go, then turned back.

"Do you need me to check your dog's paws before we leave?"

I shook my head. "They look great. That cream you gave me is doing the trick. And we've been keeping them out of the snow, carrying her everywhere like a princess."

He grinned. "You heard Gloria saying she has no interest in a mid-life baby. I get that. But I think the two of us will get a dog or two. Little ones, like your fox dog."

"That's sweet. Two fewer dogs in the shelter."

He held out his hand. "It was nice meeting you, Lena."

"You, too. Before the horror—it was fun."

He nodded, waved, and turned away, bound for Gloria and his new life.

Turning back to the room, I saw that Sam had joined Camilla and Oliver. I grabbed my coffee and donut and went to sit at the other table with my friends.

Camilla was beaming. "Oliver just told me that he is going to propose to his girlfriend."

I turned to Oliver, who said, "Things like this make you face the truth about life and death, and how short your time with someone can be. That fight between David and me—yes, it was childish," he admitted as I rolled my eyes— "but it cleared the air and made both of us think. David is going to try to get back with his wife."

"Good," Camilla said promptly. "Both of you should commit to a woman and stay committed." She bit into her raisin bagel and glanced at her phone, where I saw the name "Adam Rayburn" in her text chain.

"Speaking of commitment," I said.

Camilla smiled serenely as she texted back to Adam, her fingers nimble as a teen's.

Oliver's eyes met mine, and I realized that his charisma seemed to have dimmed like a fading light. Perhaps he no longer felt interested in generating it, or perhaps I had become immune to his charms. "Who would have won?" I asked idly.

He laughed. "Are you kidding? Camilla!! Did you see how quickly she figured out that I wrote that note to you? I was hoping to create a red herring, make it look like it was part of Sasha's web of intrigue. Camilla took one look at it and said, 'Oliver, stop playing games.' I knew right then that she was out of my league."

"Only then?" I asked, smiling.

"Okay, I've always known. The woman's mind is sharp as filed steel."

I nodded, content with his answer. "I think you're right." I looked once more into his compelling eyes. "I hope things go well with your girlfriend."

He nodded, suddenly solemn. "She's put up with me for a long time. I hope this is the result she's been waiting for. If not, I'll be very unhappy."

"You must tell Camilla and me what happens."

He nodded. "And now I will go pack. And I will not take a limo to the airport," he said firmly. "I think my friend David will drive me." He bent to kiss Camilla, then walked swiftly out of the room.

Michael came over to refresh our coffee cups. "I'll miss all of you," he said. "This place has rarely been so busy and full of guests. And the food was great. It was unusual to get treats from my guests!"

"You deserved them, for putting up with the chaos," Sam said.

Michael thanked us again and went back to his station behind the front desk.

Sam sighed deeply, then looked at Camilla and me in turn. "Who wants to go home?"

Nineteen

"We thank all of you for your support during this difficult time. Sasha Hardwick will be remembered by everyone as a beautiful, vibrant woman and a genius of the PR world. A celebration of her life will occur in the coming months, and we'll share information on Sasha's website. In addition, we thank the devoted friends and mystery writers who came to Sasha's final event. You are all winners in our book."

--from a Hardwick House P.R. press release

I woke in my room on the second floor of Graham House, surrounded by familiar sights. My cat, Lestrade, lay in a sunbeam that stretched across my bed, his large body pressed against my thigh. The room was cozy and warm, despite the delicate crystals of ice that patterned the window.

I stretched, luxuriating in the softness of flannel sheets. Green Glass Manor and its attendant tragedy seemed now like a surreal and frightening dream. A return to Camilla's house meant a return to normalcy, to treasured routines, to happiness.

With some reluctance, I climbed out of bed and

went to the window. Through the particles of ice, the frozen lawn was visible, heaped with snow still pristine and white. Beyond the lawn and the skeletal trees lay Blue Lake, cold and still, an eternal part of the landscape that had won my heart.

A draft of cold air snuck through the window frame. I shivered, then ran to the bathroom for a hot shower. Lestrade watched me scamper across the floor, his eyes half closed. He had been glad to see me, I knew, because he had followed me right up here the day before and stayed close ever since. My boy. Sam and I hadn't yet decided if Lestrade would make the move to Sam House with me, or if we should leave him in Graham House, where he now resided as royalty. Either way, I would see him every day, but I wasn't sure which environment he would prefer. Camilla and Adam had become quite fond of him, and would miss him if he left—Camilla had told me so.

I regarded him from the bathroom doorway. "Where do you want to live, my boy? Would you rather stay here and keep your amazing Graham House views? Or would you like to live at Sam House with your friends Geronimo and Arabella?"

Lestrade's eyes closed again, and he curled into the blanket to continue his winter nap. I grinned, and shut the door.

Half an hour later, dressed in a warm blue sweater, a pair of jeans, and a pair of boots lined with synthetic fur, I made my way down the graceful wooden staircase, loving everything that came into view. On the staircase wall hung the wedding picture of Camilla and Adam, standing on a bluff near a small chapel, smiling widely at the camera before a backdrop of vibrant fall color. At the foot of the stairs sat Camilla's German Shepherds, Heathcliff and Rochester, who had shambled over at the sound of footsteps on the stairs. Their ears pricked up when they saw me—they were always hoping for a walk. Behind them trotted the familiar form of Smilla; she pushed in between them and smiled up at me with her fox face. She had met the big dogs the day before, and after an orgy of sniffing between the three of them, she had apparently communicated the fact that she was in charge, and that was that. The big male dogs had become her docile servants, despite her newcomer status and small size.

"Yes, I'll take you all out," I said, bending to pat each fuzzy head.

Adam appeared in the kitchen doorway, his face as kind and handsome as ever. "No need, dear girl. I was just about to give them all a run."

I lunged forward and gave him a spontaneous hug, inhaling the scents of coffee and bacon. "Bacon," I said.

Adam laughed. "Yes, there's a pan of it in there. Help yourself. To what do I owe this prolonged embrace?" he said, hugging me back.

"I just love you. And I'm glad to be home with you."

He kissed my hair. "I share both sentiments with you."

Adam always spoke like a rather old-fashioned

gentleman. I thought that this allowed him a certain distance from emotions that might be difficult to express. Now he stepped out of our hug and said, "All right, unhand me, young woman. I need to give these dogs some exercise."

I laughed and watched Adam and his entourage of three travel exuberantly to the front door. Smilla tended to spring up and down, while the big shepherds were more about hurtling forward. They looked comical next to the always-calm Adam. Camilla appeared in the doorway, holding a cup of tea, and we grinned at the ebullient group as they made their way into the polar air.

"I do love that man," Camilla said softly.

"I just said the same thing to him, too. I love everything about this house and the people in it. You are so warm and comforting and—normal."

She smiled, brows raised. "Are we?"

I shrugged. "I mean, you have no deep, dark secrets, no dangerous unresolved issues, no violence in your past or present. I couldn't live the way Zoe did, with a giant secret weighing her down and eventually destroying her life."

Camilla's face grew solemn. She touched my arm and said, "Come have some breakfast." I followed her into the kitchen and poured myself some coffee. I made up a plate of bacon and eggs and put it in the microwave, pressing the one-minute button.

Camilla leaned against the counter beside me and said, "Zoe will be all right. I think that she and Mondo need each other, and they already had quite a good relationship." She sipped her tea and said thoughtfully, "In the end, we all just need someone to love, someone who loves us in return."

"Yes." We thought our separate thoughts for a moment, and then the microwave beeped and I took my breakfast to the table. "I belong here, Camilla. It's all so dear to me: this house, this bluff, this town. You know I'll still be a fixture here, even if I live with Sam, right?"

"I do." She sipped her tea, her face serene, and perched on the windowsill. "And you know that I will keep your bedroom as it is, for any times that you want some company, if Sam is out of town, or you're having work done at the house, or—heaven forbid—if you have a tiff and want some space."

"I do," I said, my mouth full of eggs. Camilla giggled.

I swallowed and said, "Sorry. That was rude. I'm suddenly so hungry!" I took a bite of bacon and swallowed. "We still don't know what to do about Lestrade. He's asleep up there in my room, and I feel like he would want to stay in this familiar place that he has investigated from top to bottom. But then I wonder if he'd miss me. I don't want him to be unhappy."

Camilla nodded. "We'll give it some thought."

There was a knock at the door, and Camilla set down her tea. "I wonder if Adam has locked himself—oh, no—it's Doug and Cliff."

She left the room and came back one minute later with our two policemen friends, looking tall and well-insulated from the cold. "Morning, Lena," Doug said.

"Hey, Princess," Cliff added, stealing some of my bacon.

"Get your own," I complained, pointing at the pan on the stove. He did, immediately, and he ate it cold.

"Gross," I said. Cliff swooped in and kissed me on the cheek, his mouth full of bacon. "Ew, gross again! Stop it!" I screamed, laughing, as he continued to kiss me and chew in my ear.

"Cliff is no different from those energetic puppies out there," Camilla said wryly. Doug gave her a more sedate hug, then dropped into a chair at the kitchen table. "We thought you might want an update."

"Always," said Camilla, sitting beside him. "Cliff, there are cinnamon muffins in that container near the—yes, you found them."

Cliff already had a muffin in his mouth. I looked at Doug. "Do you ever feed that animal?" Then I turned to Cliff and said, "Give me one, please."

Cliff was about to toss one to me when Camilla said, "In a polite way, please." She was barely suppressing the grin that she always wore in Cliff's presence. He was a source of endless humor, and his permanently high spirits always lifted hers.

Cliff muttered an apology and walked toward me with extravagant ceremony, lifting my hand, kissing the palm, and placing a fragrant muffin upon it.

Everyone laughed, and Doug said, "I'll have one, too. But please don't kiss my palm."

Cliff returned to the muffins. "Camilla?" he asked politely. "Would you like one?"

"No, thank you, dear." She could no longer contain her grin as Cliff grabbed two more muffins, dropped one in front of Doug, then sat down with his two and began to devour them. He really was like a big dog, I thought.

"Where's my brother?" Cliff asked. There was a streusel smudge on his lower lip, and he wiped it off with his hand. "Isn't he normally stapled to you?"

"No. And he'll be along sometime soon. He's doing a bit of work this morning."

Doug finished his muffin and grabbed a napkin from Camilla's little dispenser in the center of the table. "Sorry about the crumbs, Milla. I'll wipe them when I get up." He rubbed his fingers on the napkin and said, "Well, Angela has been booked and is currently sitting in a Blue Lake cell, pending transport to a larger facility. She has been visited by not one, but two lawyers, one of whom is going to look into the whole inheritance thing. Angela wants her daughter to get what she herself never did."

"That's good," I said. "And the other lawyer is a defense attorney?"

Doug nodded. "The most expensive-looking, spike heels-wearing, fast-talking lawyer I ever did see. Her name is Claudia J. Armitage, and she is apparently undefeated in the courtroom. I Googled her."

"That's down to David," Camilla said.

"And have David and Oliver agreed to keep in touch? Are they still in town?"

"They are both back home, but I spoke with them this morning. Oliver has offered to stay with David while he recuperates, but David asked his ex-wife if she would come to stay with him, and she agreed. She's there now."

Camilla clapped her hands. "Oh, good, good."

"And I suppose Gloria is home, too?"

Camilla said, "No. I received a text from her this morning. Charlie is taking her to Italy—an impulse thing. She's quite excited about it, and happy to get away from everything." I wondered if they would elope while they were there.

I looked at Doug. "So—Angela will spend the rest of her life in prison?"

Doug used his napkin to sweep up all his crumbs. "She murdered a woman and shot two people. She's going to jail, for sure. The question is whether a jury will be swayed by her sob story, or by the considerable skill of her lawyer. It's definitely a murder charge, but I'm guessing the lawyer will be arguing diminished responsibility, or temporary insanity."

Camilla sighed. "My poor, poor Sasha. She would have done right by both of them, once she shed the weight of her father's prejudice. And that foolish old man lost out on a grandchild. I'm surprised Selena didn't intervene."

Cliff had finally finished eating. "From what I understand, Selena was too broken up by her son's death to know what was going on around her. She didn't ever really bounce back, but she eventually re-entered the Blue Lake social scene. So says a very elderly lady who was Selena's best friend."

"It's such a saga, really, the whole history of the Hardwick clan." Camilla said with a sigh.

The front door burst open, and a multitude of doggy

toenails clicked on the front hall tile. Adam's voice spoke exuberantly with Sam's as the men entered together and Adam shut the door with a loud, decisive sound.

Cliff looked at me with a teasing expression. "Your heart's desire has arrived. I saw your little face perk up when you heard his voice."

I pointed at him. "Do you want to get me started on how subservient you are to Isabelle? I heard you drove into town in a blizzard at *two* A.M. to get the purse she forgot at the vet's office."

This silenced him momentarily. "Her favorite lipstick was in there," he said weakly.

We were all laughing when Sam and Adam entered the kitchen, their faces rosy with cold. Sam bent to kiss me, and he accepted a muffin from Cliff, who seemed to have appointed himself Guardian of the Bowl. Adam shook hands with Doug, and they chatted for a moment.

Smilla came trotting to me and settled herself at my feet, licking the snow from her paws. Heathcliff and Rochester followed, and Camilla wrinkled her nose. "It smells like wet dog in there."

Cliff burst out of his chair and hugged her from behind. "You can breathe in my secret—a manly blend of shower gel and Cliff's special aftershave blend. And hey, you smell rather delectable yourself!" He made a show of sniffing Camilla's neck and she giggled like a little girl.

"Stop!" she cried, pushing feebly at him.

Adam poured himself more coffee. "I believe you are trespassing in my domain, Sir."

Cliff stood up and made a show of backing away, his hands held up, palms out. "Listen, I don't want any trouble with you, man. I was just noticing that the lady smells nice."

Sam looked at Doug. "Cliff is in Vaudeville mode again?"

Doug grinned. "Isn't he always?" He stood up and clapped a hand on Cliff's shoulder. "Okay, comedian, we need to get going." His eyes met mine. "Belinda says that she needs to talk to you about some dress and jewelry stuff."

"Sounds good. I'll call her."

As the two policemen walked out, Cliff said, "Why is no one teasing you about Belinda? She's got you wrapped around her little finger, and—"

Doug's voice floated back to us. "Because I am Belinda's boyfriend, not her trained dog."

The sound of good-natured punching reached us. Sam looked halfway tempted to run out and join them. The Three Amigos, I thought. They would most likely be so till death did them part.

Camilla sighed, still wiping tears of laughter out of her eyes. "Oh, you youngsters do me a world of good." She stood, took her teacup to the sink, and turned to me. "Are you ready, dear Lena?"

"Ready and willing. Sam said he and Adam have some wedding business to discuss."

"Good. We'll leave you to it, then," she said, giving her husband a kiss on the cheek.

I touched Sam's hand and followed Camilla out of

the room, down the hall, and into her office. My purple chair sat waiting for me, just a foot or so from her desk, and I bundled in, leaning toward her. "Should we work on edits?" I asked. "Or should we brainstorm something new?"

"I have an idea about something new, but I'm saving that for later. Let's finish up our edits so that we can send this to Michelle before the wedding."

The words still thrilled me, every time I heard them. The wedding. My wedding, to the increasingly gorgeous Sam West. "All right, edits it is. I think we needed to decide how both Lydia and Harry can be safely in Bury St. Edmunds when the bomb goes off in Debenham."

Camilla opened her laptop. "Yes, that is tricky. It's the timing, isn't it? If Harry is seen by the kidnappers that morning in Debenham—Lena, I've lost you."

"No, not at all." But my gaze had been drifting around the room, appreciating the sight of Camilla's vase of roses (a gift eternally replenished by a besotted Adam), her neatly-stacked binders full of notes, her bookshelf of favorite titles, arranged alphabetically, her freshly vacuumed dog bed, a Christmas gift for Heathcliff and Rochester, on which they would soon come in and collapse, the pretty abalone framed reading glasses perched on Camilla's desk near her "Women Writers" calendar, the bowl of chocolates that she and I occasionally sampled when we needed inspiration for a book. The whole room, warm and familiar and mine—because Camilla had chosen to share it with me.

"You haven't lost me at all. I'm just enjoying the

ambiance." I met her violet eyes and saw that she understood.

"Yes," she said. "Now about this setting dilemma. What if Harry goes back to Debenham Station right after he makes his obligatory appearance?"

"That would be effective parallel structure. We begin and end at the train station."

"Yes—and since our title is "Danger at Debenham Station," it works well that she is in danger at the beginning, and he is in danger at the end."

"I like it," I said. "But you know what? I think she should be at the station, too. We were going to have them meet in Bury St. Edmunds, but why not have them meet on the train?"

Camilla thought about this, then brightened. "Oh, my goodness—we can have them meet in a café car—do they still have those? —and it will be reminiscent of their first meeting, when they both approach the buffet table at the dance."

We continued talking, working it through, challenging the problems, brainstorming the possible consequences. After a while the dogs wandered in, all three of them, fighting gently in a snuffling, quiet growly way, but soon enough they piled on the new bed, Smilla snugly between the other two, and became a snoring mountain. The sun was bright in the room when Sam appeared at the door.

"Might the artists be willing to break for lunch?"

We looked up, surprised. "Lunch?" I asked. "It's only—" I looked at my watch and gaped. "Two o'clock?" I turned to Camilla. "How did that happen?"

Camilla gave me a wise look. “The flow of creativity can blot out time.” Her gaze moved to Adam, who stood just behind Sam. She smiled, and he smiled back.

“Come, see what Sam and I made for the midday meal. We’re quite proud of ourselves—although we did have to call Rhonda briefly,” he confessed.

“It smells wonderful,” Camilla said. “Lena, shall we take a break?”

I rose, hungry again. Camilla came around the desk and tucked her hand into mine, and we followed the men we loved out of her snug office and into the larger warmth of Graham House.

This place was home, and these people were family.

No matter what I endured in the world outside, I knew, I could come here and be healed.

Lestrade strolled in, looking refreshed after his long nap on my bed, and he sat casually in the middle of the kitchen, in everyone’s way, licking his right paw with gentle concentration. Adam had anticipated his arrival, and he set down a bowl of tuna in gravy. Bath forgotten, Lestrade trotted to the corner to consume his feast.

We sat down to consume ours, and Adam brought bowls of steaming soup to the table.

“Perfect,” Camilla said. She looked at Sam, then me. “Do you two realize you’ll be married before the month is out? Then we’ll be two old married couples.”

“I’m counting the days,” Sam said. “It’s long since time we made this official.”

I sighed a happy sigh, warmed by the steaming soup and my fiance’s comment. Yes, at last we would be married, and I could only hope that the day was as special as we wanted it to be.

Adam poured water in all of our glasses, then sat down and said, "Here's to love."

We clinked our glasses together, murmuring agreement, and outside a new snow began to fall, its flakes sparkling like crystals in the bright winter sun.

Twenty

"I will say this: there is no mystery about how much I love Sam. He's the best man I know, and I can't wait to marry him and devote myself to his happiness. He's had enough of the opposite. From this point, we face the world together."

--Lena London-West, to reporters, on her marriage to Sam West.

Valentine's Day had never been more beautiful than it was on the morning of my wedding. It was a cold day, but not freezing, and by the time the ceremony began, in a heated tent that had been erected on the lawn behind Camilla's house, we faced Blue Lake, and our shared future, surrounded by friends. As the priest spoke, I looked around at the people who filled the pretty rented chairs. My eyes drifted to the beautiful bridesmaids standing beside me: Allison, Belinda, and Isabelle, in their amethyst gowns. I had chosen this rich shade of purple, not only in honor of Camilla's eyes, but as a reminder of my wonderful purple chair, in which I had collaborated with Camilla on many a mystery, both fictional and real.

I glimpsed Cliff, Doug, and Adam over Sam's

shoulder, standing proudly in black tuxedos with silk lapels and jewel-toned bow ties. I had walked into the tent on my father's arm, while Camilla and Tabitha, now the best of friends and serving as honorary mothers, had walked in behind us, wearing beautiful long dresses chosen to match our color theme.

Also sporting purple bow ties were Heathcliff, Rochester, and Smilla, who had made a brief appearance for a photo with the wedding party and then were ushered out by John Branch, Allison's ever-helpful husband.

Lestrade wore a tie, too, and now and again we saw him in the window, his little face curious about the strange structure in his back yard.

In the seats were friends we had made over a year-and-a-half: Belinda's brother and his new girlfriend, Patti; Marge and Horace Bick, the proprietors of our local Hardware Store and Post Office; Lane and Clay Waldrop and their two children; Rhonda, Camilla's brilliant chef and devoted friend, along with her family. Jake Elliott, a good friend who happened to be a reporter, and who happened to have been granted an exclusive story about the wedding, stood next to Star Kelly and her father, Luke. The two had grown very close in the last few months, and Luke slung a casual arm around his daughter while he chatted with Jake. At the last, most dramatic moment, Victoria West and her new husband, Tim, swept into the tent with the theatrical grandeur that always accompanied Victoria. She looked exquisite in a white coat and knee-high tan boots. She held her undeniably beautiful daughter, Athena. Victoria bustled around, finding their seats and taking off Athena's little coat to reveal a tailor-made purple silk dress that made Athena look like a tiny princess. Those assembled let out an "aww," but then the ceremony had begun.

Now I looked back at the man who held my hands in his. Sam West, the love of my life, had saved my life on numerous occasions, and I had saved his, and one dark night, also in the grassy area behind Graham House, Sam had asked me to look up at the stars. He compared me to a star in his life, and he had asked me, in a very poetic, firelit surprise, to marry him.

Now, at last, we were here, holding hands in front of our friends and family, formally making the commitment that we had made long ago in private.

"Do you, Samuel Jacob West, take this woman to be your lawfully wedded wife?" the priest said. I felt dizzy for a moment, and Sam clutched my hands more tightly as he said, "I do."

"And do you, Lena Sophia London, take this man to be your lawfully wedded husband?"

Suddenly my eyes felt hot, and a tear ran down my cheek. "I do," I almost whispered.

"Aww," said those assembled in a hushed way.

Sam grinned, reaching out with a gentle finger to brush the tear away. He gave me a tiny chuck under the chin before lowering his hand to hold mine again. We had already exchanged rings—simple silver bands—and now we were almost finished. Almost ready to begin a new life.

Father O'Brien said, "Go now, with the blessings of God, and witnessed by those who love you, both in heaven and on this earth. Ladies and gentlemen, may I introduce Mr. Sam West and Mrs. Lena London-West."

An embarrassment of applause followed this announcement, but even the loud (bordering on rude, in Cliff's case) cheering faded to the background when Sam kissed me, his hands sliding into my hair, and I tried to freeze the moment, to suspend it as long as I could, because this was the happiest that I had ever been. Based on the impossible width of Sam's smile, I thought perhaps the same was true of him.

Holding hands, we walked down the little aisle to a rather brutal assault of bird seed (Adam had assured us that this was more eco-friendly than rice) and then they surrounded us, the people we loved, and I thought my heart would burst with emotion.

Jake Elliott appeared before me and took my hands. "You are perhaps the most beautiful bride I have ever seen. And I'm not one to give compliments."

"Thank you. Audrey Hepburn said something once about how beauty was about what you felt inside. Based on my current level of happiness, yes, I can believe I look beautiful."

"Can I quote that?" Jake said, ever the reporter.

"Sure. But quote this, too: I intend to make Sam West a happy and contented man for the rest of his life."

Jake grinned. "I need to find myself a girlfriend."

The pictures came next, posed in the tent but also

outside, in the light fairy snow that added a magical look to the scene. The bridesmaids wore matching white faux-fur jackets, while Sam and I opted to go coatless, since the activity had made us very hot.

We posed with our families: for Sam, this was Clifford Blake. For me, it was my father and my adopted mothers, Camilla and Tabitha. In one photo I also held a picture of my late mother.

Next came the bridal party, three lovely women and three very attractive men. Adam, who had been paired with Belinda, was a polite and debonair partner, but he stole regular glances at his violet-eyed wife. There were photographs of duos: Doug and Allison, as best man and woman, Belinda and Adam, Isabelle and Cliff. Then the family photos: Victoria with her husband and baby, Rhonda with her family, Lane and her crew. It seemed an endless array of photo combinations, the last of which were a series of pictures of Camilla and me. She whispered, "Happy wedding, my dear girl." We both cried a little, and then laughed, and then Sam and I were being led away by a very determined photographer, and the small crowd was invited into Camilla's house while the catering staff set up the tent for dinner.

Sam and I were barely conscious of the photographer as we looked at one another, alternating between laughter and serious devotion. At one point the photographer encouraged us to try to catch snowflakes on our tongues, and we tried it, game for anything at this point. Eventually we fell into each other's arms, laughing at the absurdity of the game, and I heard the camera snapping away. Somehow, I knew that shot would be my favorite.

When the photographer finally relaxed, Sam encouraged him to go inside Graham House for some refreshment. The young man went, gratefully, and Sam took my hand and led me up the smoothly-plowed lane to a spot at the foot of his driveway, where grandfather pines towered above us, adorned with garlands of silvery snow. "This is where I met you," he said.

I held up my arm, showing him the charm bracelet I had worn with my wedding attire. He had given it to me long ago, and each charm represented something about our lives together. The night before, he had given me a tiny silver pine tree charm, which made a tiny tinkling sound when I shook the bracelet. "I thought you were so handsome, even though I didn't like you."

"And I thought you were beautiful, even though I assumed I wouldn't like you."

"And then you found me irresistible." I lifted my hands and smoothed his hair.

"I did. But I feared you would not return the sentiment. And now you've married me."

"We've married each other. Husband," I said, trying it out.

"Yes, husband. I own you now," he joked, then laughed at my horrified response.

"That sounds like a Cliff Blake joke."

"He's a bad influence," Sam admitted. "But I'm so glad he was here today."

"I am, too. Everyone, everything—it was so perfect, Sam."

"Yes." He held me against him, and I realized that I was getting cold. "Do you find yourself uncertain what to do with all this happiness?"

"Yes! It's almost—stressful. In a nice way." I leaned against him, inhaling the subtle scent of his cologne. "I'm getting cold, and hungry."

"Then let's warm you and feed you," said my husband.

"Hey, Geronimo is in the window! I can see his purple tie. Oh, and there's Arabella. What a follower."

Sam frowned. "Arabella is the idea person. Geronimo is the action person."

"Okay," I said. "Bye, guys! We'll see you tonight."

Sam took my hand and we walked back toward Camilla's house. "I'm glad we decided to take a couple of days here before we jet off to our secret destination," Sam said.

The "secret" location of our honeymoon had been chosen when Sam and I agreed we would be happy anywhere on earth, as long as we were together. Camilla had suggested that we point to a map with our eyes closed, so Sam held up a map, and I pointed. And now, in two days, we would be flying to a beautiful resort in Montenegro, on the Mediterranean Sea.

"A little time to relax before we relax," I said.

"Packing takes a while. I don't actually like it much."

"You won't need to wear much on this journey," I said, sending him a lewd look that made him laugh.

"Okay, now it sounds more fun."

We reached Graham House, and two violet visions

came out to meet us. Tabitha was trying hard not to flap her hands, probably because Camilla had a calming effect. “My darlings,” Camilla said, “it’s time to return to the tent for champagne and toasts and dinner.”

“Good. Poor Lena is a wintry wife. We need to thaw her.”

“Yes, yes, get inside the tent,” Tabitha said. Her eyes said that she feared pneumonia or some other dread disease. Tabitha still hadn’t gotten over the stress of my broken arm, the scar of which was visible at the bottom of my sleeve.

With the swift efficiency of Border Collies, the Honorary Mothers got us into the tent and on a dais of honor. Doug sat beside me, Allison beside Sam, and the rest of the bridal party fanned out to either side of the long table.

People were given champagne and trays of appetizers, and my father made his way to the microphone. He said, “I am thinking of the parents who would have wanted to be here, and cannot take part in the day. Sam’s mother and father, Lena’s mother. But they are with us in spirit, and in the beautiful legacy that is their children. Sam and Lena, I know they would shower you with love today, and I do so in their honor. Tabitha and I wish you only the best, and much joy in your lives together.” He held up his glass, and a tipsy Tabitha called “and grandchildren!”

Camilla, who sat just in front of us with Tabitha and Victoria Stratton, formerly West, called out, too.

“Yes! Lots of grandchildren.”

We laughed, and Sam kissed my cheek, and then Allison came forward to give a very pretty best woman speech. She talked of our friendship in high school, and how it lasted through separate colleges and careers, but now we were both married women who had everything in common, and would see each other all the time. We laughed at Allison's innocent desire for friendship and fun. And, after receiving a kiss from me, she sat back down next to Adam. Cliff and Doug swaggered up together, talking first about me—specifically Doug's first meeting with me on a stormy October day which also happened to be my first day in Blue Lake, and a day I just happened to meet my idol, Camilla Graham, and discover a dead body. "That was all one day," Doug said, and the audience laughed. "And that's kind of what life with Lena London is like. Never a dull moment."

Cliff grabbed the mic and told the story of coming to Blue Lake to take a job with the police, but really to meet his long-lost brother. He didn't mention that he had ended up saving Sam's life and almost dying in the process, but he did say that his life hadn't really felt complete until he had met Sam. "I don't think of him as my half-brother," he said, in a rare serious moment. "Sam is my brother, and I love him." He held up his champagne. "Congratulations, Sam and Lena. You are truly perfect for each other."

Camilla and Tabitha came to the mic together. My eyes filled with tears before either of them spoke. Tabitha began. "Neither of us had the pleasure of raising Lena. Her dear mother did a wonderful job of mothering her into her teens. But we are both privileged to see Lena as a daughter now. I feel privileged to know her, and Sam, and I thank you, Lena, for making my husband Eric so proud of you." She handed the mic to Camilla while people applauded. Camilla said, "Lena, you know how special you are to me, as a daughter figure, but also as a friend, a collaborator, and a mischief-maker." Everyone laughed. "And Sam, Adam and I think of you as a son, and we are so happy to know that the two of you have found such joy in each other. We wish you every happiness."

Before more people could wander up to the microphone, the D.J. began to play soft music, and the wait staff, specially selected by Adam, began to serve our dinner.

For a time, there was a lull. People ate their food, gently clinking silver and glassware. Sam and I kept looking at one another in disbelief, as though we had gotten away with something big. The photographer was walking around with the video camera, letting more people make comments for the bride and groom. I saw one of Lane's children speaking into the camera, and my eyes welled up again.

"You okay?" asked Sam, his blue eyes concerned.

"Ugh. I keep crying. Let's make this our last sentimental event."

He laughed and kissed my shoulder. "That doesn't work if you're a sentimental person."

"Darn."

Someone started clinking a knife against a wine glass,

in that annoying wedding tradition that attempts to force the bride and groom to kiss, I suppose as a way of entertaining those assembled. At first, I was irritated at the sound, but then I realized that this very tradition would give me a chance to kiss my husband in some very public displays of affection. I turned to Sam, whose eyes were twinkling at me. "The people have spoken," he said.

I pulled on his lapels until his lips met mine, and we stayed that way for a pleasurable while, listening to the distant sound of whooping and catcalling.

Eventually we pulled apart. I said, "Soon, my pretty, I will have you all to myself."

"I think that's my line." He grinned. "But I do feel pretty, especially with the purple boutonniere."

The photographer stood before us then. "The D.J. says it's almost time for the first dance. Ready for some pictures?"

Moments later we were outside the tent, waiting to be "introduced" as husband and wife. First, according to tradition, the emcee introduced my father and Tabitha, Camilla and Adam, Allison and John, Cliff and Isabelle, and Doug and Belinda. "And now . . . Mr. and Mrs. Sam West."

Sam looked at me. "Sorry. He made that all about me."

I took his hand. "You are so sweet. I am fine being known as the wife of Sam West. As long as people know you are the husband of Lena London."

We smiled, and then walked in to the sound of applause and music.

For our first dance, the emcee played *Dream a Little Dream of Me*, and Sam and I swayed gently; occasionally he would spin me outward and pull me back in, but mainly I stayed tucked up against him. "I always dream about you," he whispered, and his face was serious.

Others began to dance around us, but I barely noticed, nor did I pay much attention to the changing songs. I did rouse myself from my love stupor when my father tapped Sam's shoulder, and we switched partners. Sam twirled off with a chatty Tabitha, and my father smiled down at me. "I'm so happy for you," he said.

"Thank you for everything, Dad. And Tabitha—I know she worked so hard."

He smiled fondly in his wife's direction. "She's going to sleep for about three days. It wasn't just the anticipation and the worry over every detail, although that took some energy."

"But?"

"But she also had a lot of champagne," he said, and I laughed. We finished dancing to a moody Sinatra song, and then I found myself dancing with Doug.

"Hey," he said. "Nice wedding."

"Thanks." I grinned at him. "It means so much that you're here, to me and to Sam. You've been such a good friend to him—"

"And he to me. I'll always regret the way I treated him in the beginning . . ."

"Hey. It's forgotten. You know Sam isn't a grudge holder. And he knows you were doing your job. That is water so far past the bridge that it's out in the ocean by now."

"I think that metaphor got away from you," he said with a brotherly smile.

"Whatever. The point is I love you and Belinda, and we are glad to have you as friends."

"Sometimes I think you're my best friend, Lena. But don't tell Sam or Cliff. They'd pitch a fit."

I didn't laugh. "That means a lot. Sometimes I feel the same way. And if you tell Allison, I will murder you."

"Okay. We agree to mutual murder threats on both sides."

I laughed, and he spun me around the floor.

During Robert Palmer's "Simply Irresistible" Sam found his way back to me, and we leaped around. I realized that Tabitha wasn't the only one who would sleep for three days.

I edged close to his ear. "You are an incredibly sexy dancer."

Sam sent me a slow smile that started a slow burn in me, making its way up from my toes. "Come with me," he said. We made our way across the dance floor and out of the tent, where we found a secret spot in the snowy darkness. Sam held my hand, but he was looking up at the Blue Lake stars. Just in front of us, we could hear the comforting, regular breathing of the waves. "At one point, Lena, I thought I would spend my life in jail. I also thought I was alone in the world."

"Sam," I said, squeezing his hand.

"From that to this." He swept his hand to indicate the glittering night, the tent full of warmth and laughter. "It's quite a contrast."

I flung myself at him, wrapping my arms around his neck. "You deserve every good thing you have, including me."

"I'll certainly try to deserve you."

"Should we go home now?"

"I think we should say our thanks and goodbyes to all the guests. We don't have to open those presents, do we?"

"No—Tabitha says we can do that tomorrow, with just the family."

"Good. I only want to unwrap one present tonight."

"I approve of that plan. Oh—there's Camilla. I think she's heading inside to let the dogs out."

"Camilla," Sam called. She came over to us, a pretty blue jacket over her purple dress. "Hello, young lovers." She gave us both a hug. "What a memorable night."

"It is. Thank you for everything, Camilla. I'll remember every delicious moment of this day."

"I think everyone enjoyed the Valentine goody bags you passed out. Who doesn't love a present?"

I smiled. Sam and I had in fact filled the bags—elegant, red, velvet-look things—together, tucking in expensive chocolates, a heart-shaped picture frame, a card that said, "The Wedding of Lena London and Sam West" with a little picture of us, and then, for women, a heart bracelet, for men, a lottery ticket, and for children, an action toy or an art set—their choice.

"That's good," Sam said. "We had fun making them."

"You know," said Camilla with a dreamy expression, "I've been thinking about your honeymoon."

"Me, too," said Sam.

Camilla laughed. "I mean the setting. Montenegro. You will take many pictures, won't you? I've been on the Mediterranean, but only via Italy and Greece. I think Montenegro has a ring to it, don't you, Lena?"

A light went on in my head. "Oh, I see. You're thinking that maybe "Murder in Montenegro" sounds like a promising title."

"I am," Camilla said, with a mischievous smile.

"There's no escaping the machinations of mystery writers," Sam said. "But this time I can help Lena with the plot before she even gets home. You'll have to add "Sam West" on the cover."

Camilla patted his arm. "Feel free to submit a writing sample, dear."

We laughed, and Camilla walked back to her house to let the curious dogs out on the lawn.

Sam took my hand and began to lead me back to our wedding party. "Maybe you and Camilla should try writing a romance. "Moonlight in Montenegro." I can help you work out all the racy scenes."

I giggled and followed him through the doorway, festooned with fairy lights. "I think Camilla and I will stick with murder. But you and I? We'll stick with love."

"That sounds about right." We walked in, and Sam snagged a glass of champagne for each of us.

"You know what? I haven't eaten much tonight. Too much going on. Do you think there's any wedding cake left?"

Sam sniffed. "With that giant cake that Belinda's

brother made? We had fewer than fifty people, and that thing could feed two hundred. The only people I saw going for seconds were those two little cuties of Lane's. Oh, and little Athena got a big finger full of frosting before her mom whisked her away. She got it into her mouth, though. She looked happy."

I laughed. "She's so beautiful. Oh, and here she comes!"

Victoria whisked up to us, baby in arms, and Tim followed with their coats. "My lovelies, we must go. We're headed to New York early in the morning. But I am so, so glad to have seen your wedding. Thank you for inviting us. You know I adore you both." She kissed my cheek, and Athena took the opportunity to grab some of my hair. "Oh, you schnook," Victoria said fondly, disentangling my hair from Athena's plump fist.

Sam shook hands with Tim, and Victoria kissed his cheek and whispered something in his ear. Then they moved swiftly out the door, leaving a slight vacuum behind them.

Sam and I returned to our seats with plates of cake, which was truly delicious. One layer had been a light, spongy lemon, the next a delicious cherry cake, and the bottom tier was banana. All of them had been frosted with a decadent cream cheese mixture. I rolled my eyes.

"You're making your better-than-sex face," Sam complained. "Now I have this cake to live up to."

I laughed. "Maybe we could bring some cake with us. Sort of a threesome."

Now Sam laughed. "I have my pride, Lena."

Doug and Belinda were the next to go, clutching their red gift bags and telling us what an enjoyable time they'd had. Belinda squeezed my hand and said, "You'll come over before you leave, right? Maybe give us a hint of the honeymoon destination?"

Sam pointed sternly at her. "That is top secret." Then he smiled. "But maybe."

Belinda gave him her pretty smile and then turned back to Doug, who had been watching her. Their engagement had to be on the horizon—Doug was smitten.

Cliff and Isabelle followed on their heels, saying they had to let their dog out. "Your little Smilla is a real sweetheart, Lena. I'm so glad you rescued her out of the snow."

In twos and threes they left us, thanking us, congratulating us, wishing us well. Soon the tent was empty of everyone except the staff who were efficiently tidying up, my father and Tabitha, Adam and Camilla.

My father gave me a final hug. "I'm taking Tabitha back to Camilla's so that she can start her long winter's nap."

I laughed at his poetic reference, and I kissed the tipsy Tabitha on her cheek. They headed toward the house, Tabitha leaning heavily on my father.

Camilla and Adam strolled up, arm in arm. "Go, you two. You did your polite duty, more than you had to, even. Now escape to your snug home down the road, and we'll see you tomorrow."

More kisses and hugs, and then we were out in the

cold night, making our way past Camilla's house, where Smilla was going to spend the next two weeks, and onto the rocky pathway that led down the bluff.

We could see Sam's house through the trees—just a dark shape with some glimmering landscaping lights and at least two glowing windows. It looked familiar and welcoming.

Sam must have thought so, too, because he looked at me, and without a word spoken, we both began to run down the road, toward the pines where we had met, toward the house where we would live, toward the future that held our hard-won happiness.

The snow crunched beneath our feet, and our laughter floated up toward the silvery stars that hung over Blue Lake like precious stones.

We reached the steps, and I looked down, laughing, at my snow-dampened hem.

"Let's get you out of those wet things," he said, pulling me to him.

"Let's get you out of those dry things."

He laughed, and kissed me, and we climbed the steps. "Shall I carry you over the threshold?" he asked.

"No. I've been over this threshold before. Let's start a new tradition."

"Okay, you carry me over the threshold." Sam unlocked the door and turned to look at me, his face expectant.

I giggled. "Try again. Why don't we both make a promise, and on every anniversary we'll come back to these stairs and make new promises to each other."

"Okay." He took my hands in his. "I promise that you and I will be happier as a wedded pair than we ever were apart."

I smiled. "I look forward to it. And I promise that you will never go one day without laughing from pure joy. I'm going to make you happy, Sam West."

"You already do, Lena London-West."

We stepped over the threshold, and Sam's cats came to congratulate us, still wearing their purple bow ties. Sam bent to greet them. "Let me just feed them. And then Project Wedding Night can commence."

I laughed again; my face was sore from laughing and smiling all day. Sam followed the cats into the kitchen, and I moved toward the stairs. On the sideboard sat the day's mail and both of our phones. We had decided that no intrusions from the outside world would be allowed on our wedding day, and we had enjoyed the freedom our decision had engendered.

My phone buzzed on the tabletop, and I glanced toward it, tempted to look at the message. I shook my head and ran upstairs. If Sam and I wanted, we could make Blue Lake what we had always hoped it would be: a haven, an idyll, a home.

For as long as we could, we would keep the world at bay.

***

Later that night, I lay curled against my husband, warm as toast beneath the covers and staring at the flames in Sam's bedroom fireplace. My eyes drifted to the window. "It's snowing."

Sam rustled and rested his chin on my shoulder so that he could see the snowfall, delicate but determined. "Enough snow," he said. "I'm staying in this bed until spring." He pulled the covers over our heads and pressed his lips to mine.

The snow fell, quiet and soft, until we were back asleep, and in the morning it shone blue-white, blanketing Sam's yard and reflecting the sun in painful, glittering crystals.

Sam walked in, holding both of our phones and a basket of muffins that Rhonda had dropped off early that morning, using a key that Sam had given her.

"There's coffee, too," Sam said, "and little bacon sandwiches."

"Mm. I'm starved. Is that my phone?"

"I thought we could steal twenty minutes of real world time and then hide them again."

"Throw it here."

He tossed me the phone and handed me a plate with a muffin on it. "I'll set your coffee here on the table."

"Heaven," I said, scrolling through my texts and then my e-mails.

Sam was doing the same, trying to make the most of his twenty minutes. I bit into the muffin and said, "Oh, Rhonda. You spoil us. Where did she find such fat blueberries?"

"Blue Lake's pride," Sam murmured. His brows drew together. "Did Cliff send you an e-mail? He says something about a gift he told you about."

"Cliff?" I thought back to the night before, chaotic

and wonderful and unforgettable. "He told me something when we were dancing together. Something about a present we'd find in the morning. I was so distracted..."

"Oh. If it's a present, I assume it's waiting with the others at Camilla's house."

"I suppose. I think he said it was big. Is it terrible that I was barely listening?"

"Not if you were distracted by my handsomeness."

"Well, of course. That always distracts me." I inched toward him and kissed his cheek.

"Good," he said, his voice smug. He was scrolling through his mail, but finally seemed to reach the end of the new correspondence. "There." He tossed his phone aside and looked at Rhonda's basket.

I was on my second muffin, and I looked at him guiltily. "Will you fall out of love with me if I gain twenty pounds on our honeymoon?"

He grinned. "I'm pretty sure you'll work off the calories you consume."

"Perfect. Then I can eat all these muffins." I popped the rest of the one I had in my mouth, and Sam dove toward me.

"No way. Give me some of those."

Sam's phone buzzed. And he glanced at it, chewing hugely at the whole muffin he had shoved into his mouth.

"Gross, Sam," I said, my voice mild. I picked a fat blueberry out of a third muffin. "I think that Rhonda must—"

Sam sat up straight and said, "Shh." He listened, so I listened, too, leaning forward in the bed. Had that been the sound of footfalls?

"Sam," I said, clutching his arm.

He was off the bed now, grabbing a baseball bat that lived in the corner of his bedroom, and moving toward the door.

"Sam! Don't you dare!" I hissed.

He pointed at me. "You stay there," he whispered. "I'm just going to check it out." Behind him, I thought I heard the sound of the front door closing, clicking softly shut.

Sam left the room on quiet feet. He went into the hall, and both of his cats materialized behind him, wanting in on whatever action Sam might find.

I dove out of bed and crept toward the door, stiff with anxiety. Surely there was no one who wished us ill, after all of the good cheer we had shared with our friends the night before? Surely there could be no more malefactors lurking in the shadows, waiting to ruin Sam's life, or mine? I stood in the doorway, irresolute, listening.

Then I heard Sam's voice, strange and solemn. "Lena, can you come down here?"

Uncertain, I donned my robe and slippers and padded into the hall, then down Sam's polished wooden staircase. "Sam? Where are you?"

"The living room," he called.

I found him standing next to a tall wooden structure that resembled an old-fashioned lamppost, and in fact there was a charming old frosted glass orb at the top with a light inside. Beneath this elegant structure were what looked like two street signs with the street names burned into the polished wood. One said "London Lane" and the other, perpendicular to the first, read "West Way."

I stood staring. "It's beautiful."

Sam held up a card. "It's from my brother," he said with a smile. "He made it. He said it's a symbol: the intersection of London and West."

"It's gorgeous! Cliff made that? What an amazing and thoughtful present. I don't know whether we should keep it outside, by the pines, or inside, as a conversation piece."

Sam sighed. "It has to be inside, I think. I want to see it every day. To remind me that Fate brought us to this intersection, and our paths have crossed permanently."

"London Lane," I said dreamily. "You know, a year and a half ago, you didn't know Cliff, and you didn't know me."

Sam pondered this. "And I wouldn't know either of you if I hadn't come to Blue Lake and befriended Camilla."

"All roads lead to Camilla," I said, smiling. "Do you know--? I think those little pegs on the sides are for people to hang their coats on. I think this is a perfect and whimsical coat rack."

Sam grinned, nodding. "I love it. I need to find Cliff. He's probably lurking outside; I heard him leave."

"He probably went to Camilla's. We should think about heading over there, too."

He pulled me against him. "In a while. I want one more intersection of London and West."

I giggled, and the cats strolled around the new furniture. The snow shone blue-white and sparkled in the sun. A sudden gust of wind blew some crystals against the window like a silent blessing.

We *were* blest. And on that February day, the first day of our married life, we embraced beneath Cliff's lamppost and dared to dream of Ever After.

The End

Other Work

If you liked this novel, check out the other Writer's Apprentice mysteries!

A Dark and Stormy Murder
Death in Dark Blue
A Dark and Twisting Path
Death Waits in the Dark
Death with a Dark Red Rose
A Dark and Silent Night (A Christmas Short Story, available in e-book format)

And stay tuned for more information about Book 7, *A Dark and Starlit Sea.*

Also by Julia Buckley:

The Undercover Dish Mysteries
The Hungarian Tea House Mysteries

As Veronica Bond:

The Dinner and a Murder Series

Author Info

Julia Buckley has written a variety of mystery series, four of them with Penguin Random House (the fourth penned as Veronica Bond). She taught high school English for three decades, but retired early to teach remotely and write more frequently.

She lives with her husband in a suburb of Chicago, where she loves to watch the seasons change and enjoy her menagerie of animals, consisting of three cats and a beloved black Labrador. She has two grown sons that she hopes will one day become writers, too.

Her hobbies include reading, writing, painting

landscapes, corresponding, and discussing novels with her three book groups. Her partial vision loss in 2020 resulted in her discovery of, and addiction to, audiobooks, especially in the mystery genre.

Contact Julia at **julishka64@gmail.com**, or follow her on Instagram (jellenbuckley), Twitter (@juliabucks) or Facebook (Julia Buckley Mystery Novels). You can sign up for her newsletter at **www.juliabuckley.com**.

Made in the USA
Columbia, SC
01 June 2024

36479769R00174